Illusions

D0862421

Illusions

DEVON SCOTT

Kensington Publishing Corp.
http://www.kensingtonbooks.com

To the extent that the image or images on the cover of this book depict a person or persons, such person or persons are merely models, and are not intended to portray any character or characters featured in the book.

DAFINA BOOKS are published by

Kensington Publishing Corp.
119 West 40th Street
New York, NY 10018

Copyright © 2005 by Devon Scott
Published in arrangement with Strebor Books, www.strebor books.com.
Distributed by Simon & Schuster, Inc., 1230 Avenue of the Americas, New York, NY 10020. 1-800-223-2336.
Dissolve © 2005 by Jonathan Luckett
ISBN 1-59309-041-2. LCCN 2004118376
First Printing July 2005

All rights reserved. No part of this book may be reproduced in any form or by any means without the prior written consent of the Publisher, excepting brief quotes used in reviews.

If you purchased this book without a cover, you should be aware that this book is stolen property. It was reported as "unsold and destroyed" to the Publisher and neither the Author nor the Publisher has received any payment for this "stripped book."

All Kensington Titles, Imprints, and Distributed Lines are available at special quantity discounts for bulk purchases for sales promotions, premiums, fund-raising, and educational or institutional use. Special book excerpts or customized printings can also be created to fit specific needs. For details, write or phone the office of the Kensington special sales manager: Kensington Publishing Corp., 119 West 40th Street, New York, NY 10018, attn: Special Sales Department, Phone: 1-800-221-2647.

Dafina and the Dafina logo Reg. U.S. Pat. & TM Off.

ISBN-13: 978-1-4967-0243-2
ISBN-10: 1-4967-0243-3
First Kensington Mass Market Edition: December 2016

10 9 8 7 6 5 4 3 2 1

Printed in the United States of America

*For my mother
Esther Margoshes Luckett*

"In a mad world only the mad are sane."
— AKIRA KUROSAWA

"There is always some madness in love.
But there is also always some reason in madness."
— FRIEDRICH NIETZSCHE

1

The place was close to perfect. A large studio, it was set on the top floor of a majestic old brownstone in Brooklyn. David Sands loved it. He stood in the center of the large room staring around at the tall ceiling, skylights, and brick fireplace, beaming with joy. God, there was so much to do. But so much to work with. He sighed happily. This was going to be a great apartment.

The landlord of the place, an elderly man named Mr. Whittaker, sat on a metal crate full of CDs and sipped a cup of hot tea. He had shown David the apartment only a few days ago and now felt content, for Sands had just signed the lease. Not that the old man needed the money, but it was sure nice to have someone else in the building. His two kids were all grown up, and after his wife passed away from cancer five years ago, he had rented the apartment upstairs, keeping the bottom two floors for himself. Sands looked like a good character— another artist (a painter, no less), but that was all right with him. After all, this place was made for painters.

"I can't get over these windows," Sands said, facing the rear of the building. There were two windows, large floor-to-ceiling glass panels. They were almost eight feet high and twice that in width, allowing an unobstructed view of the backyard, and the buildings beyond. Sunlight blazed in, falling on a thick off-white rug, warming the floor.

"Oh yeah," Whittaker said, pausing to slurp his tea, "one of the tenants put all this stuff in a few years back. An artist, this one was," he said, pointing a bony finger in Sands' direction. "Guy was a painter, just like you. Kept on making all of this fuss about there not being enough light in here. Said it affected his creativity!" Whittaker let out a sharp yelp that barely resembled a laugh. He was grinning though, and holding his stomach with a callous hand. The other trembled slightly, spilling a bit of tea on the rug. "Shit, sorry," he mumbled softly.

Sands watched him with amusement. He liked the old guy. He sure could talk though. He had kept Sands for two hours the other day just rambling on about the place and the neighborhood. Sands knew that he was just lonely, looking for someone to tell his stories to. And that was okay with him.

"Sure seems like this painter did an awful lot of work to the place," Sands said, his eyes traveling around the loft.

"Oh yeah, this guy was a real handyman. And I figured, what the hell. He showed me his plans and I said go for it. And boy did he! Knocked out a bunch of walls, put in the skylights and the windows, and installed hardwood floors throughout the entire place." Sands shook his head. This place didn't look like any of the brownstones he had seen, including the one he had grown up in just a few blocks away. He could understand though how a painter had done all this: the wide-open loft; light streaming in from dual skylights and twin windows. He felt a sudden urge to kick the old man out and get to his easel. But he hadn't even unpacked yet. There was plenty of time for his craft later.

Sands stood at the windows admiring his new view. He was a tall man, dark with short black hair that always looked combed, even when it was neglected for a few hours. His brown eyes were set into a soft, youthful face that hid his true age of thirty-five. He glanced ahead at the building that faced his. It was the same height as his building and built of dark stone the color of mud. Sands also noticed that each window was covered with a plastic shade, giving the impression that the occupants were not around. Perhaps they were on vacation. He looked down into the backyard, his eyes following the neatly cut grass and gray flagstones set in the ground back to a metal fence. The other building's yard extended to the same fence, the two yards hugging each other back to back. Below him, the yard was well kept. Despite the cool autumn weather, Mr. Whittaker had planted a row of flowers on either side. An oval pool in the center surrounded by small flagstones beckoned flocks of sparrows and an occasional blue jay. The other yard, on the other hand, had tall grass and unkempt vines, their lanky tendrils climbing up the fence toward the sky.

"You keep the yard in excellent condition," Sands remarked to the old man, who had risen and now stood by the window. The sun was beginning to descend, sending its brilliant light filtering through the massive branches of several large oak trees.

"Well, I've got time to kill now," Mr. Whittaker said, pausing to reflect on a thought. "Besides, I like to put in a few hours outside, as long as it doesn't get too cold. The tenants before you used to do a little themselves, so we just got in the habit of keeping it nice and neat."

"It shows. What's the story on the yard behind us? Are those people away or something, because theirs needs some tender loving care, if you know what I mean?" The old man just smiled and tipped his mug up to finish the last of his tea. He set the mug down in the palm of his hand and turned to look at the building with the unkempt yard.

"Strange story about that house and its occupants. But, to answer your question: no, they aren't away. Actually, no one lives in that house anymore. A brother-in-law, I think, of the original owner comes around once a month to check up on the place and tidy up the yard. Yeah, no one lives there anymore." He walked over to the side of the main room where the kitchen was located and placed the mug carefully in the sink. "Well, I got to be going; thanks for the tea." He disappeared out the door and down the steps before Sands could question him further about the house or the occupants. It didn't matter much. There would be plenty of time later to sit and shoot the breeze with the old man. He found himself looking forward to that next time when Whittaker would come to talk. For now, there were things to do. He wanted to finish unpacking his things and fill the water bed before the evening so he could sleep in comfort the first night in his new home.

By nine, Sands had managed to sort out the majority of his belongings. Boxes lay everywhere. Large ones marked "bedroom" were stacked in one corner of the loft, while others marked "dishes" were in the kitchen and dining room area. The bed had been filled in a little under three hours. The heater had kicked in, but it would be a while before the bed was completely warm the way he liked it. A diamond-studded night filled the windows, sending disturbing shadows and eerie moonlight through the panes of glass. He had managed to start a fire an hour ago. The small pile of wood that Mr. Whittaker had left had since burned down to reddish-brown coals sizzling in the evening, painting the room in shades of soft firelight. More than three-dozen paintings leaned against different walls, waiting for Sands to mount them. Multitudes of colors, they were dazzling images that represented his life's work. He had also tacked up a two-meter square canvas on one wall and pulled out his paints in preparation for beginning his next project. He had an idea floating around in his head: a single vein of a concept—and he thought he might try to run with it to see where it ended up.

Sands flopped into a deep rattan chair facing the windows. His drink lay at his side, a tall frosty glass filled with squares of clear ice and Jamaican rum. He put the glass to his lips, shut his eyes, and savored the flavor of the smooth liquid as it shot down his throat. He felt incredibly good. He looked out at the buildings before him. The one in front was completely dark, almost black. Its sheer face seemed one-dimensional in the moonlight. He shivered without thinking; then returned his gaze to the room in which he sat. As he glanced around his loft, he smiled proudly. This was all his. He had worked damn hard for it, and now he had what he had always dreamed of. It was perfect. In the heart of Prospect Heights, only blocks from where he grew up. That was important. He wanted to be close to his "roots." Sands had drawn much inspiration from the city and his childhood, depicting in his paintings the hardships of growing up in the ghetto, learning to be a man, and surviving. In addition, he loved Brooklyn. Prospect Park, the library, and the Brooklyn Museum—they had all been subjects of his paintings. His students in the P.S. 9 art classes found his work intriguing.

He stared at the canvas tacked to the wall. He wanted to start painting now, for there were so many images to capture here. But he was tired. Sitting in the chair with his drink, he was mesmerized by the fire and its dying embers. He began a new train of thought, concentrating on the red hot coals, their texture, and unique form. He drifted off to sleep, painting a fresh picture of their life and death in his mind.

Sands awoke quickly, opening his eyes without difficulty. A few moments were needed to adjust his vision to the darkened room. The fire was out and the moon was high overhead in a starlit night. There was enough light for him to note the time: eleven forty-five. A flash of light had caught his eye. Was this why he had awakened? He wasn't sure. He turned his head and glanced out the window. A light had come on in a third-floor window of the building across the yard. Yellow light coated a thin window shade, yet Sands couldn't see shadows or movement. He twisted in his chair trying to stretch while contemplating his move to the water bed. He would go in a second, as soon as he found the energy. His eyes fluttered for a brief moment and they would have shut completely had it not been for a movement behind the yellow shade. Sands sat up with interest and stared at the window. A figure moved behind it, first coming into focus as it moved toward the window, then blurring as it walked away. Sands guessed it was the brother-in-law, coming to check on things and take care of the yard. It was about time, he thought.

The figure moved into focus again and seemed to stop directly in front of the window. Sands wondered what the person was trying to decide. For a second the figure didn't move, then bent forward and pulled the shade down a few inches. The figure let the shade go and it went flying upward, rolling itself tight as it went. Light poured out into the darkness of the backyard and Sands had to shake his head to make sure he wasn't asleep. The figure was a woman. She was tall; full of hips, but far from fat; curvy, meat on the bones, the way he liked, he could tell even from here—with an enormous shock of black hair worn '70s afro style. She was dressed in a black-lace teddy, practically see-through, as far as Sands could tell. A thin chain of gold adorned her neck, settling quite nicely into the valley of her upturned breasts. The woman wore a pair of black sunglasses set atop high cheekbones. Her face reminded Sands of some exotic African model he had seen in several fashion magazines. She was bending down, reaching for the window and with two thrusts, she pushed it up. Her hips moved to a syncopated beat, one Sands could feel even though he could not hear the music. She seemed so carefree and totally unaware that she was being watched. His heartbeat quickened.

The woman stuck her head out the window and into the night, inhaling the fresh, cool air. Her hair seemed to undulate and dangle over her face for a moment, but with a quick flip of her head she caused it to sail over her face, exposing her dark forehead for a brief instant. Sands looked on in disbelief as she bent over the windowsill and stared out. He could see her large breasts, forced between her elbows and the windowsill, straining sensuously against thin lace, trying to escape their confines. She looked up again, this time toward Sands, her dark sunglasses reflecting rays of stray moonlight.

For a brief moment, it seemed that she was staring straight through him. Then she stood up, closing the window and pulling down the shade in a quick motion. Her figure remained in front of the yellowing shade for a moment longer and then she was gone, her image fading out of focus as the light was extinguished.

2

David Sands awoke just after dawn; the morning sun rising into a blue-filled sky.

He stretched briefly, before settling back down into the confines of the water bed. Sands lay there, pausing to stare up at the skylights and the sky beyond. Since he had neglected to put up drapes the night before, the loft was too bright for him to be able to go back to sleep. His gaze swept around the room, taking in the white powder of burned-out coals, and next, the window and what lay beyond. His thoughts traveled back to the night before and to the mysterious woman he had spied on. Actually, he told himself, it wasn't spying; he just happened to glance out his window when she leaned out for a breath of fresh air. For all he knew, half of Park Place had witnessed the same event, and were lying in bed right now with a hard-on, fantasizing about the strange woman with the dark sunglasses.

God, she was beautiful. He'd have to pay more attention to that window in the future. This might be a nightly ritual with her, and Sands planned on being in the front row for the show!

Sands climbed out of bed, suddenly aware that he didn't have anything on. He was used to sleeping in the nude; he enjoyed the feeling of his body pressed against the warmth of the water-bed mattress, and was accustomed to sleeping in a room where the shades were drawn; of no possibility that anyone would see him.

He felt a sudden twitch of excitement.

What if she was sitting by the window right now with the curtains drawn, watching him?

What if she was spying on him the way he spied on her the night before?

Sands walked to the kitchen slowly, purposely avoiding the middle of the room, glancing toward the window every few seconds. His heart was pounding as he scanned the windows on the third floor. He stepped away from the dining room table purposefully, and stood in the center of the loft, his toes curling into the soft cushion of the rug.

His breathing was arrested.

He felt himself growing hard.

What if she was watching him right now?

Texture.

That's what intrigued Sands most about the building. Its face was rough or smooth depending on the angle of the sun, and when you viewed it.

Sunlight bounced off its vertical wall and window sills, creating a kaleidoscope of patterns. He would capture all of this in time, he promised himself as he dipped his brush rapidly between two trays of acrylic and oil paints. The square canvas was beginning to take shape—the building, as seen from his window, filling the whiteness. He was detailing the windows on the third floor, using a thin brush and charcoal to form an outline of a woman who was peering out from behind a curtain. In another window, he had begun to pencil in a second woman; this one stood squarely in the frame pushing up the glass. Details of their faces, forms, and dress (or lack thereof) would come later.

Perhaps all of the windows would be filled by nightfall, each one telling a story of a woman the painter had never met.

Dusk came quickly; Sands had spent most of the day in front of the canvas, neglecting everything but his painting. He paused at five to light a small fire, using cardboard and the cut-up remains of old crates he had used for moving. The fire hissed and crackled, sending an array of sparks up dark chimney walls. Warm light fell on his back as he worked, while sounds from an old Al Jarreau record filled the loft, causing him to smile with nostalgia. He remembered other nights like this one, spent in front of a nice warm fire with a woman friend, and Al crooning in the background as only he could.

Sands felt good. His painting was coming to life, and he liked it. Already, his mind was whirling with another scene, another collage of images that he couldn't wait to set down on canvas. This one was almost finished; by ten or eleven he figured it would be complete. That was important because he wanted to make sure he was still up around eleven-thirty. Hopefully, the mysterious "afro" lady—something out of an Erykah Badu video—the one with her hair worn wild—afro style—would reappear in front of her window, just as she had last night. Sands smiled. He might have spent the whole day painting, but his mind never strayed from the previous night and what was possibly in store for him tonight. There was no rational reason why she should show herself again tonight. What he had witnessed the night before was probably a one-time deal; at least that's the way it always turned out. It was too good to be true; and yet he felt that this time, things would be different. He didn't know why, but he knew she would show, just as beautifully and mysteriously as she had the previous night.

Nine, ten, eleven.

The hours came and went quietly without disturbance.

Sands retired his brush for the night, feeling quite satisfied with his latest work. It could use some more color; a touch of gold to the woman's lips, a splash of blue to soften the night-time scene, and finally, yellow, to bathe the windows with light. All these things would come later, perhaps even tomorrow.

He added more slabs of broken-up crates to the

fire, and settled down into the rattan chair with a glass of Jamaican rum to watch the flames as they came alive. He glanced at his watch. Eleven-thirty.

Soon now, he hoped.

At precisely midnight, his watch chimed the new day, and David Sands opened his eyes. The room had grown dark; the small burning mound giving off warm, flickering light in small doses.

Shadows of an occasional flare-up danced on the far wall behind the chair where Sands sat. He stood to stretch, and reached for his drink, focusing his attention out the window. The building was dark. No light spilled from any windows tonight. He went to his window and stood with his face pressed against the cold glass, searching for any sign of her. Unfortunately, he saw none.

One, two.

Hours passed effortlessly as Sands slept, opening his eyes only when he shifted to get comfortable in the chair.

By three he gave up trying, and drained the watery remains of the rum in one quick gulp. He climbed into the water bed, grateful for the warmth of the heater. Sands fell asleep quickly, failing to notice the single light that had come on across from him. A shapely woman stood behind the panes of glass, staring through dark sunglasses at the loft across from hers. She smiled to herself while extinguishing the lights, leaving the telescope on its tripod in front of the shade.

3

The brightness of a new day forced Sands out of bed at seven.

This time, however, he grabbed a large sheet from the front room and placed it over the windows, cutting down the light. He returned promptly to his water bed where he slept until noon!

An hour later, he showered and made some breakfast.

By two, he had straightened up the loft, and began the tedious process of hanging his works of art.

Mr. Whittaker stopped by for a short chat a little after three. He was preparing to take a stroll around the neighborhood, and wanted to know if Sands cared to join him. The painter declined, saying that he needed to hang all of his paintings before dark. Whittaker understood and stayed for a while, delaying his walk to look at Sands' art, and to shoot the breeze. At six, Sands lay down exhausted and famished. So, he decided to treat himself to some take-out Chinese food down on Vanderbilt Avenue.

For some reason Sands felt irritable. Actually, he had felt that way all day. He thought he was just overtired. Or, maybe it had something to do with last night. He pushed the thought out of his head. It was senseless to dwell on the woman. Sands had happened to be at the right place at the right time when she had appeared the night before last. It had nothing to do with him.

Nothing.

It was all an accident. Anyway, he was a grown-ass man; he needed to stop spending his days thinking about a woman he had seen only briefly one night. Sands had far more important things to do. Art projects were being lined up, and he planned on getting more involved in the community. He couldn't let himself get bogged down with enticing fantasies, no matter how tempting they might be.

Sands let the thought drain out of him while walking down Park Place to Vanderbilt Avenue. He reached the corner and immediately the smells of sweet and sour sauce intermixed with the aroma of fresh shrimp and stir-frying assaulted him.

He would forget the woman, he promised himself.

Afro-lady with designer sunglasses was history . . .

A new moon burned a hole in the dome of the sky, while a quick blur overhead signaled the end to a star's life. The fireplace was ablaze in warm light, sending dancing flickers of shadows around the loft. Sands lay on the thick off-white rug sipping a drink, his smooth face a pale blue from the reflection of the television. He pressed the buttons on the remote, scanning the channels for a movie or anything else of interest. The news dominated the airwaves at this time of night, and most of what was being reported was dull and depressing. Finally, he found something of interest on one of the local channels and he decided to give it a shot, at least until something better came on. During the long commercial breaks, Sands found himself staring out the window and to the dark building beyond. Every few moments he would glance at the window on the third floor before returning his attention to the TV. At eleven-thirty a talk show came on, and Sands settled back, prepared to watch that until he fell asleep.

At precisely eleven forty-five a single light came on in the building across from his. Sands' peripheral vision pickcd it up immediately; he stood quickly and went to the window. He stared at the third floor, his mind and pulse racing. It had to be her, he thought. Who else could it be?

Sands turned the television off, keeping his eyes glued to the lighted window. For a moment he saw nothing.

Then, he thought he could perceive shapes moving behind the yellow shade; a pulsating form, like the night before last.

He extinguished all the lights and used the metal poker to kick the coals around in the fireplace, decreasing the light emanating from the white-hot embers. He completed this task rather quickly, not wanting to miss any activity unfolding in front of him. David grabbed his drink and took a wild swig. The dark liquid spilled onto his cheek and ran down his shirt. He wiped it off and stared at the building.

God, he hoped he wouldn't be disappointed this time.

A dark form materialized in front of the shade, swimming in and out of focus. Then it became still, and Sands saw the outline of the woman.

For a moment, she stood perfectly still; then her hands went to the shade and pulled it up, allowing an unobstructed view of her body.

Sands let out a harried breath, instinctively moving away from the middle of the window to the side, where he would be out of her direct line of sight.

As on the first night, she wore a black-lace teddy, her eyes adorned with dark sunglasses. She reached for the window and opened it without effort. Her head jutted out into the night air and her oversized afro, like a pendulum, swept from side to side in time to her hips.

Sands squinted his eyes, trying to use his vision like a pair of binoculars to focus in on her smooth chocolate skin. His gaze followed the gold chain down into the valley of her breasts and David swore he caught a hint of a nipple as she stretched toward the moon high overhead. The woman seemed amused, for she continuously tipped her head from side to side and laughed, as if she knew someone was watching her. Sands found that she concentrated her stare in his direction. He stood still by the window as she went through her ritual dance. Finally, she closed the window and stood in front of the glass for a few seconds, facing his direction. The woman was smiling now, and Sands felt his eyes lock with hers.

He felt himself shudder.

A moment later she was gone. He stood by the long sheet of cold glass, straining to see into the room across from his, to catch even a fleeting glimpse of the woman. Yet, he saw no hint of movement or shadows.

But the light remained on and he felt compelled to stand there all night if he had to, until the bulb burned out.

A knock at the door broke his spell.

It was late.

David held his breath waiting for the second knock.

It came, momentarily.

He reached the door, silently putting his ear to the wood, listening for a clue. Soft breathing answered from behind the door. Sands turned toward the window and saw that the light was still on. He inhaled a breath before opening the door.

She was standing there, leaning against the woodwork, smiling.

Sands was speechless.

He stared at her unblinking for a moment, then swept his glance away, embarrassed. The woman wore a full-length black leather coat that went down to her knees. Her feet were adorned with black spike heels with no trace of nylons. She wore a black Bogey hat, which was tipped forward over her forehead, hiding her funky hair. Her right hand was gloved in soft black leather; it clutched her coat closed, level at her breasts. Her left, Sands noticed, dangled at her side, holding two crystalline wine stems gingerly between long fingers. He mumbled a low "hi," found himself staring at her features for an embarrassingly long second before standing aside for her to enter. She strode past him into the dimly lit room, and Sands remained where he stood by the door, savoring her strong intoxicating perfume. As he closed the door, she reached the center of the floor, stopped, and turned to him, waiting. He tried to speak, but nothing would come out, as if conversation would shatter the moment, and the fantasy. The woman stared into his eyes silently as a grin began forming on her full lips. She walked over to the water bed and placed the wine glasses on the headboard, testing the mattress with her ungloved hand. She smiled as it undulated like a serpent to her touch. She returned her stare to Sands, who stood in the center of the room, his hands at his side.

"I've been watching you," she said softly, and Sands smiled at the accent he could not place. In the near darkness, she had not removed her sunglasses. They rested on high sculpted cheekbones. Her face, now that he could see her up close, was beautiful, and Sands noted her strong ethnic features. He took a step toward her, his heart pounding hard against his chest wall with the fury of a caged animal.

"Funny, I've been watching you, too," he remarked. She was still clutching her coat and the hat hadn't come off yet. She was glancing around the room, carefully examining each one of his paintings with a critic's eye. "My name's David, by the way," he said, putting out his hand toward her. She accepted it, the flesh soft and warm, but she remained silent.

"You did all of these?" she asked.

Sands nodded silently.

She took a step toward him, dropping her right hand. The coat opened and a single blade of light reflected from the gold hanging at her neck. As Sands strained to see what she was wearing underneath, she grabbed her hat with a gloved hand and pulled it off, sending it spinning to the bed.

"Like my hair?" she asked, and Sands saw it was neatly cornrowed. He unconsciously looked out the window, remembering back to a moment ago, the Erykah Badu afro, swaying in the moonlight.

He didn't understand.

She saw this and laughed.

Her left hand reached into a deep pocket and pulled out a bottle of wine. She handed it to him and Sands felt the cold drops of ice water descending down the sides. He looked at the label as the woman threw her coat onto the rug. She stood there, in her black-lace teddy and heels, and gave Sands the most sensuous smile he had ever seen.

"Drink," she whispered; falling backwards onto the water bed. She reached for his hand silently, and pulled him down to her. He lay on top, the bottle at their sides, as her long fingers went to his

face. She stroked his cheek with a polished fingernail. David closed his eyes and kissed her neck. His
lips touched hers slightly, and for a brief second
they remained there, poised a millimeter apart.
Then she grabbed him from behind and closed
the narrow gap. Her tongue invaded his mouth
and he tasted her for the very first time. His mind
whirled—just what the hell was going on here? A
dream? Or a fantasy come true?—and yet, when
he touched her soft skin, he felt the flesh, instant
feedback and knew—this dream was real.

Her face appeared to have been dipped in oil.
He inhaled the sweet aroma, a mixture of fruit and
flowers like the incense bought on Fulton Street
from the Muslims. He licked her cheek. She groaned
softly. He licked her again. Her hand groped for the
bottle and brought it to his neck. He flinched
against the cold as she laughed. She opened the
bottle; Sands reached for the glasses. She poured
the sparkling liquid into his glass quickly, spilling
some on the bed. He shrugged his shoulders and
smiled while she filled hers. They toasted each
other silently, and took a sip, both groaning with
pleasure as the wine descended down their throats.
The woman sat up, and placed her glass on the
headboard. Sands, eyeing her silently, finished his
drink in one quick gulp.

"Easy, darling," she said, taking the glass from
him, and placing it alongside hers. She pushed him
onto the bed and made him lie back. He silently
obeyed; her gloved hand went to his stomach, sliding her hand up and down his taut muscles. She
reached underneath his belt and pulled out his

shirt. Using both hands, she grasped each side of his shirt and pulled it apart. The buttons popped away from the material with a low, machine-gun sound. She straddled him effortlessly, running her hands over his smooth, dark chest, her hips gyrating against his pelvis. She bent toward him, and kissed him hard on the lips. The gold chain left the cleft of her breasts and touched his chest. His hands went behind her head and felt her hair. It was neatly done, parallel tracks that ran between his fingers. He reached for her sunglasses, but she pulled away.

"Don't," she whispered, and he nodded solemnly. She moved off him and lay beside his body, unbuckling his belt. He pushed himself up off the bed as she grabbed his jeans and boxers, sliding them down his thighs. She threw them on the floor and grinned as he lay naked on the bed.

Black-gloved fingers wrapped around his penis as the other hand reached for the bottle of wine. Sands lay on the bed, his mind spinning as the woman massaged his growing member. She stroked him using long full strokes up and down. He grabbed at her breasts, but she pulled away, smiling. Sands didn't mind. The feeling of the soft leather against him was sheer heaven. He had never felt anything like it. When he was fully hard, she gave him a slight squeeze and put the chilled bottle to her moistened lips. She tilted her head back, filling her mouth with wine. Sands watched quietly, moaning whenever she squeezed his balls. She bent down toward his thighs and without warning let the cold liquid stream out of her mouth and splash over his hardened dick. Sands flinched in pain and tried to twist away, but the woman lowered her mouth down on him, and swallowed his entire length deep into her throat. He moaned with pleasure as she first licked the shiny drops of liquid off the sides of his shaft, then plunging his cock into her warm mouth, daring him to come. He grabbed her head and pushed her down onto him, staring up at the ceiling, eyes unfocused.

His hand reached for her breasts once more.

This time, she let Sands grab them.

She freed them from the confines of the silk and rubbed them across his chest. The nipples grew hard immediately, and the sweet-scented oil that adorned her body drew lines across him where her breasts touched his. He squeezed them gingerly, and it was her turn to moan with pleasure. Keeping a nipple between his fingers, he snaked one hand down her taut stomach to her thighs. Sands' fingers danced lightly over the silky material of her panties. Her hand met his and unhooked a clasp covering her mound. Sands rubbed lightly and she pushed her hips to meet his magic touch. He let his fingers rest on the outside of her moistened sex, teasing and tantalizing her. She thrust her hips to one side, then the other, begging him to enter her tunnel. He did so, finally; Sands heard her gasp sigh of relief. The woman increased the rhythm of her sucking, increasing the pressure as she felt him twitching in her mouth. She slowed down, not wanting him to come yet, yearning for him to fill her insides with his beautiful penis, wet with saliva and a touch of Spumante.

The woman rolled off of David silently, and sat at the edge of the bed, staring down at him. She drained the last of the wine from her glass and then stood up, legs apart, with her hands on curved hips. She remained there quietly, waiting for Sands to make a move.

"Take it off," he told her, the surge of authority that coursed through his veins making him tremble—propping himself up on one elbow as she began her sensuous undress. The camisole fell silently to the floor, and Sands swallowed hard as the warm firelight danced off her well-formed shape. Her rounded breasts were large, yet firm, and thick dark nipples poked up from chocolate skin. She moved toward him as he unrolled a condom onto himself. She mounted him slowly, using her already damp thighs to lube him up. For a moment, she poised herself straight over his stiff cock, letting the hardness of his thickened shaft slide between the crack of her ass and her thighs. Finally, when neither of them could stand it anymore, she thrust down upon him, feeling him open her up, as he plunged deep inside her cavern.

The woman rode him good; she squirmed on top as he held onto her breasts from below, lifting his buttocks off the bed to meet her slippery thrusts. Her head fell back as she rode him; her dark sunglasses pointed toward the ceiling, plastic frames and lens covered with a film of sweat and sweet scented oils. They worked each other good, locked into a wonderful bond of pleasure. They moved to the same beat, a syncopation of rhythm each one of them could feel. For Sands, the painter, he became someone outside of himself, this artist, existing for only one reason: to satisfy her. He could feel the passion rush through his loins. So he increased his rhythm, feeling the pressure building deep within the base of his sexuality. She felt it, too, pressing her hands down onto his chest hard, meeting his strokes with her own quick, full thrusts.

What was happening here?

Sands had no time to analyze his response—his mind was a spinning top, his body a frenzy of activity below—the woman gyrating and undulating above him as they crashed against one another. He held on, grasping the flesh of her breasts, pinching her nipples, watching her respond in delight, snaking his hands down her sides, feeling the fullness to her, the supple form of her curves, reaching back and sliding his hands down to her full heart-shaped ass, squeezing the cheeks as if they were fresh, sun-ripened melons. He could feel himself buried deep inside of her, and he marveled at this feeling, concentrated on it as she rode him, feeling his orgasm about to crest.

With a high-pitched scream the woman came moments later. She held him tightly as she unleashed her fury onto him; little bombs of pleasure exploding deliciously, one after another, with no break in between.

In seconds, he joined her, flooding a stream of warm milk that washed into the latex. She moaned with pleasure when he came, arcing her sharp fingernails across his chest, as the last of her orgasm began to ebb away. When it was truly over, she slid off him and lay by his side, removing the condom and squeezing the last of his creamy sap between long fingers. She curled up beside him and fell asleep almost instantly. Sands remained awake for a few moments more, stroking her braided locks; attempting to sort through the details of what just occurred, the . . . *insanity* of it all . . . while inhaling the fragrance of spent sensuality . . .

4

When dawn erupted, David Sands found himself alone.

He sat up disoriented, quickly searching the room for the afro-lady with the dark sunglasses. As images from the previous night crept into his mind, he got up and walked around the room, surveying the loft through groggy eyes. An empty bottle of wine lay in the trash can by the bed.

The wine glasses, however, were gone.

She had gone during the night without leaving a note.

His eyes scanned the building across the yard. The shades were drawn on all of the building's windows, the way they normally were. He sighed to himself.

Perhaps it had been all a dream, Sands mused. But he knew that wasn't true. She had visited him in the night, and they had made love. Sands never knew that a woman could make him feel that good. His first impulse was to grab his brush and easel

and paint a portrait of the woman who had mysteriously come into his life. Of course, that would
come later.

The first order of business was to find her. Sands
smiled to himself.

And he didn't even know her name . . .

Sands showered and dressed quickly. He was
eager to see the woman again. He wanted to talk
and make love again. He left the house, running
down the steps like a child, and headed for Prospect
Place where the dark house faced his.

Sands returned home an hour later, depressed.

The front of the house had been boarded up. It
appeared to be vacant. That was silly, he told himself. That couldn't be right. He had seen her in
the window. Twice, as a matter of fact!

Too many things didn't add up. He reached the
stoop of his brownstone as Mr. Whittaker was opening the front door.

"Hiya, Dave," Whittaker said, grinning through
yellow teeth. "Had some company last night, didn't
you?"

"What are you talking about?" Sands asked, not
in the mood to joke around.

"Oh, you know damn well what I'm talking about.
Practically knocked the plaster off of the freaking
ceiling! But, that's OK. If I were your age, I'd be
doing the same thing." He laughed hard, holding
his stomach with one hand. After he calmed down,
he stared at Sands and noticed his uneasiness.

"Something bothering you, Dave?"

"No, just a little tired, I guess. Didn't get much sleep last night, if you know what I mean." He managed a weak smile as Whittaker nodded his head in agreement.

"As long as it was worthwhile, then I guess it's all right."

"Yeah. Hey listen, Mr. Whittaker, you never finished telling me about the people who lived across the way from us."

"You mean the ones with the messy backyard?"

"Yeah." Sands took a seat on the stoop and Whittaker followed suit. The old man stared at the ground for a few seconds before tipping his head up and continuing his story.

"They were a young couple. A beautiful young woman from one of those Caribbean islands, which one, I couldn't tell you because it's been a while. Her name was Nona. She reminded me of a model, because of her exotic good looks. She was married to a hard-working boy named Malik. He worked in the city doing construction work. She stayed home and tended to the house and the chores. Well, Nona started venturing out of the house on a more frequent basis, and, at some point, became interested in art. She began spending the majority of her time down in the Village and SoHo. She hung out with the artsy crowd: painters, like you, and other artists. Her husband didn't like the idea, but he really couldn't keep a good eye on her, since he worked all day. The way I heard it, she would wait for him to leave, and then jump on the subway and head into the city." Whittaker paused before continuing.

"I guess the husband began to notice that things were changing."

"What do you mean?" Sands asked, genuinely interested.

"Nona was spending a great deal of time in the city. The house was not being kept the way Malik demanded. Chores weren't being completed. Malik assumed that his wife was having an affair." Mr. Whittaker stopped to take a deep breath before continuing. "You've got to understand those people." When Sands raised his eyebrows, Mr. Whittaker immediately continued. "I don't mean any disrespect—Malik, as I recall, was part Trinidadian, part West African—and many of the men there are insanely jealous; they want their women to stay home all day and take care of the little ones. It was actually quite tragic," Whittaker said and grew silent.

"What are you talking about?" Sands asked, the tension in his voice quite evident.

"He became psychotic. The straw that broke the camel's back was when he became convinced that she was sleeping with my tenant—can you believe that? The one I was telling you about—another painter, just like you! It really was pathetic. So sad."

"What!" Sands exclaimed, grabbing the old man by the shoulder. "What happened?"

"Malik figured that if another man had had his way with his wife, then she was somehow spoiled. If he couldn't make Nona into what he wanted her to be, then no man would ever set eyes on her again. I'm told it was a terrible thing. He cut off all of her hair, her trademark, believing that would make her undesirable. Then, he disfigured her beautiful face."

"Oh my God," Sands whispered, thinking back to the night before, not wanting to hear anymore, but knowing he needed to learn the rest.

"Yes, it was indeed horrible." Whittaker wiped the corner of his mouth with his sleeve. He shook his head morosely before hanging it low. In the ensuing silence Sands witnessed his eyes watering.

"She died then," Sands said. It was more statement than question.

"That's the most puzzling thing," Whittaker replied, raising his head to meet Sands' stare. "They found the hair, and I'm told other evidence, but they never found Nona's body. Some say Malik buried it somewhere safe where the cops wouldn't think to look for it. Others speculate that he hid her body in the walls of the house. I guess we'll never know."

Sands was rising now, using the old man's shoulder for support. He hobbled up the stone steps to the door slowly while Mr. Whittaker watched him in silence. When he reached for the brass handle Mr. Whittaker cleared his throat, and spoke to him in a low tone.

"Sorry to upset you, Dave, but you wanted to hear the details . . ."

His voice trailed off as Sands stumbled into the house, shutting the door quietly behind him.

5

Nona Scott-Walker sat in an oversized rocking chair and used the ball of her foot to rock slowly back and forth. She had been there for the last hour, staring into the space above a small color TV set. Her gaze was almost catatonic; she neither spoke nor moved. Occasionally, she turned her head to one side while running a hand through her long, unkempt hair. That's what she did when she was troubled, and deep in thought—she played with her hair—picked it out, then curled it about slender dark fingers, pressing it to her scalp, feeling it expand outward again, like a sponge, not held down . . . just like her . . .

Meanwhile, one talk show bled into another without notice. Nona was lost in thought.

What went wrong?

It was a simple question.

Why then so impossible to answer?

Things between her and Malik had gone steadily

downhill; lately, it had gone from bad to worse. How on earth had that happened?

Nona wiggled her toes, shifted her weight to get comfortable as she contemplated her situation.

Remembering the good times brought an arresting smile to her face. That time on the Staten Island ferry, two summers ago—seemingly a lifetime ago—2 a.m., a handful of people sequestered on the lower deck inside . . . yet she and Malik had ventured outside . . . her black party dress raised up by Malik's powerful hands . . . right then and there he took her from behind, holding her head between his palms, thrusting upwards and inside of her with fiery passion that excited her even to this day.

But where had those times gone?

What had changed?

Nona knew . . .

In the beginning, Malik had been this different person—caring, giving, attentive to her needs. But shortly after the marriage, things began to sour— her plans for going back to school at night were nixed—Malik didn't want her riding the subway after dark—too dangerous, he said, too many distractions for a beautiful black young woman like her.

Just what the hell did that mean?

Then she was laid off.

Financial difficulties never help an already strained marriage. She found a part-time job, but was forced to quit because of the hours—again, Malik didn't approve of her being out of the house after dark. So, she found another one—retail at the Fulton Mall . . . but that, too, didn't last long . . .

Neither did the next one . . .

Malik nixing every decision she made.

As if she were back in high school . . .

Nona brushed the thoughts away.

Instead, she chose to focus on a different subject—self-satisfaction, something she was fast becoming an expert in. Lately, Nona found herself constantly fantasizing about new ways to get off. In her mind, sex was like eating or drinking. It satisfied an urge she just could not deny. She found the subject creeping into her head at the weirdest times: at the supermarket in the middle of picking fresh lettuce, on the subway going uptown, and in the mornings when she got out of the shower and sat down at the long oak vanity to paint her nails and pick out her hair.

By nine, her frizzy hair had dried in clumps, yet Nona hadn't noticed. Her body was wrapped in a white terry cloth robe—Malik's—the kind that came down to the knees and was held together by a thick white belt. She was nude underneath, her body long since dry from her morning shower. Several times, Nona broke off her thoughts long enough to bury her nose into the folds of the robe, inhaling the scent of Malik's fresh cologne.

Nona stretched her legs and yawned. A TV commercial flashed on the screen inviting the viewer to switch from one fabric softener to another. The robe fell away from her as she moved in the chair, revealing long legs and strong thighs. She flicked her gaze down to the pubic hair that crept out from the confines of the robe. That thick patch of dark hair brought her back to the subject at hand.

Why is it, she thought, as she absent-mindedly fingered her pubes, that men can go running the streets, sticking their dicks into anything that moves without a care or a worry, and yet, when women do it, it was a different story?

Why, Nona mused, is it that most of my friends can't talk about sex without lowering their voices; and then only if there is no one else in the room?

God, what is wrong with everyone?

Am I so different, she wondered, because I derive joy, real joy, from getting off?

Are there other females out there who really enjoy a good hard fuck like me, or am I the only one?

Of course there are, Nona answered silently. But they are known as that . . .

Nona grabbed her pick, the one with the molded black fist for the handle off the vanity and ran it through her hair. She stared at herself in the mirror and smiled. Yeah, I'm decent looking, OK, more than decent, I know that, she told herself, but I'm not conceited about it. I keep those thoughts to myself. I share them with no one.

Men find me attractive.

I like that.

Nona put the pick down and grabbed the lapels of the robe, pulling them apart. She thrust her bare breasts out at the mirror, holding each one in hand. She winked seductively and laughed, watching her bosom hcave with each intake of breath.

Yes, she thought, men definitely find me attractive.

Just the other day, Nona was in the Washington Avenue A&P. It was early that day, warm and comfortable, one of those picture-perfect days that you hoped would never end. Nona wore a pair of cutoffs and one of Malik's tee shirts (no bra because, well, just because). She was in the beverage aisle selecting a six-pack of Coke when she heard someone clear their throat, so she turned around.

"Hi, I don't mean to be bold, but I've got a hundred dollars, and I'd really like to spend it on you." A white man, forties with good looks, carrying a carton of eggs and a half-gallon of milk in his hands, stared at her.

"Excuse me, but are you talking to me?" Nona asked and looked around in disbelief. She couldn't believe her ears.

"That's right, honey. What do you say?" His eyes flickered from her full breasts to her crotch.

Now I know my shorts are a little tight, Nona thought, *but where are your manners, for Christ's sake?* "First of all!" Nona exclaimed, placing a hand on her hip, "I'm not a whore, but if I were, I'd charge at least triple what you're offering me!"

"That can be arranged," he responded with a gleam in his eye.

"In your dreams!" she said and walked away.

Goddamn men!

There are ways to ask a girl for the coochie, and then there are ways!

Nona's fingers lightly brushed her pubic hair as she smiled. The funny thing is, I would have considered his proposal, given her current situation, she admitted, if only he had known how to ask . . .

Nona was painting her toenails and was in the process of switching feet when she glanced over to the right and noticed Malik's razor lying on its back. The twin blades' gleam seemed to focus all energy in her direction. She stared down at her crotch. A full bush covered her sex. She began to think about her pussy. Nona giggled with delight and said the word aloud. It's my pussy, and I can shout it from the rafters if I please . . .

Bet Malik's won't recognize it, Nona mused, *when I'm finished.*

She grabbed the razor and twirled it in her palm. Her heart began to increase its pumping; her face flushed as her breathing increased. Wiggling out of the robe, she sat up proud, her dark nipples erect and upturned as Nona profiled in front of the mirror. Her fingers went to her sex and rubbed the already-moist flesh, her thighs opening wider in response to her touch. Vaginal walls contracted around a finger, sucking it in. It felt good, awfully good, but the razor's gleam once again drew her attention away. Sliding out her finger with a sigh, Nona went to the bathroom, returning quickly with Malik's shaving cream. She did not waste any time lathering herself up. In fifteen minutes she had shaved herself clean—so smooth, like that of a baby's, except for the fleshy dark lips which hung impatiently, waiting for a man's—her man's—touch.

Nona felt alive, more alive than she had felt in months. She sponged herself off with warm water before covering her skin with baby oil. Satisfied, she stood up in front of the mirror and stared at the bare patch. It looked funny to her, since she was not used to seeing herself like that. At the same time, she felt incredibly sensual and beautiful. Malik's going to love this, she thought, flopping back down into the rocking chair. For the moment, her troubles were gone, evaporating into the brilliant sunshine.

With both legs up, dark slender fingers going to work, opening herself up; Nona brought herself from one fantastic orgasm to another.

Nona climbed the stairs slowly, savoring this new feeling between her legs. She had taken the subway to West 4th Street, the Village, in order to walk and get some shopping done. She always liked this area, its carefree atmosphere and laid-back lifestyle where anything was possible. Today she was feeling extra good. Taking purposeful strides, Nona stopped every so often to glance in a merchant's window. Here in the Village she saw everything in the reflection of sheer glass: sleek leather jackets and skirts, flowery ties and scarves, and electronics gadgets—some so high-tech, she didn't even know what they were for. Fast-food joints and eateries littered Broadway. Heading uptown, she stopped in front of the red brick and glass windows, inhaling the pleasant scent of fresh bread, croissants, and jams.

Malik had warned her about the Village once.

"It's full of fucking faggots," he had said one

evening in a rapid diatribe, his accent becoming more pronounced whenever he became angry; this after she mentioned to him that she wanted to go there.

"It's no place for a woman like you," he quipped, pitch rising, pointing a large finger in her direction. What on earth did that mean?

Something about the place had fascinated her from early on. Perhaps it had to do with the art galleries and studios that lined the meandering streets, with the thoroughfares weaving in a confusing maze that never ceased to amaze her. It was here in these streets that she would find herself walking for hours, scanning the gallery windows and studio foyers without purpose. Nona was no artist. Nor did she possess a creative spirit. But it still interested her nonetheless, and it grew to an intense fascination. Perhaps it was not the galleries at all, but rather that pleasurable feeling she got whenever she visited this place. She loved its streets, the way a soldier loves his country, and constantly looked forward to exploring its never-ending matrix.

Nona strode down a side street, past a vegetarian restaurant where the smell of pasta and pungent spices permeated the air. She was dressed casually today: a short, black leather skirt and black tee, matching pumps, and an oversized biker jacket that belonged to Malik. Resting atop high cheekbones was a pair of black sunglasses. She didn't wear nylons today. It excited her to walk down the street, passersby pausing in conversation to nod as she went by smiling. Little do they know that today I'm completely free . . .

Nona paused in front of a woman's boutique, admiring herself in the window's reflection. She arched her back and opened her legs a little wider, enjoying the rush of cool air that escaped from a sidewalk grate. I hope no one is watching, she reflected, as she rotated her hips, allowing better access to her inner thighs. Then again, I hope they are . . .

Nona had a beautiful face. She was endowed with the "exotic" looks that were so popular in the fashion magazines these days. Nona's rich chocolate skin, her high cheekbones, long, frizzy hair, almost bohemian in appearance—but in a seductive kind of way, along with her lengthy eyelashes and a seductive smile made her an eye opener everywhere she went. At twenty-eight, she was still young, and didn't possess the experience to deal with all of the attention that came her way. Sometimes she became overburdened when too much fuss was made over her looks. Nona had a kind of naiveté that drove men wild. She knew what their whispers were about, but most of the time she just smiled and played dumb.

Last summer, for example, she had been walking the streets of the Village on a hot August day when a photographer caught her in mid-stride on Bleecker Street. She had been wearing a vibrant yellow mini-skirt and matching heels. Nothing much to fuss at, she believed, but the photographer had thought differently. The next day, her face and outfit, along with the caption "Hot fun in the Summertime!" had adorned Page Six of the *New York Post*.

For a brief strand in time Nona became a celebrity around the neighborhood. Even the guys at Malik's job had paused in mid-sentence when they had seen that shot. Luckily for her, she faded from their minds as quickly as she had sprung up. Malik had not enjoyed having his wife spread out for all to awe over.

Nona crossed a narrow street to glance in the window of an antique shop. The storefront was littered with odds and ends; an ancient sewing machine made of heavy metal caught her eye, as did a round oak table with a base of dark mahogany. She passed this place quickly; she knew that she could become caught up browsing for hours if she was not careful. Her stomach was beginning to growl, signaling time to eat. A few blocks away were a bunch of good delis. Perhaps she would go for a hot pastrami on rye or a gyro from that Greek place down the street.

A left turn sent her down an equally narrow passageway that was unfamiliar. She loved exploring these side streets. Nona felt as though they were timeless. Looking upward, she marveled at the wrought-iron balconies that adorned many of the brick buildings. Lush ivy and strong vines the size of a man's forearm snaked their way up the

face of the structures. She fantasized about standing on one of those balconies on a moonlit night,
her gorgeous lover below, staring with lust-filled
eyes at her moist sex beneath colorful silk panties.
He grabs the vines with both hands and begins to
climb toward her, the muscles in his arms bulging
with each grasp of the cold metal. The swelling in
his pants brushing against leaves makes her re-
sound with excitement. Soon now, she whispers,
he'll be inside me.

An art gallery farther down the street captured
her attention. It was a narrow place, inconspicu-
ously sandwiched between a tavern called Pete's
Place and a for-lease building. She would have almost missed it if it had not been for a painting in
the window. It was a strange image. Nona couldn't
see all of it, because the glare from the sun was
blocking half of it from view. But, something about
it drew her near.

The painting took her breath away.

It was mesmerizing, like standing on a crowded
railway station and witnessing your twin, the one
you never knew existed, disembark, for the very
first time.

Nona stood still and didn't breathe. The street
was deserted, so no one spied her dazed confusion
in the shop door's reflection.

The portrait was of her.

Perhaps not exactly of her, but someone so similar in appearance that Nona thought it had to be
more than just coincidence.

The large picture hung alone in a six-foot square window. The painting itself was large, at least five feet tall by two feet wide. A beautiful woman, thick, chocolate, like her—stood amidst a background of a color mosaic. The colors seemed to flow from one geometric shape to another—blues, reds, greens, browns—and yet they were faded in comparison to the woman in the foreground. She had a thick bushy hair that spilled into the background geometry. In one gloved hand she held a small pillbox mirror, in which her facial features were captured. The woman's face was made up of soft lines, her arching eyebrows charcoaled, a touch of color on high cheekbones, and a sensuously curved mouth dressed in bright red lip gloss. What stunned Nona almost as much as seeing this woman's face was the outfit the painting's model wore. The woman was adorned with a red suit of exquisite leather. The jacket was open practically to her navel, held together by a single large button. Her breasts peeked out from either side of the lapels; curves of soft flesh tantalizing, teasing the viewer with a hint of dark, distended nipples. The skirt was equally sensuous: dangerously short with a slit in front rising three quarters.

Nona found the suit incredibly sexy.

Not only was it beautiful, but it made a bold statement about feminine sexuality.

The striking similarity between the picture's subject and Nona was unnerving. Was it just coincidence, or something more profound? Nona intended to find out.

6

Nona's entrance was announced by a bell that hung over the glass door. The gallery's interior was spacious and tastefully decorated. Contemporary images hung on walls skillfully lit by recessed track lighting. A number of marble and bronze statues took their spot in the center of the room, sharing space with a soft leather loveseat. A thin man with short blond hair and round frame glasses emerged from the back room, strolling over to Nona, whose back was to the storefront window.

"Holy cow!" the young man exclaimed, his hands forced into his pockets as if searching for change. "Don't tell me," he said, "I already know!" A bony hand escaped his pocket and wiped at his nose. His distant gaze and unsteady stance told Nona he was high.

"What?" she said.

"The painting, right?" he said, pointing the bony white finger past her toward the street. "Christ, I can see that!" Every word seemed to be forced out—as if under duress.

"Tell me about it and the artist," Nona asked, suddenly feeling extremely nervous.

"The artist?" the man replied, pointing toward the loveseat. "Why don't you sit down. And, can I get you some coffee or tea or something?" His hand went to his nose again, beads of sweat forming on his forehead from seemingly out of nowhere.

"Thanks, no. Just the painting, please."

"Sure." He sat down very slowly next to her and placed his hands flat on his lap. His face had a sullen look to it, a hollowness to the cheekbones and orbits around the eyes. His lips were thin and moist from constant licking. The man's shirt was of starched white cotton, plain and buttoned to the neck. His pants were more stylish: a shiny material, probably polyester, which blended blue and black stripes into an interesting expression of art. Black kung-fu slippers completed his attire.

"My name's Jai and I manage Cityscape Gallery." He paused briefly and snorted before continuing. "You have a striking resemblance to the painting in my window. Undoubtedly, this is why you are here."

"Ahhh . . . yeah, go on."

"All right. I acquired 'Red Leather Bitch' last week from a relatively unknown artist by the name of Brehan. I promised to give it some air time in return for, well, the details of such business arrangements are, I'm sure, no interest to you." He smiled briefly, showing perfect rows of yellowing teeth.

"Brehan," Nona repeated. "Where can I find him?"

"Are you interested in acquiring this piece?" His eyes flickered for a moment—a candle wavering, almost being blown out—Nona decided she disliked this shell of a man immensely.

"Perhaps, what is its price?"

"Eight thousand dollars."

Yellowing smile again.

Nona exhaled slowly, trying not to show her discomfort. Her mind was racing. Images of the painting flooded her brain.

"Perhaps, but only after I have spoken with its artist."

A quick pause.

"It can be arranged. Wait here." Jai rose, disappearing to the back of the gallery. He reappeared a few minutes later holding a folded piece of paper. Nona took the note and unfolded it, reading the inscription.

"Masquerade. Friday, July 19th. 6 p.m. What is this?"

"A gallery opening. Masquerade, three blocks west of here. Brehan will be there. So will the rest of his work."

Nona was standing by the door, staring at her likeness in the window.

Friday, July 19.

Six days from now.

"You sure Brehan will be there?"

"Definitely, he wouldn't miss it for the world." Jai snorted before continuing. "And judging by your interest in his painting, neither should you . . ."

* * *

Four blocks away on Broadway, Nona found a dark-skinned boy with a camera. He was young, no more than twelve, holding an old Polaroid camera and beckoning for onlookers to have their picture taken.

"Photos for a dollar," he yelled to passersby. Nona caught up with him and rummaged through her purse for some cash.

"I'll give you ten if you'll accompany me down the street."

"Ten dollars?" the boy asked, his eyes blinking.

"Ten dollars. Down the street. I need a photograph of something."

In her hand she held a crisp ten-dollar bill.

The young boy hesitated for only a moment. Silly woman, he thought as he snatched the money and pressed it into the folds of his jeans. Heading off with her, this dark woman with a 'fro, the boy was all smiles.

7

The sign above the window spelled out "Jake's Leather-N-Lace" in colorful neon. Nona glanced up and down the busy street on East 68th before going inside. A metal desk fan on the counter sputtered noisily, blowing racks of lingerie around on white hangers. An elderly man sat on a wooden stool behind the counter, hunched over a small color TV set. With the channel tuned to *The Price is Right*, the owner barely noticed Nona as she strolled over to the far wall, examining a rack of leather skirts.

"May I help you?" came a soft voice. Nona spun around, expecting a deeper sound. The man was standing in front of her and smiling, dressed in an old white tank top and a pair of baggy dark pants.

"Uh, I'm just looking," Nona answered, thinking to herself: *This is the ninth damn leather shop I've been to in the past three days. If I don't find that outfit soon, I'm going to go out of my mind!*

"Well, take your time," Jake, the proprietor said, rubbing his sweaty neck and sneaking a glance at Nona's curves. She wore faded Levis that fit her to a tee; a matching jeans jacket gathered at the waist with a thick black belt. Underneath, she wore nothing but a black-lace bra. She had seen the look in a French movie once and quickly mirrored the style. Of course, she got plenty of stares whenever she dressed like this. Then again, she got stares no matter what she was wearing.

"We've got some really good stuff this year," Jake said, smiling.

"Really?"

"Oh yes. Perhaps I could show you something in white?" His right hand held a flimsy teddy, barely large enough to contain a teenager. Nona laughed.

"I don't think so." She walked to the far end of the shop, her hand gliding against suede jackets and soft leather pants. This store had a good selection, both in leather attire and the more sensuous items like panties, nylons, and bras. She paused to admire the sexy outfits that hung on the shiny racks. Sexy thongs and g-strings, erotic hose, a few nasty adult toys under glass. *If I weren't looking for something in particular,* she reflected, *I could have a great time in here. Malik would cum in his pants at the sight of me in this stuff.*

"Do you fancy leather or lace, or is it both?" Nona again was fascinated with the softness in Jake's voice. She was staring at a black lace thong— wickedly nice. Her fingers absent-mindedly fingered the sheer material, her mind way off in the distance, in the midst of a delicious fantasy. She hadn't sensed his presence until he spoke.

"Oh, I'm sorry. I was thinking about something."

"Quite all right. I was just curious. Do you have a particular fancy for leather or lace? I can normally spot a woman's preference right off the bat. Comes with the territory, if you know what I mean." He crossed his arms in front of his chest and cocked his head to the side, as if studying a museum statue. "Now, I'd say you're a lace person. Yup, it's written all over your face. Bet this on it," Jake remarked, and reached for the hanger that held the thong Nona had eyed previously.

"Sorry, my weakness is for leather. I'd wear it always if I could afford to."

"Really?" Jake asked. Grinning widely, he pointed the edge of the hanger at her. His eyes never wavered as the metal slipped between the folds of her jacket and gently nudged them apart, exposing the black lace bra. His smile grew in intensity as Nona brushed the hanger away and turned on her heels toward the door.

"Miss! Wait! I didn't mean . . . Hey wait!"

Nona brushed past a rack of suede bikinis, almost knocking them over.

"Listen one minute. Hey miss!"

Nona stopped short of the door and spun around, glaring at the old man. Suddenly, all of the frustration of the last three days welled up inside of her and readied to burst forth. She felt like crying or hitting someone. This asshole was of no help to her. She knew that it would be no simple task to find the outfit shown in the painting. For all she knew, the red leather suit only existed in the mind of one talented painter named Brehan. However, she felt she had to at least try and find the thing. Nona had searched nine stores without success. This was the last one, so taking shit from some aging white man was the last straw.

Besides, this "thing"—searching for gear that may not exist—was getting out of hand. She had never obsessed over anything before.

What was happening to her?

What was she doing?

She would meet Brehan sans the outfit.

Thoughts of the inevitable made her feel better immediately, as if the pain had suddenly passed, and she could take a deep breath and sigh.

Nona stared at the old man and nodded.

"What?" she said simply.

"Look, I've been in this business thirty-three years. Seen all kinds, believe me. And if there's one thing I can spot, it's a connoisseur of fine erotica. Now come on, honey! Let's stop playing this game. You came here for something, I can tell. Let me help you find it. And if you don't see what you are looking for, then ask. Because you might be pleasantly surprised."

Finishing his sermon, Jake flapped his arms to his side and stood silently, waiting for Nona to digest his words and deliver her response. For a moment she said nothing. Then she reached into the breast pocket of her jacket and pulled out a photograph—a slightly bent-up Polaroid—and handed it nervously to him.

Studying the photo for a moment, lost in thought, the old man's thumb rubbing the Polaroid incessantly before he cracked a smile.

"Now we're cooking," he said with a gleam in his eye. "Now we're cooking with gas!"

Three days. That's what Jake had said.

It would take three days. He had seen the outfit. Oh *yes*, he could get it.

But it would take three days.

And it was gonna cost her . . .

Nona, deciding against the subway, took a cab to the East 68th Street store. She arrived at 10 a.m., racing out of the house shortly after Malik left for work. The store was empty this time of morning, save for Jake, who was huddled over the TV, just as before. He turned and grinned when Nona entered, and quickly shut the set off.

"Well, hello there! Today's Friday and I did promise you something, right?" He stuffed his hands into his baggy pants and frowned.

"You've got it, don't you?" Nona asked. A look of sudden panic came over her. She was in a hurry. Tonight was the gallery opening. She would meet Brehan tonight. It amused her to think that she didn't even know what she was going to say when she met him.

The previous week had become a blur. She cared for one thing, and one thing only.

Find the outfit and meet Brehan.

She didn't know why she was being propelled toward this meeting.

She only knew that it had to be done.

"I ran into a slight problem," she heard Jake say in his soft voice.

Nona's panic-stricken expression was replaced by a look of white fear.

"No!"

"Hey, just kidding." He grinned. "Don't you know how to take a joke, Miss? Wait here while I fetch it. You can use the dressing room in the back." Jake went off leaving Nona alone in the store. It took a moment for her heart to cease its racing.

She glanced around at the assortment of fine leather and sexy lace. Three days ago, she browsed the store, fingering the laces and feeling the cool leather, but not today. Nona needed to get the outfit and leave. She didn't like this place. Jake made her nervous. Actually, he scared her. Maybe it was the way he stared at her—his eyeballs rotating in white orb sockets as he smirked; his stare taking in every curve of her brown body. Other men did that, too, but it was somehow different with Jake. He wanted her; that much was obvious. But, she wasn't sure what he'd do if he got her alone . . .

Jake returned quickly, holding the leather suit on a wooden hanger covered in dark plastic. Nona quickly lost her train of thought when she saw it. She laughed lightly—nervous mirth as she shook her head slowly. At last—the search was over. Jake handed her the suit and gestured toward the dressing room.

"Try it on for size, Miss. You're gonna love it!"

Nona tore the plastic away like a child at Christmas, gasping when she saw the red leather. She touched it gingerly and sighed; it was incredibly soft; supple. The jacket was expertly tailored just the way she remembered it from the painting. She gently took the jacket off the hanger and marveled at the sleek skirt hanging underneath. Her fingernail traced the slit up the front of the skirt, imagining for a moment, the soft touch of her lover as his finger retraced her steps, stopping at the entrance to her moistened sex.

"Just what the doctor ordered, huh?" Jake asked. His eyes gleamed, but the look was lost on Nona. The suit was even more beautiful than what the painting had portrayed.

"Come on, come on! Try it on, will you?"

"All right!" Nona took the jacket and skirt and went into the shallow booth that Jake called a dressing room. A set of chestnut-stained saloon doors kept Jake's roaming eyes at bay. But just barely. The doors were three feet high, covering the area from her neck to her knees. Nona shrugged. It was better than nothing.

"Size nine, right?" she asked.

"Just like you asked," Jake responded.

Nona undressed quickly, throwing her jeans and blouse on the single hook. The jeans didn't stay and fell onto the floor. *Fuck it,* she thought. *If I bend down now, Jake will get the thrill of his life, and that's the last thing I need!*

The skirt slipped effortlessly over her calves and thighs, fitting absolutely perfectly. Nona had worn a pair of sheer nylons underneath her jeans and her favorite red pumps purposely for today. The heels went well with the skirt. She slipped on the jacket, but quickly took it off again when she saw the reflection in the mirror. Her white bra just didn't cut it. That would have to go if she was going to rock this outfit.

"Everything okay?" Jake asked, nuzzling up to the dressing room.

"Yes. Would you mind?"

"Sorry, just trying to help."

"Yeah," Nona quipped, under her breath. "I bet." Nona slipped off her bra and hung it on the hook. Her nipples became hard when she put the jacket on, savoring the feeling as the supple leather caressed her body. She closed the jacket with the single button and faced the mirror.

"Wow!" It was her only response.

"Come out. Let me see you."

Nona stood in the dressing room for a moment and studied her reflection in the mirror. She profiled, offering first her right, then left side for inspection. The verdict was in. She simply loved the suit. It was perfect. It was beautiful. And it was definitely *her.*

Nona stepped out of the dressing room and strolled to the center of the store like a model. Jake could do nothing but stand still and whistle. His catcalls added fuel to her fire. She thrust her head back and laughed, rocking her hips back and forth until it became a sensuous dance. Nona closed her eyes and spun around smiling.

She felt wonderful!

This outfit made her feel special; incredibly sexy. She spied Jake looking at her like a piece of succulent steak, just waiting to be devoured.

"What do you think?" she asked, gliding over to him. Jake looked her up and down, nodding in approval as he went.

"Fantastic. It's you, I swear! No one could wear it better!"

"Thanks, Jake, really. Thanks for this, and for everything. You did a rush job for me and I appreciate it." The glow that radiated from her face portrayed just how happy she was. Jake nodded and blushed, still staring at her. His eyes had settled on her breasts filling the jacket, swollen and half exposed by the open front. For a moment, his smile was stuck on his face, frozen, as if in time. Then it slowly disappeared, replaced by a new expression, one Nona knew only too well. It was unbridled obsession.

Frenzied lust.

Jake cleared his throat and said: "There is, of course, the matter of payment."

"Oh, don't worry, Jake," Nona replied, trying to contain the rising angst. "I've brought the money— five hundred dollars. Let me change, real quick, and we can settle up." Nona quickly turned toward the dressing room as Jake grabbed her forearm.

"Not yet," Jake said softly, while beads of perspiration meandered down his forehead. "You see, we've got a slight problem." His tongue emerged from between his lips and moistened them slowly.

Nona focused on this action, likening the act to the way a snake extends its forked tongue.

"What problem, Jake?" Nona asked cautiously.

"The problem of payment for services rendered." He smiled. Nona suddenly felt sick. "You know what I'm talking about, Miss. Five hundred dollars just ain't gonna cover this suit." His fingers reached for her lapel, but Nona recoiled—a cobra facing off against a mongoose.

"What are you talking about?" Nona exclaimed, voice rising, tears filling her eyes. "You told me five hundred dollars would cover it. Five hundred dollars! That's what you said!"

Nona's chest was heaving, Jake observed, and her oversized hair slumped against her dark forehead was damp with sweat.

"I'm sorry, Miss, but things have changed. The outfit was difficult to acquire—the price higher than originally quoted. Bottom line—if you want the suit, you'll pay the price." Jake's eyes had narrowed almost to slits.

"Goddamn you—you promised!" Nona shouted. "You're a goddamned snake, that's what you are!"

Jake just grinned.

"You're not the first one to make that accusation, but the fact still remains. This, my child, is business," he said softly, cracking a smile. "Pay the price or I'll sell it to someone else!"

For the first time Nona suddenly wished that her pussy was filled with sharp razors. She would tug on his skinny little dick with her hand, watching him swell until he couldn't stand it anymore.

Then she'd guide him into her box and clamp down on him when he shrieked, locking him in. She'd yell: "There, I've paid the fucking price!" as Jake lay there, blood squirting from a stump where his dick used to be . . .

The thought brought her mild comfort.

"You bastard! What's the new price?"

Nona already had an idea brewing, and was merely stalling for time. Her mind raced, looking for an opening, a clean solution—an easy way out. She wasn't going to fuck this old guy, that was for damn sure! He didn't turn her on in the slightest. Anyway, that had nothing to do with anything. Even if he had turned her on, it wouldn't make a bit of difference. She enjoyed turning men on, but she had never crossed that line and been unfaithful to her husband.

Nona was a prick teaser—that and nothing more. The thought of actually sleeping with another man frightened her. She could fantasize all day about fucking one, but when the situation turned real, Nona tightened up quick.

"What I want," Jake said, licking his lips once again, "is to bury my face between those long dark legs of yours and suck the sweet juice out of you until your entire body turns pale like me!" He paused, wiping the sweat from his brow and brushing the rising erection in his pants. "Then, after I fuck the living shit out of you, pardon the expression, the suit is yours . . . in fact, fuck me and the outfit is free!"

Nona stood motionless, fighting a rising urge to

beat this old man into unconsciousness. A whole micro-fantasy played out in her mind, where she bludgeoned the man to death while he clawed at her nipples. She derived a split-second of pleasure from imagining his skull cracking open; the thought of this cracker forced her blood to near boiling—another asshole white guy who had played the race card. At the end of the day, they were all the same—not looking beyond her midnight smooth skin to what lay beneath. Fuck what she's made of—all they're interested in is that black pussy. Wanna see if her black coochie is still pink inside . . .

The momentary reflection made her sick.

Nona cut this thought off abruptly. It didn't have to come to that. She cleared her head and thought about what was happening. Jake had something Nona desperately wanted. He knew how much she wanted the red leather outfit or he never would have pulled this stunt. On the other hand, Nona had something that Jake wanted just as badly. If only she could turn things around and play the same game Jake was playing, she'd get what she wanted without giving up the obvious. Nona let these thoughts mull around in her head for a minute. Jake was silent. He took her pondering to mean that she was giving his proposal serious consideration. *Good,* he thought. *She'll come around. She wants the outfit too bad to resist.*

Nona folded her arms across her chest, presenting Jake with a hard stare before softening it into a smile.

"Jake, I won't let you fuck me," she paused for effect, "But I'll give you one hell of a show you'll never forget. But only if you give me your word that the suit is mine."

Jake rolled his tongue. For the first time, he felt himself growing nervous, thinking he might have lost the upper hand.

"A show?" he asked, his voice almost a whisper.

"The best girlie show you've ever seen!" Nona bent forward slightly, exaggerating the fullness of her breasts. Jake took the bait, becoming mesmerized by the heave of her bosom when she exhaled. "Your word, you snake, or I'm out of here right now—history!"

"A show," he mumbled. "I don't know . . ."

Nona's finger hovered over the single button holding the jacket closed, circling around the way a helicopter does prior to landing. Jake's eyes followed her movement. She unbuttoned the jacket slowly, methodically, letting it hang open, exposing her hardened nipples.

"A show, Jake, all for you," she whispered. Her breasts were engorged . . . spilling towards him.

"All right, Goddamn it!"

"Your word," she said, covering her breasts with one hand.

"Yes! Shit! You have my word. You can have the suit!" Jake rubbed the bulge in his pants nervously.

"That's better," Nona said, suddenly enjoying the upper hand. Jake was now visibly uncomfortable. Nona was going to play with this prick, letting him know just how good of a bitch she could be.

Nona removed her hand from her breasts and peeled the jacket lapels apart.

"Now go close those shades and get your ass back here before I change my mind. And if you hurry, maybe I'll let you lick these," she teased, pinching the flesh of her mounds together. Jake moved like he was twenty years old again!

8

She backed into the dressing room, letting the swell from her bare tits draw Jake near. He would have followed her into the tight space had she not put up her hands at the entrance, forcing him to stay at arm's length. He pushed the doors completely open and propped his body in the doorway, filling its width. Nona had removed the jacket and leaned back against the cool glass. Jake was taken back by her dark body that glistened with sweat.

"Jesus," Jake gasped, "you're incredible!"

"Yeah? You think these are nice, wait 'til you see my shaved pussy." With the sound of the last word, Jake shuddered, touching the front of his pants nervously.

"Take it out, Jake baby. Let me see that snake!"

Jake hesitated, a look of fear spreading over his face. He hadn't expected this. Nona had looked so quiet—a submissive black girl, one whom he thought wouldn't question him or his motives.

Yet, she was different.

She had turned the tables on him, and a black girl at that! He found himself powerless to do anything about it. Now she wanted him to show her his thing!

His face flushed. She was moving too fast, things way out of control—*his* control. He felt ashamed.

"Come on. Jake, time's a wasting!" Nona chuckled and reached for his pants. She pulled the zipper down slowly and reached into his underwear. His member was swollen, but still limp. "Is this the best you can do?" she asked, cocking her head sideways and rubbing his dick between her fingers. "Jake, Jake, Jake . . ."

Nona peeled off the skirt, letting it fall to the floor. Her nylons came up to her waist and she wasn't wearing any panties. Jake gasped when he spied her shaved vagina held captive beneath the sheer nylon.

"That's right, Jake, check out this luscious pussy. How'd you like these lips wrapped around that dick of yours?" Nona laughed and grabbed his penis again. Jake pushed her hand away and replaced it with his own. His fingers wrapped around his shaft and began a rhythmic massage. He closed his eyes and exhaled slowly, reopening them as Nona began peeling the nylons down her thighs.

"Oh God!" Jake cried, his voice barely above a whisper, increasing the tempo of his hand job. Nona took Jake's other hand and placed it on her breast. For a moment, he left it motionless. Then, he grabbed her soft flesh and squeezed hard. Nona put a finger to her sex and slipped it inside. Jake groaned once and jerked himself mad. His hand was a blur—a frenzy of activity down there. Nona didn't care. He moaned again as a single glob of semen spurted out and ran down the leg of his trousers. He collapsed back, hanging onto one of the dressing room doors and panting like a sun-whipped dog. The entire episode had taken less than ninety seconds.

Nona dressed quickly, taking the suit and wrapping it in the torn plastic.

Jake remained where he was, speechless as his breathing took several moments to return to normal. His eyes were closed and his forehead was damp with sweat. Nona said nothing as she swept past him, grabbing the Polaroid off the counter, and leaving as fast as possible before Jake regained his strength to come after her. It took him a long time before he mustered the strength to even contemplate just that.

By that time, Nona was already home, the suit tucked away in an ancient grandmother's trunk that was sequestered in the attic underneath a pile of outdated clothes.

Jake finally reopened the store at half past twelve, returning to his stool and the small color television set behind the counter to wait for his next customer.

9

The hum of the engine, high-pitched and screaming as he downshifted to take a curve, excited
him. The roar of air was a dull inevitable throb in
his head; windows were cracked and the radio up
high, but details lost. David Sands concentrated
on the road, its slick tarmac glistening from a late-
night autumn shower, reflections of light spilling
over every crest, the city taking on a different kind
of glow—the kind he liked—the kind made for
driving.

F.D.R.—East Side Drive, midnight, Saturday.
The city was alive and Sands knew it. He could see
the pulse at every corner, every intersection. Felt
its rumble as the automobile-hum assaulted his
bloodstream, pumping adrenaline to every capil-
lary, synapses firing like a well-oiled engine. His
fingers tightened around the leather of the steering wheel, the veins in his dark hands bulging,
flexing; his breathing shallow. Heading toward
Brooklyn, the bridge on his left, standing majesti-

cally in the cool air, her arches well lit, beckoning drivers the way a lighthouse calls to ships. The fish market below the highway seemed to glide underneath him as he slipped the car into the left lane, bypassing his exit and heading for Battery Park.

Sands was a man of mixed emotions. In one sense, he felt energized—his new loft shaping up quite nicely. On the other: drained, emotionally spent; all wrung out from activities of the previous week.

The task of moving in was complete, but there still remained a few things left to do. Sands had tried to accomplish all of these before returning to work, but once he did, he found himself having a hard time concentrating. The images of the woman in the window haunted him, her addictive aura creeping into his thoughts at the strangest hours. None of it made sense—it didn't add up—one moment, a curious sight in a window she was—this exotic black beauty—an aberration that came to him as if in a dream— when the air and the rest of block was still—save for him and his breath that caught in his throat as he gazed across that seemingly endless expanse of backyard that separated them. The next moment she was his lover—her flesh pressed against his flesh—her sweat on his sweat, tongues intertwined as they moved against one another—harried, frenzied thrusts of unbridled passion.

And now?

Nothing but a boarded-up building. A home that hadn't been lived in . . . in years . . .

Didn't make sense . . .

Sands tried to block it out, especially after returning again to find the house abandoned.

Perhaps Mr. Whittaker was mistaken?

No.

What else to do?

Nothing.

Nothing to do but move on.

He couldn't continue on like a high school boy with a hard-on—distracted . . .

David Sands was a rational man. An adult with responsibilities. There were children in his elementary school art class to think about. Bringing out the creativity in youngsters took concentration and a devotion to the task at hand. There was no room for diversions, especially from a strange woman in a window.

So he had taken the car out tonight.

Gone out cruising.

The air would do him good. He needed a change in atmosphere. A change of pace.

Sands hadn't felt like being around people—so the local watering holes or doing a club uptown was out—didn't feel like dressing up, dealing with pretentious folks—the "beautiful people"—who held up walls with their backs and asses while talking shit about what they got or ain't got! Instead he followed the sparkling asphalt around the city, exploring its veins and arteries, hoping for something to distract him, perhaps finding someone to help him forget . . . *her* . . .

East Side gave way to West Side; the soft glow from the instrument dash providing comfort. It was as if he were flying solo in a tiny Piper aircraft, cruising at eight thousand feet, the cityscape lying before him like a giant doormat. It was a consoling thought. Sands turned up the volume on the CD player, Grover Washington Jr. blowing on his sax, hot jazz on a cool night, coaxing him to remember the good times: times spent with Lisa a few years back, crazy times when nothing made sense except for when they were together; when the darkness of night had given way to daybreak, and they had lain awake; this unforgettable song looping over and over again, the melodic drawl of the saxophone giving him the verve to slip inside of her one more time, fearful that this new day would be his last.

Freeway lighting, fierce and harsh, created strange patterns of light. Bold yellows illuminated the slick road, but beyond the edge, the colors faded into darkening shadows. Sands concentrated on the obscurity of darkness, edging the car toward the shoulder, seeing just how close he could get. Deepening shades of yellow gave way to browns and then black. It was as if the light had been stopped short, abruptly pulled back from the edge by an invisible hand. Overhead, Sands' attention was drawn by two bands of black separated by an injection of twinkling stars. He recognized the pattern immediately, remembering a painting of his own that used a similar stratification.

The painting was simple in design and implementation. Two bands of solid black surrounded a middle band depicting the face of a woman. The image detailed the middle of her exotic face: thin nose, fire-engine red lip gloss, and eyes covered by a sequined party mask. Thick cornrows could be

seen curling away from her forehead in perfect parallel bands. Although conservative in appearance,
the painting retold much more than it showed. For
Sands, the image released a flood of memories: a
hauntingly beautiful woman, silent behind her
mask, yet communicating more with her eyes and
body than words ever could.

New Jersey lay to the left, her villages and towns
twinkling. Sands hunched down in his seat, letting
the car propel him onward to an unknown destination. Suddenly he had a thought. Since he didn't
believe in cell phones—he abhorred those elec-
tronic things, and the constant tethering they im-
plied—he steered the car off the highway and
found a pay phone near Tenth Avenue. Rummaging through the glove compartment, he found his
address book and flipped through the worn pages
looking for Lisa's number. His watch informed
him it was now twelve thirty-five. He dialed the
number rapidly, his heartbeat pounding against
an already rising anxiety.

Two, three, four rings. He thought about the
song as he waited for her to answer—and the curves
of her wonderful flesh—following an imaginary
line from the space between her shoulder blades
down to the rise of her full ass—he liked to do that
as he lay on his side, pelvis pressed against her
thigh—trace her flesh with the tip of his fingernail—watching her twitch and move seductively.
He hung up on the fifth ring, slamming the phone
down on its cradle, cursing silently. Lisa did won-
ders for his foul mood. She knew just what to do!

Just what he liked—after a time, lovers did that for one another. Why, he wondered, wasn't she home?

Could it be another man? Someone else in her bed?

Of course it could—and the thought made Sands regretful for picking up the phone and dialing her in the first place.

Continue with the drive, he told himself, *don't think about her.*

Get back on the highway, and head uptown. To Times Square perhaps, the pomp and circumstance of the area, cleaned up by Giuliani, now looking more like Disneyland on steroids than what it used to be, a haven for pimps and pushers; big-tittied woman wearing two-sizes-too-tight skirts with slits up to their asses and fuck-me pumps.

But no more.

Now it was just harsh lights, everything to excess, digital camera-toting tourists, with their loud-ass children, meandering up and down the sidewalks, obstructing traffic to catch a glimpse of *GMA* being taped.

Hands gripping the steering wheel, he let the car accelerate to 70 before sighing heavily and taking it back down to 45. *Take it easy,* he told himself; *calm down, let the ride take you, draw your tension away.*

The anxiety was like the tides, ebbing and flowing in his chest wall.

His thoughts were on Lisa, a younger woman whom Sands had met at a teaching conference a while back. She was cerebral, into art, librarian looks—conservative—but killer body once the clothes came off! Lisa was the kind of woman who knew how to satisfy her man. And she very much enjoyed satisfying him.

Tonight I could just fold into her, he thought. *Fall into her familiar* . . . that's what he had loved about being with her, the way it just felt right when they were together—they rarely fought, gave each other their space, knew intuitively when enough was enough . . .

So what had gone wrong? Sands really didn't know. He knew he was partly to blame. He had let things slip—fall away, like sand in his palm—men did that too often; found the relationship firming up, stabilizing, taking shape—and they pulled back, lest their intentions be misunderstood.

Problem was, he could have settled down with Lisa—when he finally took the time to consider the possibilities, it was all there . . . in front of him—and the imagery scared him. By that time, Lisa had retreated, determined not to allow Sands to play with her emotions . . . so she made herself unavailable. Chase me, she was saying to him—come and sweep me off of my feet—if you truly want this.

But Sands hadn't gone after her.

Remembering her wire-frame glasses, the way she used her forefinger to push them up onto the bridge of her nose every few moments. The way she'd scrunch up her nose to get them to move without intervention, when her hands were not free. Her smile, as she unbuttoned her blouse, revealing her white-lace bra against flawless chocolate skin—transforming herself without words from a fourth-grade teacher to this unconventional siren—commanding him with her whisper-like voice, doing things to him that belied her demure exterior.

Tonight, I could fold into her, he thought. *Fall into her familiar.*

It wouldn't be right, though. He hadn't called her in well over three months. It had been just sex then when they reconnected—two or three late night dinners that were fronts for souped-up booty calls, a way to ease the damp loneliness of winter; then that stopped altogether—as if they both recognized that this new thing between them—friends with benefits, as the young kids called it nowadays—served no real purpose other than to keep them locked into this cycle, spinning, not moving forward, no progress, no evolution.

She didn't even have his new number. Probably would be shocked when she heard his voice. It didn't matter, though. Not now. Now, he'd do just about anything for a good woman, someone familiar, someone who knew him, what he liked, knew what he needed to ease the angst he carried like a cross.

Give it a few minutes, Sands decided; try her again then.

The stars had come out by one a.m., the veil of heavy moisture-laden clouds blown east toward the Atlantic. Sands found himself staring at the sky while he drove, concentrating on the patterns, identifying the constellations as he had done when he was a kid. He stopped several more times to phone Lisa; each time the all-too-familiar steady ring caused him to seethe. Finally, at ten minutes to two, he decided to call it quits, heading home to Brooklyn. A drink and a shower would do him good, help him unwind. Sands made it all the way to Flatbush Avenue and was turning left onto Park Place, when thoughts of Nona invaded his head. He tried to turn them off, squeeze the flow off like a faucet; he ached to forget the vacant building and all that it represented, but it did no good. Sands found himself slipping past his brownstone and turning the corner toward Prospect Place and the dark house facing his.

10

Nona was always at a loss for words when she stood in this place. The room featured a vaulted ceiling, a pair of lovely French doors that opened from the second-floor hallway, and a coat of fresh white paint that at times seemed overpowering. It was tastefully decorated with a white Italian leather sectional, a thick off-white throw rug, a polished aluminum and glass coffee table, and matching end tables. A Yamaha piano, bone white in color, was positioned against the far wall facing the window. On the walls hung a number of AA paintings—Romare Bearden, Monica Stewart, Charles Bibbs, a Gordon Parks original, and in the corner stood a full-size statue of a nude man with thick-hanging dreads, cast in ivory.

The house belonged to her down-the-street neighbor and good friend, Chantal, who lived alone. It was a large house for one person, but Chantal designed each room to convey a different emotion or subtle mood. The backyard reminded Nona of a section from the Brooklyn Botanic Gardens. Everything was manicured just so; the placement of the trees, bushes and flowers was choreographed to perfection, creating an ensemble of light, shade, and colors. Nona loved the place; she found peace whenever she was here.

The two had known each other for years and shared many secrets. Nona—although several years younger, and without the financial inheritance Chantal enjoyed—offered her a refreshing outlook on life with her carefree ways, and the sultry, tantalizing fantasies that she spun.

A light rain had begun to fall shortly after four. The disappearing sun cast an ominous haze upon the white room. The rain streaked the panes of glass, the steady drumming therapeutic. Nona strolled from the window to the center of the room; Chantal reclined in the V of the leather sectional clad in a FUBU sweatsuit, sock-covered feet resting comfortably on the coffee table as she followed her movements with quiet envy.

"Well, what do you think?" Nona asked, spinning on her heels to face her friend.

"Absolutely fantastic," Chantal replied. "Frankly, I'm jealous. I've always wished I had your figure."

"Oh, girl, stop that, you look fine," Nona said, knowing that the words weren't enough. She added, for good measure, "Besides, I wish I had your ass—ass for days, girl—and you know the fellas just love ass for days!" Nona laughed, feeling on top of the world. She just loved this new outfit. She maneuvered around the sofa, listening to her heels echo against the hardwood floor.

"It's tight—you're lucky to have found it," Chantal said.

"Yes," Nona responded, recognizing that look in Chantal's eyes. Perhaps it had been a mistake to come here, but she really didn't have much of a choice. In order to get out of the house and attend the gallery opening this evening, she had to lie to Malik, telling him that she and Chantal were going shopping and catch a movie afterwards. Her husband didn't suspect a thing—or so she prayed. Anyway, Friday was traditionally poker night with the fellas from the construction site. Nona would just get in the way of their boys-night-out language and behavior after a few too many Coronas. Besides, she had used Chantal for excuses so many times before that it had become second nature to her.

"What time does the party start?" Chantal asked.

"It's a gallery opening, not a party, and it starts at six." Nona shook her head imperceptibly and felt the tension spread. Maybe she should have invited her. Chantal knew about the painting and its painter, Brehan. She had to understand how important this meeting was to Nona. Nonetheless, Chantal seemed aggravated about something. Nona thought she needed to get out more, meet some decent men—any man for that matter.

"Hey, why don't you come with me? It's gonna be mad fun up in there."

"No, that's all right," she replied. "Don't wanna spoil your fun. You go and do your thang—knock 'em dead, sis." Chantal smiled weakly; Nona spotted her pain.

There were things Nona would never understand about her girl. She was a pretty woman, obviously well-off, in a better position than most people to enjoy some of life's more exciting pleasures, and yet Chantal never took advantage. She stayed in most of the time; top-floor home-office was where you'd find her most often, burning the midnight oil, working on her burgeoning clothing line, going out only occasionally when the mood suited her.

Her past and background were equally mysterious. Chantal didn't speak much about her parents or her upbringing. From past conversations Nona had been able to piece together details of a life with a South Carolina-bred father and her Georgia mother. They had met in dental school—Howard University, before moving to New York and getting married, starting a practice, somewhere along the line having babies. The house was her parents'—willed to her after they passed away. She had a brother somewhere, who collected exotic birds or some thing, but that was all Nona knew.

Nona sat beside Chantal, rubbing the supple leather absentmindedly between thumb and forefinger. She turned to her, patting her friend's thigh as she gave Chantal her full attention.

"I'm serious, girl—you need to come with me tonight. The more I think about it, we should have planned this from the beginning."

Chantal sat there, her back pressed into the sectional, eyeing her friend, remaining silent.

"It's a Friday night—and forgive me for saying this, but once again you have no plans—"

"Hold up—"

"Naw, let me finish," Nona quipped. "It's true—you haven't been out in a while—right?" A two-second pause. "I know, I know, you've been working hard, finishing up the line and all, but come on—this has more to do with ReyShawn than anything else."

"Trick, please! You know I'm not tripping over that nigga!" Chantal rose, went to the window where she paused to glance out at the streetlamp that had blinked on, bathing the rain-laden sidewalk with false light. "That fool's history—he's a has-been, you hear me?" she said, face inches from the cold glass.

"Listen," Nona began, volume lower, putting on her calming voice, "you know you're my girl and all—I'm just saying. You need to get out more—"

Chantal interrupted with a loud sigh.

"As I was saying, before being rudely interrupted . . ." Nona flashed a smile, then continued, "It's important that you move on—get out and meet someone new . . . and what better way than to head to a gallery opening—so much better than doing the tired-ass club scene—'cause that shit is played out!"

Chantal turned to face her friend. "I have moved on." Nona nodded but said nothing. "I *have*, Nona. Just because I don't feel like running the streets every single night doesn't mean that I'm sitting here alone lamenting over his ass."

"Oh, so you've been entertaining company?" Nona asked with a raised eyebrow.

Chantal blinked and smiled. "Well, yeah, I have. And check you out all up in my Kool-Aid!"

"He got a name, this playa?"

"He's rich, thick, and chocolate . . ." Chantal said in singsong.

"Who, bitch?"

"Jack, bee-yatch!"

"Jack who?"

"Jack Rabbit!"

"Oh please! You wearing the hell out of that thing—aren't you?" Nona asked, referring to Chantal's vibrator. "Your ass needs to invest in Duracell, as many batteries as you run through!"

"Don't hate!" Chantal retorted.

ReyShawn was an MBA student at Columbia. Chantal had met him six months ago at open mike in a black-owned spot on Flatbush Avenue called Chocolate Monkey, which she and Nona used to attend regularly—one of the few places that Malik allowed his wife to go because it was walking distance from their house—and because Chantal tagged along. He was interesting—quiet intelligence with this militant tongue that emerged whenever he was in front of the mike. ReyShawn was drawn to Chantal's eyewear—like him, she was bespectacled; her quiet style, and high-yellow skin. ReyShawn, himself, was dark-skinned, tall and lanky, like a ball player, except he couldn't twirl a basketball on his fingers or dunk a ball to save his life. Her struggle with her weight didn't seem to faze him in the slightest.

Everything in the beginning had been cool between them—wonderful, in fact. Chantal was happy again—for the moment anyway—except now that she once again had a man in her life, she constantly tripped off of her eating habits and her weight, knowing in her heart that what men really wanted most was a *thin* female—that shit about give me a woman with a big-butt and a smile be damned!—and it was only a matter of time before ReyShawn displayed his true colors and moved on. So she starved herself, spent four nights a week in the gym sweating her ass off, carried a gallon jug of water wherever she went, refusing to consume any carbs—the devil, as she came to call them—no bread, cereal, pasta, soup, sugar—except for the days that he wasn't in her bed, late at night when she'd binge on fat-free Oreos and ice cream. ReyShawn was supportive at first, telling her constantly that he dug her soft, spongy middle, making her laugh when he tickled her navel, encouraging her to wear belly shirts that showed off her curvy flesh.

"You a beautiful black sistah whom I like just the way you are," he'd tell her repeatedly, "A fine Nubian queen with an ass that would make any black man proud!" he'd add as he palmed her backside through tight Apple Bottoms jeans. But as time went on, he grew tired of her constant complaining, and her struggle, which seemed to point to a deeper issue.

He'd probe about her seeming obsession, and she'd shut down. Just that quick.

To him, their conversations, their activities, their very world began to revolve around her quest to lose twenty-five pounds!

Three months into the relationship, ReyShawn bailed. Actually, he never said a word—instead he just stopped calling, and showed up at the C-Monkey one night with a slender brunette—a white girl from his Economics of Strategic Behavior class. That was that.

Chantal got the hint.

That was two months ago.

"I appreciate you covering for me again," Nona said, purposely changing the subject.

"Don't worry, girl. Your tab is bursting and one of these days I'm gonna collect, that's for damn sure!" Chantal said this with a smirk, and Nona blinked, wondering how true her words actually were. She waved the thought away as she stood up.

"Whatever, Chantal—I've made up my mind, you're coming with me tonight—it's gonna be off the chain. You'll have fun, you'll see! Shit—you might even meet someone! So no backtalk from your ass, you hear me?"

Nona glanced at her watch—plenty of time for them to get ready. Anyway, one needed to arrive fashionably late. Didn't want to appear pressed . . .

This was New York City.

Who the hell arrived at anything on time these days?

11

The taxi dropped Nona and Chantal off in the Village in front of the gallery called Masquerade. The rain had stopped an hour ago, but the streets were still slick, reflecting reds and greens from taillights and traffic lights. They stood outside for a moment taking in their surroundings. White light from inside the building splayed outside onto the darkening ground. Nona checked herself in the window; glanced over at her friend who was clad in a pair of low rider jeans, sequined top, and tan boots, before heading in.

The place was crowded. Masquerade was larger than Cityscape gallery and its rooms convoluted around one another like a maze. Nona and Chantal brushed past hordes of people holding glasses of champagne and finger foods while smooth jazz enveloped them like a thick wool scarf. Most were fashionably dressed—an eclectic crowd: mostly white, some blacks, Latinos, and Asians; a whole clan of European men in Armani; their women, trendy in Dolce & Gabbana. Yet men and women alike turned as Nona walked past. "Red Leather Bitch" was hanging on a far wall, well lit from above by bright track lighting. She walked over to the painting with Chantal in tow, and spied Jai, the gallery manager, standing with a bunch of people. He stopped his conversation short when he spotted Nona. Excusing himself from the guests, he grabbed her by the arm and whistled.

"My God, look at you. I can't believe it," he remarked. Nona laughed.

"Jai—this here is my friend, Chantal. Chantal, Jai, from the other gallery." Jai eyed Chantal and nodded imperceptibly. "Do you think Brehan will be surprised?" she ventured.

"Shit, will he! Let's go find him right now!" Jai took her by the hand and led her through a mass of people and paintings down a darkened brick hallway to an equally large room. A crowd had assembled by a tall painting depicting a nude black woman on her back, hands to her breasts, legs splayed. Her charcoal skin blended into a background of earth tones, giving way to a starlit blue. Nona fell in love with the painting immediately.

"Brehan, there's someone I want you to meet," Jai announced, touching the shoulders of a man with his back to them. Nona felt a twinge of anxiety as the man paused an instant before turning around. A second passed and he was facing her. He was a good-looking man: close to six feet, butterscotch skin, chiseled jaw, clean shaven, and blue eyes surrounded by a pair of aristocratic-looking tortoiseshell frames. He wore his light brown hair in dreads that were pulled into a single bunch of locks that cascaded halfway down his back.

"Hello," Brehan said, voice soft, almost unsure, and smiled as the realization of who he was looking at set in. Standing next to him was a light-skinned woman with a shock of frizzy, bronze-colored hair. Her arm was loosely slung around Brehan's, but she tightened her grip soon after spotting Nona. Brehan disengaged himself and removed his glasses, staring at Nona for what seemed like a full minute.

He seemed to want to say something—he'd open his mouth, then change his mind, closing it quickly. Finally, after shaking his head in disbelief, he said one word: "Unreal." Turning to Jai, he asked, "Where on earth did you find her?"

"Actually, she found me. She was searching for you. Let me introduce you to—what did you say your name was?"

"Nona," she added, extending her hand, "I'm very pleased to meet you at last."

"Brehan. The pleasure is indeed all mine." Brehan took her hand and shook it gently, grasping it a little longer than custom would dictate. "This," he added, "this here is Angeliqué," gesturing to the woman beside him.

"Bonjour." She weaved her arm back through Brehan's and blinked at Nona.

"My friend, Chantal," Nona pronounced to Brehan and Angeliqué. The artist took her hand while Angeliqué merely nodded. Nona glanced at Angeliqué. She reminded her of Lisa Bonet, from *The Cosby Show*. Same bohemian look, same sexy-sultry features.

"I'm at a loss for words. Surely you've seen the painting?"

"Yes. It's wonderful."

"*New York Post*, last summer." Statement, not question.

Nona nodded solemnly.

"I still have the Page Six photo tacked up in my studio. Hope you don't mind me using you as inspiration."

"No, it's all good. It stunned me, when I saw it." Nona smiled as Angeliqué stared blankly at her.

"When I saw your photo something in me clicked. I'd wanted, for some time now, to emblazon on canvas what I felt was a departure from what people see in their minds when they think of the new millennium woman— I'm tired of looking at force-fed images of emaciated white women with blue eyes and blond hair brought to us by CNN! I know there are plenty of sensuous and exotic-looking women of color out there—but when I saw you— the curves, the high cheekbones, the smooth dark skin," he said, reaching out to stroke the flesh of her face; Nona blushing, and not rushing to shut down his action, as Jai nodded vigorously. "I knew I'd found what I wanted."

Nona gulped.

"This is so freaky, man!" Jai exclaimed. "Imagine my reaction when she came into Cityscape. I freaked right the hell out!"

"True."

A pair of black waiters came by holding trays of sushi and champagne. Angeliqué grabbed two glasses, handing Brehan one. Nona and Chantal each took a flute—Nona shook her head at the selection of hors d'oeuvres; Chantal, on the other hand, studied the tray, frowning as the waiter described each item—*hotategi*-scallop, *kani*-crab, *buri*-yellowtail, *masu*-trout, *tako*-octopus. Having not eaten in several hours and discovering that this was the only food being served tonight, she swiped a napkin off the tray and grabbed four pieces of raw fish, putting each one in her mouth and chewing slowly, glancing at Nona as if she were conducting a taste test. Brehan sipped his champagne slowly, dark eyes riveted to Nona's. She glanced away while smiling.

"Your name, Brehan," Nona said. "It is . . ." searching for the right words, "interesting . . . and unique."

He nodded. "It is an Ethiopian name, meaning light."

"Are you from Ethiopia?" Nona asked, taking a moment to gaze at his features—the piercing blue eyes set into a creamy butterscotch façade. The skin was smooth—unblemished—and she resisted the urge to touch him the way he had her moments ago.

"No," he answered, shaking his head, but venturing nothing further. Nona nodded, sipping at her champagne as her mind raced.

The woman beside him, Angeliqué, frowned, disengaging her arm from the artist. "Think I'll get some air," she announced to no one in particular. She moved away, her unkempt hair bouncing off her shoulders as she moved.

Brehan seemed to dismiss her without so much as a wave. His hand found the small of Nona's back instead, keeping it there for a moment, applying slight pressure to her torso.

"There's much we can speak about," he said to her, his stare locked with hers.

"Agreed," she responded, feeling her heart rate flutter. "I don't know where to begin," she added.

"Perhaps at the beginning?" Brehan asked, applying further pressure to her back; and suddenly, Nona was gliding away, as if skating on a sheet of clear blue-ice, Brehan steering her towards a hallway opposite the one Angeliqué had just taken, leaving Jai and Chantal standing alone.

The next three hours would be forever etched in Nona's mind, but at half speed—a cerebral, slow-motion DVD. She would later remember specific details, but not complete events. It was as if the rest of the evening was a gray slate, with bits and pieces of color splashed throughout.

Certain events became pinpoints of light, while others were unfocused and inaccessible.

One thing was ice clear. She had fallen in love with the evening and all that it offered.

Brehan was a doll: a true renaissance man: a gentleman, intellectual, and romantic who had captured her heart with his words, his thoughts, and his art. He propelled her from one painting to the next without intermission, giving her the slightest of summaries, just enough to tantalize, to tease, before moving on. Brehan was a talented artist, and extremely modest. Through his paintings, he had captured the raw essence of sensuality. Nona became fascinated with his style of expression— from his artwork to the way he explained his motivation or inspiration for painting them, using carefully picked words, in hushed tones.

Nona smiled while recalling him explaining his latest work, "The Act."

"To me," Brehan said to her while a small audience gathered around a painting of oversized phallic appendages and orifices awash with vibrant colors; an audience that seemed more impressed with the beautiful woman by his side than by his words, "this is at the crux of what I believe artists are trying to emphasize. 'The Act' signifies happiness, passion, and the spirit of eroticism conjoined in a wonderful bond of delicious pleasure!"

Brehan was an engaging host. Nona would forever remember his introductions of her to strangers as the inspiration behind "Red Leather Bitch." She would recall the never-ending flow of libations and hors d'oeuvres, good weed, and even a little cocaine (she tried one line.) She fell in love with the atmosphere and the people of Masquerade. She adored their conversations, their free-for-all politics, and their zest for life and all things beautiful. Nona didn't fully understand everything she saw or heard, but she was able to separate things into neat little boxes and decipher their meanings by association.

Nona received two gifts that evening:

One, a pencil drawing of her made on the back of a napkin by Brehan was extra special, because it was spontaneously produced, and like "Red Leather Bitch," pushed the exact right buttons within her.

The second was a kiss from the painter himself—they had shared a deep and lingering one before she left—and he had "captured it" with Nona's coral lip gloss on the back of the napkin used for her drawing; coral lip gloss that was smeared around the flesh of Brehan's soft sensuous lips . . . igniting, like a match struck, a feeling of scorching passion within Nona that shot out from her epicenter to her very extremities . . . like an explosion . . . never experienced before . . .

12

The cab dropped them off in front of Chantal's home at 1:30 a.m. They ran up the stairs and were ushered inside. All Nona could think about was Brehan and their evening together. He had asked her to model for him; Nona had reluctantly accepted, both excited by the thought of seeing the painter again, and frightened by unforeseen circumstances that could lead to her fantasies coming true. Brehan was like no one before him—and she desperately wanted to see him again. Yet, when she was back in the confines of familiar territory, Chantal's home, she wondered whether it was the artist himself that she craved, or the mystique surrounding his paintings, the whole artsy crowd, and the gallery atmosphere.

Chantal was playing the piano when Nona came downstairs from changing back into jeans and an oversized sweatshirt. Suddenly, Nona ached to be back in her own home again. She was fired up from the evening and was incredibly horny, and she knew Malik would be, too. A night of card playing, drinking beer, and shooting the shit with the fellas always did that to him. Nona needed Malik badly tonight. She was hot; her panties were wet; she wanted her man.

The card game was winding down when Nona returned home. Malik eyed her with disdain but said nothing, glaring at her as she walked by with the shopping bags left at Chantal's from the day before. She spoke briefly to Malik's friends before heading upstairs to the bedroom on the third floor. There she took a quick shower before climbing into bed, giving in to her tired body. Nona was thankful for the soft cool sheets surrounding her. Malik had left one of the windows ajar, allowing the night air to permeate the room with its soothing wind. The yellow drapes fluttered in the early-morning breeze and Nona watched them gyrate in the near darkness for a while. The building directly across from hers had its top-floor lights on, radiating harsh white light into the darkness. Nona sat up and could see a stranger moving about the room. Details were hard to decipher, but she could tell the stranger was a man, one whom she didn't recognize. Perhaps, he was one of Mr. Whittaker's sons. He had several boys in college, if her memory served her correctly. Mr. Whittaker was a super nice guy, but he seemed kind of lonely, for he was always talking to her from his garden. Nona spent a great deal of time outside sunning herself in the backyard, and it seemed that Mr. Whittaker was always there at the fence, scolding her to be careful and not take in too much sun.

Malik's entrance erased any thought of the stranger or Mr. Whittaker from her psyche. He had taken his shirt off at the doorway—and Nona found herself staring at his body. The light from the hallway illuminated his large chest and strong dark shoulders. Years of construction work had sculpted his muscles well. Regardless of what was going on between them, she felt desire stir in her loins.

Malik was a good-looking man. He wore his black hair short and brushed back, and sported a thin mustache. His contagious smile and well-sculpted face made him a favorite among Nona's lady friends. Nona did love her husband; but lately she wondered if she was still *in love* with the man she had married. Malik was a good provider, but his old-fashioned ways were creating a wedge between them. He still refused to allow Nona to work unless she could find a 9 to 5. They could use the extra money for sure. Even the sixteen-hundred dollars he collected each week came and went relatively quickly. He had softened his stance on her returning to school— Malik now allowed that—only though if her classes were held during the day. The worst part, however, was Malik's insane jealousy. Just the thought of men looking at his wife drove him crazy! He was extremely possessive of her. In public, he always kept her close by his side; usually his arm never left her waist; never allowing her to run off by herself unattended.

All in all, Malik was a good man, and he did love his wife. But something had changed—their relationship wasn't the same as it once was. And she had changed. She was no longer the confident, in-control woman she had once been.

Now she held her tongue. Better to let things lie, she figured, lest her husband really gets angry and loses control.

Her new M.O.

But how long could that last?

How long before things came to a head?

How long before things spiraled out of control?

Nona found herself wondering—is this all that's in store for me? Nona always saw her life panning out differently—college, a career, and a family down the road.

Perhaps in time all of that would still come.

They were still young.

Life was still unfolding . . .

Malik settled into bed facing away from her. The smell of beer and corn chips hung from his breath. She moved closer, allowing her legs to touch his. For a moment she remained there, neither talking, just limbs connecting before she moved in, wrapping herself around his frame. She hugged him, hoping that tonight he wouldn't push her away.

Malik turned, facing her. Nona kissed his lips softly, testing the waters. For a moment neither spoke.

"What are you doing?" he asked, his voice low, yet steady. There was no malice—and for that she was thankful.

"You are still my husband. And I am still your wife."

Silence.

Nona moved closer still.

"So tonight, Malik, we do what husbands and wives do."

He opened his mouth to speak, but her hand was there to stop him.

"No talk," she whispered.

Nona rolled over and spread her legs wide, beckoning him to enter.

"No foreplay?" Malik asked, amused.

Nona shook her head sadly. Instead, she took his hand, guiding him to her moistened sex.

Moments later, she was enveloping him with her sexual juices.

13

Sands brought his vehicle to a stop a few doors down from the abandoned house, cutting the engine. He sat still for a moment, listening to the night sounds. At the end of the block a pair of tomcats battled it out as their cries pierced the calm of the early morning. Otherwise, there were no sounds. Sands glanced up and down Prospect Place; all the buildings were dark, their occupants fast asleep.

He removed a flashlight from the glove compartment and grabbed the tire iron from the trunk. Quietly, he walked to the house, glancing up at the vacant windows to see if anyone was watching him. The stoop of the dark house ascended to the parlor floor with a boarded-up door at the top. Plywood-covered windows masked the face of the brownstone. Sands slowly climbed the stone stairs running his hand over the rusting banister. He reached the top and stepped into the dark shadows, once more glancing around to make sure he was not being watched. Satisfied, he turned back toward the door and began working on getting inside.

A large slab of wood had been nailed over the front door, presumably to keep homeless people and bums from making a sanctuary of this house. Sands ran his hand along the edge of wood, feeling for an indentation, a sign of weakness. Near the doorknob was a two-inch space where the wood had buckled from age and rain. Sands slipped the tire iron into this space, working carefully to ensure he had a good fit. With the iron in place, Sands worked it against the wood, feeling it give under his pressure. Soon, a space had widened enough for Sands to get at the brass lock freely. He slipped the iron between the lock and the door frame, and pushed against the iron with all of his weight. The door creaked for a moment and then gave way, the deadbolt ripping away from the door frame. Sands paused for a moment, wondering if anyone had heard the sound. He cupped the flashlight in his hand and peered through the space into the hallway. With his shoulder against the door, he pressed as quietly as possible, the door creaking against his weight. The space widened as the door bowed inward enough for Sands to edge inside.

Several minutes later, Sands stood in the center of the hallway, having closed the door against the slab of wood. Save for the flashlight beam arcing across the gray walls, the house was pitch black—the boarded-up windows not allowing any stray light to enter. He carefully examined his surroundings. Except for a thick layer of dust that covered the stairway and floors, the house seemed to be in good shape. Sands dug his shoe into the floor, drawing circles as if he were playing in the sand at the beach. Hardwood floors the color of honey were well preserved. A pair of French doors opened into a large room with a black marble fireplace. Sands walked around the room slowly, the flashlight beam illuminating the way. A large door with arc-shaped pieces of glass and beveled edges set in gray wood led to a back-room. Sands assumed it was the library, judging from the floor-to-ceiling bookshelves that lined the walls. Sands felt spooked in the dark house, the old floors creaking under his footsteps as he searched the second floor. The house was empty; no furniture or household belongings remained. All that survived was dust and loneliness.

Sands made his way down the staircase to the first floor. The worn wood squeaked with every step, making him self-conscious. At the bottom he paused for a moment, concentrating his energy on listening for noise. When he was still, the house was silent, but as soon as he began moving, the sound of his footsteps seemed to echo throughout the house.

Once in the kitchen, Sands shone his light near a porcelain sink, causing a pair of bugs to scurry for darkness. All that resided in the sink were strands of hair and dirt, and a bluish-green stain shaped like a teardrop. Sands quickly left the kitchen, finding no point in remaining.

Sands climbed the stairs again, consciously trying to stay to the very edge of the wood in order to make the least amount of noise. This time the des-

tination was the third floor. It was here that he
hoped to find some sign of her. It was from here
that Nona had first appeared to him that night,
thrusting up the sash; swaying her hips to a silent
beat.

Sands made his way up the stairs, allowing the
thin flashlight beam to guide the way. At the top of
the stairs he paused. A hallway ran the depth of
the house with a bathroom poised in the middle.
The master bedroom faced the back of the house,
while two smaller rooms faced the front. He peered
inside the two front rooms and quickly left, finding
them bare and depressing. Walking to the back of
the house, he stopped at the closed door to the
master bedroom. Taking a breath, he opened the
door and went inside.

Large, oversized drapes, white in color, almost
reaching to the floor, fluttered in the early morning breeze. Sands instinctively jumped back when
he saw the changing shapes, amoeba-like, angling
toward him. He splashed the light over the room,
arcing it about in a frenzy until finally satisfied that
he was alone. The room was large, but not bare. By the
two windows sat a lone rocking chair that creaked
slightly as it rocked back and forth, gently pushed by
an invisible hand of wind. To the side, scuffed with
age and misuse, was an old grandfather's chest
made of black vinyl. Along the wall was a recessed
walk-in closet with twin doors of painted blue oak.
He dragged one door open and peered inside. As
expected, it was empty. Sands shone the light on

the ceiling and along the floor, searching . . . for something. The interior of the closet went back about five feet to the right.

At the end of the closet a slab of wood had been sloppily nailed over what appeared to be a hole in the wall. Sands gazed at the wood for a moment, scratching his head in thought. He was tired—it was the dead of night. And yet, the possibility of learning something, anything about her, drew him onward. Seconds later he pulled the closet door shut and returned his inspection to the windows.

Sands shone the light on the floor and almost failed to notice a white telescope that lay fallen on its tripod. Beside the windows, it was nearly obscured by the fluttering drapes. Sands touched the cool metal, then picked the instrument up, and spread its black legs so that it would stand alone. Sands found it was awkward holding the flashlight in one hand and trying to manipulate the scope with the other. He finally succeeded in righting the scope, pointing it out the window at his building. Sands pulled up the chair and sat down, looking through the eyepiece and focusing. The lamp in his living room came into focus immediately. Sands smiled, thinking of Nona.

Sands sat back and stretched, allowing the chair to rock him for a moment. His thoughts went back to the grandfather's chest. He shone the flashlight on it, studying its exterior through tired eyes. What time was it anyway? His watch provided the answer: 3:45 a.m. Sands got up and stretched again, yawning as he walked over to the chest. He set the light down on the hardwood floor, shining it on the chest. He ran a hand over the brass buckle and unhooked the two fasteners holding it closed. Raising the cover, he grabbed the light and surveyed the insides.

The chest was filled with an assortment of magazines, notes, and memorabilia. Sands rummaged through the chest, removing the contents and spreading them carefully on the floor. There were photographs, black and white and color, which he placed in a pile to his left: photos of Nona and Malik, the house, the backyard, and sexy snapshots of Nona. Sands studied these carefully, spending a great deal of time on the photos of Nona. She looked beautiful in each of them, and Sands suddenly realized how much he wanted her.

The pictures displayed in front of Sands represented the life of a woman that he yearned to know— a woman whose images were burned into glossy Kodachrome; a warm, vivacious woman judging from the contagious smile and sensuous gaze in the photos. Sands felt the desire in him stir, more than words could express—for that smile, for the warmth, for passion she brought out in him.

Sands returned his stare to her eyes.

There was a sensuality that she expressed with her dark and exotic eyes; the way she held her hand on her waist and grinned at the camera on a snow-filled day. The photographs told a story of a life. He saw her grow and mature before his very eyes, changing like the seasons. Mood swings were captured here; the way she wore her hair, sometimes long and unkempt, and at other times braided like an African priestess—always beautiful beyond compare.

Sands picked up a bent Polaroid—a woman clad in a sexy red leather suit. He compared it to the others, marveled at its similarity, although he was convinced it was not of the same woman.

Other things in the chest—men's magazines, some adult DVDs, several Zane novels. He flipped through the magazine pages, pausing to admire the beautiful woman contained among them. Picking up another and quickly leafing through it, David noticed a passage had been underlined in black ink.

> *"His tongue caressed my skin like knife spreading butter, bathing my hard nipples with wetness till I screamed. I arched by head back and sighed heavily. 'Do it,' I moaned softly, grabbing his dark bald head in my hands. 'Fuck me with your fantastic tongue!'"*

Sands put the magazine down, acutely aware of the rising bulge in his pants. What else was in this chest?

Odds and ends: a napkin from a party, a pencil drawing of Nona on the front, an imprint of lipstick on the back. More freehand drawings on tattered, folded paper. More Polaroids; all of her. Sands glanced back in the chest and ran a hand along its insides. At the bottom, underneath a stack of magazines was a pair of silk panties. Turning them over in his palm, he stared at the lace fabric, shaking his head as he fingered the narrow crotch. His digits ran up and down its length slowly. The swelling in his pants caused him to recall the night they made love. Where was she? Sands desperately needed to know.

4:15 a.m. The wind had picked up, whipping the undulating whiteness around at the windows. The howl of the night echoed throughout the house. Sounds enveloped the room. Rising and falling pitch changes and soft wind songs created the illusion that Sands was not alone. For a moment, he put down the items from the chest and concentrated on just listening. He reminded himself that violence had erupted in this house, perhaps in this very room.

Sands shuddered momentarily.

A husband had beaten his wife.

Primal violence, by his own hand . . .

A woman cut, disfigured . . .

The thought made him sick.

Ghosts were out tonight, haunting him with their cries of grief and pain. Sands shivered as the air chilled his skin, his flesh welling up with goose bumps.

Try to wipe the thoughts from your mind. Focus on the night—that night she came to you. Remember that night—let it blossom in your brain until it consumes you—that incredible feeling while making love. More than just physical—something that invaded your soul, something you can't put your finger on, but can't let go of either.

Look at her, Sands told himself, *look at her photographs and remember that time.*

Sleep called to him. It tugged at his sleeve like a restless child, there at every turn, whispering to him hypnotically, seductively drawing him in like the woman in the window. Sands was feeling exhausted and was no match.

Sit down.

Catch your breath.

A second or two in the rocking chair; gather your strength before heading back to the car, home to bed.

The caress of the water bed—gentle and comforting.

Go, in just a second.

The allure of sleep, however, was overpowering. Sands drifted off effortlessly, the addictive wind songs enveloping him, rocking his worn body in the chair the way a mother hushes the cry of her newborn baby.

Cinematic blue.

Enthralling, affecting blue that reminds one of those rainy days with a lover, legs and arms intertwined amid lust-stained sheets.

Dark hair splayed over designer eyewear.

The rise and fall of soft dark flesh.

Disorientation.

The room seemed to spin on a vortex: tall columns of white that slowly changed shapes rhythmically. Sands dispelled the urge to leap up and scream. Instead, he lifted his head slowly, the room coming into focus only after intense concentration.

His back and sides ached.

The floor, long golden hardwood slabs, seemed so close. He reached out, touched them, blinked twice and sat up.

He had been on the floor for God knows how long. His aching muscles told him that he probably fell asleep there. Eyes blinking, he tried to remember the circumstances. His watch swam in and out of focus in front of his eyes. 8:22 a.m. Sands stood up, groaning in pain as he adjusted to the new equilibrium. Slowly, he shot a glance around the room. Save for the rocking chair by a pair of open windows, the room was empty.

The chest and its contents—gone!

But that can't be. They were right here.

Right there, next to me . . .

The pain began as a dull throb. Sands searched the room again thinking this must be a dream.

He went to the windows, peered out toward his home. A forceful sun burst in, temporarily blinding him. He pulled back into the sanctuary of blue, squinting to adjust his vision as she shook his head.

A reflection, a glimmer along the floor boards fixed his attention. Sands bent down, his fingers connecting with glossy plastic. He picked it up and held it inches from his face—a Polaroid—an image of Nona.

All that remained . . .

14

Nona opened her eyes to the sound of hammering. She got out of bed wrapping her body in a white sheet before going to the window, and peeking out from behind the yellow shade. The harshness of the sun caused her to squint, but she quickly became accustomed to the light. Several shirtless Mexican workmen on scaffolding were hammering and measuring windows on the building across from hers. The men were well tanned and Nona enjoyed watching their muscles flex. Mr. Whittaker, she recognized at once. He stood in the middle of the garden conversing with another man who was light-skinned, wearing sand-colored cargo shorts and a faded navy tee shirt. The man was a stranger to Nona. He continually pointed to the men on the top floor as he referred to a large blueprint that he kept under his arm. He must have been the man whom Nona had spotted several nights before. He carried a relatively thin build; but in good shape, no paunch, standing tall, well defined calves; Nona guessed his age at thirty or so, with dark hair worn closely cropped, and normal features, neither attractive nor ugly. He seemed very sure of himself, for he appeared to be supervising the workmen. What were they doing anyway? Putting in new windows? She didn't know.

Today was going to be another hot day. The past week had been fairly hectic in preparation for meeting Brehan at the gallery opening, and Nona planned on taking it easy today. Besides, she hadn't had a chance to fully analyze the entire evening's happenings—she felt a tingle between her legs that caused her to smile—partly from her husband last night, partly from meeting the painter in her dreams.

Sunning herself seemed like the best course of action. She had not spent a full day at home in a while. Besides, with the workmen around, she would have a little fun sunning herself; perhaps give them a little show.

Nona took a leisurely shower, washing away the remnants of the previous evening's lovemaking. She remained under the steaming water for a long time, thinking back to last night. She wondered whether Brehan was thinking about her, right now. Would he have forgotten her already? If that bitch Angeliqué had anything to say about it, Nona was sure he would have. No. Brehan wasn't like that. He seemed different—a man of his word. It was about the art with him—this was deeper than just pure physical attraction. He'd call her; Nona was sure of this. And she would be glad. Because Nona wanted to see him again.

Nona possessed an extensive collection of

bathing suits. Malik loved her in bikinis and sleek one-pieces—it being one of his most favorite things to do—buying her sexy swimsuits and lingerie. Her weight rarely fluctuated, so the ones she purchased two years ago still fit her like a glove. Nona searched through her drawer for the white skimpy one. This one was French cut, high-waisted with a thong back, displaying her ample heart-shaped ass. The top was equally skimpy, doing a less than adequate job of containing her breasts. The bikini was incredibly sexy and Nona loved wearing it, first because it allowed her to tan on virtually every part of her body, and second, and most importantly, because she got the most lust-filled stares when she donned it. Of course, Malik would kill her if he found out she was actually considering wearing it outside of the bedroom. But Malik wasn't home . . .

The lounge chair was already in her favorite spot when she got outside. Along with the latest issues of *Cosmopolitan, InStyle,* and *O* slung under her arm, Nona carried her black sunglasses atop her forehead. Ignoring the whistles and catcalls while spreading ample amounts of baby oil all over her body, Nona lay back and closed her eyes, feeling the stares caress her from every angle and saturate her to the bone.

Nona, with her radiant dark skin, didn't need to tan. Regardless, within a few hours, her deep rich blackness shone strikingly against the white nylon fabric of her bikini. She had heard the occasional catcalls and whistles from across the way. Nona responded with a smile, turning on her stomach, allowing the sun to caress her back, legs, and tight ass.

Nona nodded off from time to time, but always managed to awaken before too much time passed, before her skin burned. Generally after an hour of lying still, she got up and reached for the garden hose by the house. Turning it on full blast, she pointed the nozzle toward the sky and stood underneath the fallout. Screaming loudly, Nona shook her head wildly as the cold water met her skin. It took only a moment for the onslaught to soak her completely, but that instant brought her immense gratification. The only consequence to this action was the fact that her swim suit became almost completely transparent. The workmen across the yard eagerly applauded her hourly show; Malik, on the other hand, would hardly find it amusing.

Shortly after one, Nona awakened gently, conscious of the lack of hammering. She glanced up at the window from her lounge chair, placing a hand over her eyes and squinting until she became accustomed to the bright sunlight. The workers seemed to have quit for lunch or maybe even for the day. She lowered her gaze to ground level, noticing the stranger whom she had seen with Mr. Whittaker earlier. He was sitting in a plastic chair with his head tilted back, eyes closed. His bare chest was smooth and hairless. Nona's eye was drawn to his left nipple which was pierced. The ring of circle that cut into his flesh captured her attention. She was, for a moment, aroused. Then Nona glanced away.

She got up and stretched. The sun beat down hard, and Nona felt the urge for yet another spray from the hose. The water arced upward in a delicious kind of way before falling upon her like a sudden August rain, quenching her thirst. She tilted her head back and opened her mouth, sucking hungrily at the droplets of spray. Nona kneaded her hair, knowing that it was unkempt, like some nappy-headed child, yet she didn't care. This was her time—her moment in the sun! She felt good, glad to have stayed home—neglecting everything else, especially her chores; instead relaxing, using the time to gather her thoughts. A night of powerful lovemaking had primed her, revitalized her spirit. Nona was always at her best when she was good and satisfied.

The light-skinned stranger was sunning himself thirty yards away. Nona thought of Brehan, the artist, his piercing blue eyes, his dreads meandering down his back. She found herself wondering if *his* chest was pierced, too—wondered what he looked like naked and engorged. She shook her head as Angeliqué entered her mind's vision, ridding herself of that annoying thought. Nona's curiosity getting the best of her, she walked over to the fence that separated her yard from Whittaker's.

"Sun's gonna fry you . . ." she said, then continued once the man opened his eyes. "Your skin, that is, if you're not careful."

The man bowed his head, glancing down at his reddening chest.

"True," he replied, raising his arms to stretch before rising from the chair. Nona observed his biceps flex. "I guess I dozed off," he remarked. "Good thing you woke me."

"Yeah, you'll be hurting for days if you're not careful!"

He glanced down again, running a hand over his chest and stomach. He winced slightly and smiled.

"Damn, you're right. I didn't plan on dozing off. Guess I'm more exhausted than I thought," he said, walking over to the fence.

"Rough night?" Nona asked teasingly.

"Something like that!" He winked before continuing. "Naw. Actually, I'm in the process of moving." He paused a second before finishing. "Moving in."

"Guess that means we're gonna be neighbors!" Nona wiped her hand on her bikini bottoms before extending her hand. "Nona Scott-Walker."

"Michael Thompson. Pleasure to meet you." The man smiled and eagerly accepted her hand in his.

"Where you from?" Nona asked, leaning over the fence, placing her elbows on the warm metal. Her full breasts hung from thin straps attached to small patches of bikini nylon. Nona expected Michael's eyes to travel rapidly to her cleavage, but she found herself pleasantly surprised at his lack of attention. Instead, his eyes were locked onto hers.

"Born and raised in the ATL! Lived there all my

life, but several months ago I decided it was time for a change. You feel me?"

"Feel ya. Never been to Atlanta, but heard all kinds of things," she said.

He laughed, raising a hand to his near-bald head, rubbing his hair. His face was covered with a thin layer of stubble that Nona found appealing in a ruggedly handsome way.

"What have you heard?" he asked.

Nona grinned. "Well, for one, every brutha down there is on the down low!"

"Oh Lawd, here we go!" Michael exclaimed. "Ever since that freaking book came out, bruthas have had to defend their damn selves!" He pursed his lips, moved closer to the fence, leaning against it before grinning at Nona. "Truth be told—a big percentage of black males down there *are* on the down low. And you know what? It makes meeting women that much harder for a two-hundred percent heterosexual male like myself!"

Nona eyed him. "That why you moved up here? J.L. King messing up your groove?"

"You a trip! Naw—I came to NYC because of my art. The other stuff was secondary, though important."

Nona's stare narrowed. "You an artist?" she asked, her voice rising.

"Yeah," he said off-handedly. "Atlanta's cool, but the connections are here— the galleries, the museums, the business opportunities."

"An artist," she found herself repeating. Words that sent a shiver down Nona's spine. Thinking back to last night; thoughts of Brehan again, his soft, yet sensuous voice invading her psyche, the whole gallery scene gliding through her veins, infusing into her being until she was consumed.

"A painter actually." He smiled, noticing the intense expression on her face.

"Really?" Nona said. She proceeded to tell him about the gallery opening at Masquerade, and a talented young artist named Brehan whom she had just met. "It's weird, because I never paid the slightest bit of attention to art before. Now, I find myself intrigued . . ." She let the sentence hang, like her thoughts, which had yet to fuse into anything concrete.

The heat had caused Nona to sweat; beads of perspiration formed in her cleavage, sliding between her breasts. She resisted the urge to rub the oily flesh. "I think that's wonderful. I'm always impressed when a sistah shows an interest and appreciation in art."

Nona observed Michael as he spoke. She found him handsome in a nontraditional kind of way. He had an unsympathetic look to him—dark eyes, thin lips, ultra-short hair, until he smiled; then that, and his long eyelashes gave him an appealing edge. She stole a glance at his nipples—marveling at the curved piece of metal that bisected his left side. His body was toned . . . stomach flat, arms well defined—it was obvious he worked out— lived a healthy lifestyle. She was all for that.

The heat had affected Michael, too. He wiped his forehead with one hand; licked the salt from his lips. Nona watched him intensely, waiting for his composure to slip, for him to steal a glance at her tits. Men were wired like that—like dogs or something—they stared at women's breasts as sure as the sun rises. When an opportunity presented itself (and even when it did not) no man could resist a peek; in fact, she had grown so accustomed to men staring at her chest that it became a way of life—annoying as hell— but a fact of life. Deal with it!

So, why then, wasn't he looking?

Was he not attracted to her?

No, that wasn't it.

Men could care less about attraction when it came to tits and ass.

Maybe he wanted to seem polite at their first encounter.

Regardless, Nona found herself wondering why she was preoccupied with this particular train of thought. Why did she care whether Michael stared or not?

Nona wiped the sweat from between her breasts, allowing her fingers to linger in her valley a fraction longer than necessary. Michael, however, didn't take the bait. Instead, he pivoted his head toward the top-floor scaffolding before turning back around.

"How long have you been married?" he asked, eyes locked with hers.

The question caught Nona off guard. "What?"

He gestured to the ring on her left hand. "That *is* a wedding ring, I presume?" Nona detected a smirk, and pursed her own lips in response.

"Three years. You?"

Michael waggled the fingers of his left hand in front of her face. "No wedding ring," he announced.

"Doesn't mean shit," she retorted.

"To me it does," he fired back.

Nona nodded. "Touché. So, let me ask you something. Is there a 9-to-5 or do you just paint?"

"Actually, I've received a grant from the Brooklyn Museum to be an artist-in-residence for two years. My work will be exhibited there and at other spots around the city."

"Wow, look at you, blowing up and shit! Congrats!"

"Not Andy Warhol, yet . . . Katie Couric or Matt Lauer ain't blowing up my phone just yet . . ." he rejoined.

"Modest, I see. Look—I'm interested in seeing some of your work," Nona said with a smile.

"And I'm more than happy to show you. Perhaps you and your husband could swing by once I'm settled. The place is a real mess right now." Michael gestured upward. "Renovation and such . . . plus, most of my works are still in storage in Atlanta. But as soon as I settle in, I'll have the two of you over. Cool?"

"Cool," Nona replied, feeling a twinge of disappointment.

Nona glanced back at her house before straightening her top, stretching the nylon fabric over her oversized breasts. "Well Michael, I'm glad you're moving in. Seems like you're good people . . . like we have something in common besides lying out in the hot sun." She grinned. "Look forward to our continued conversations."

"For sure—and back at ya, Nona—you're cool peoples . . . I'm digging your style, Nona. Your free-style!"

Nona turned and waved to Michael, who stood for a few moments watching her sashay her ass in that flimsy G-string bikini of hers. She moved on a few yards before stopping, pivoting her bare feet on cool grass to face him again.

"Question," she asked.

"Shoot."

"That hurt?" she asked, point to the piercing with her finger.

"Yeah, at first," Michael responded, tugging lightly on the ring, distending his nipple as Nona watched, enthralled. "But sometimes pain can be a good thing—especially if it leads to a new level of passion. Feel me?"

"Yeah, dude," Nona said, nodding slowly, embracing his words and their deeper meaning, "feel you for *real . . .*"

15

Nona's cell rang later on that afternoon—a polyphonic rendition of Ciara's *Goodies*. She checked the Caller ID, saw it was Chantal, and flipped it open.

"What's good?" she answered.

"Red Leather Bitch!" she heard her friend exclaim.

"Excuse me? I know you didn't just call me a bitch, *bitch!*"

"Calm your ass, trick. You sitting down?" Chantal asked.

Nona glanced around. She was in her living room, flipping through a New York University catalog.

"Yeah, why?"

"'Cause your boy called . . ." Chantal let the weight of that sink in.

A pause.

"Who?" Nona asked.

"Painter-dude. Brehan. How quickly we forget."

Nona's heart rate spiked.

"You kidding, right? When? Why didn't you three-way me? Damn!" Nona was pacing the hardwood floor, glancing out the window at the backyard. Her new neighbor was nowhere to be seen.

" 'Cause I ain't nobody's secretary, that's why! And you best stop trippin' before I hang up on your ass!" Chantal laughed out loud.

"Okay. Okay. So, what did he say? Tell me . . . damn, tell me everything." Nona returned to the couch, the university catalog forgotten.

"Not much to tell you. He asked for you. I told him you weren't here, and was there a message? Homeboy said he enjoyed meeting you, and that he very much wanted to get you into his studio."

"Ah shit," Nona exclaimed, breathing heavy.

"What? You wanted him to call—well, he called."

"I know, Chantal, but I didn't expect him to call so soon. I mean, what happened to giving a girl two or three days between meeting her and calling?"

"Trick, please—you can't be serious! You wanted this man to call and now you're tripping over the fact that he did? Don't make no kind of sense to me!"

"Chantal, it's not that," Nona said, her voice growing quiet, "it's just, I'm scared, I guess . . . scared of where this whole thing might lead. You know?"

Nona rose, went to the window again, staring out at the expanse that separated her home from his . . .

Michael . . .

Her new neighbor . . .

Another painter . . . .

"Listen, Nona—I'm your friend—and I'm telling you that your ass needs to be careful. Malik is not the kind of man to fuck with. He's already over-the-top with jealousy when it comes to other guys simply *looking* in your direction. If he finds out you're modeling for painter-dude—he's gonna fucking kill you!"

A pregnant pause, followed by another. Nona sighed heavily before speaking. "I know, girl. Lord knows I know." She shook her head, and then glanced across the yard at the third floor windows covered by scaffolding. "I'm just so damn tired of having to ask permission for everything—that shit is played out, and it's not even me . . ." Nona reflected on her own words and then added, "Well, that *used* to not be me."

"So, what you gonna do?" Chantal asked.

"What would you do, given my situation?" Nona retorted.

"Girl, don't even get me started on your situation. 'Cause you know how I feel about that—your situation is whacked!"

Nona could just see Chantal shaking her head; could hear the sarcasm dripping from her voice. She began shaking her own head as well.

"I know, right? This shit is whacked out of control . . ."

Another pause, while both women composed their thoughts. It was Nona who spoke first.

"Chantal," she asked, "did painter-dude leave a number?"

"Of course, girl," Chantal replied, "you know I got you!"

A day later Nona found herself in one of those *designer* coffee shops, as she liked to call them, a trendy new spot between 6th and 7th Avenue, walking distance from Washington Square Park. At its core it was *just* a coffee shop, but with an upscale décor, earth-tone colors, low lighting, soft, comfortable lounge seating, free Wi-Fi access, premium salads, croissants, bagels, the works. A steady stream of patrons flowed through its doors while Nona sat against the window, latest copy of the *Village Voice* in her lap, a steaming mug of spiced apple Chai in her palm.

Nona glanced at her watch, trying to contain her rising anxiety. It was shortly after one p.m. She sipped at her Chai, glancing down at her attire—Diesel low-rider jeans, teal Kenneth Cole leather pumps, and a set of formfitting tank tops—inner, purple, outer, forest green. A pair of black sunglasses was on the sofa beside her.

Afro picked out nicely; shapely.

Makeup, minimal—eyeliner; lipstick—something new she was trying out called *Fetish*, a rich brown with copper shimmer. That was it.

Definitely not trying to look made up.

But wanting him to know she's not playing either.

He walked in at twelve past the hour. Washed-

out baggy jeans, white linen shirt, open halfway
down his chest, a black cord around his neck,
gleaming metal at its apex. Black open toe sandals.
His dreads were hanging free, thick whips of hair
swinging languidly behind him. iPhone in his hand,
his head bopping to a beat she could not hear. Blue
eyes found her effortlessly. He walked over, removed the earbuds as she stood, holding out her
hand. Brehan smiled, straight white teeth drawing
her in as he pressed a hug into her space, ignoring
her outstretched hand.

"It is good to see you again, Nona," he said
softly, eyes piercing hers with the intensity of their
purity.

"It is good to be seen again, Brehan. And to see
you as well."

He took a seat across from her, placing his
phone on the coffee table between them.

"What are you listening to?" she asked. "Saw you
bopping to something as you came in."

Brehan smiled while grasping his hair with both
hands. "My tastes are eclectic. You probably
haven't heard of the music I listen to—nothing
mainstream; nothing that you'd hear on Hot 97 or
KISS-FM!"

"Try me."

"Jimmy Cliff, Paul Hardcastle, Incubus, Jamiro-
quai, Haydn, John Mayer." He paused. Nona blinked.

"Okayyyyyyyyyyyyyy, you got me! I have heard of
Jimmy Cliff—but the others? Naw."

He smiled. "Radio has become so commercial-
ized, and much of what we listen to is the result of
what they want us to hear—like the images of our

people on television and the stuff we read in the papers—all filtered . . . all *processed*. I'm not trying to sound 'conspiracy' or anything like that—just stating a fact. Some of the best-made music will never be heard by the masses. Why? Because it doesn't fit into this nice little mold of what is mainstream." Brehan tilted his head back; let his dreads fall down his back. He flashed another smile. "Sorry, I'm not trying to school you . . . or get prophetic. I'm just passionate about this kind of thing."

"I see. And I love it! Do go on," Nona urged, her mind whispering, *School me, boy . . . School me for days . . .*

Brehan nodded and rose, moving to the sofa beside her. He picked up his phone, rubbing the gleaming thing between his thumb and forefinger. "Ever hear of Bob Baldwin?"

Nona shook her head.

"This guy is an amazing jazz pianist and composer. Worked with everyone from Herbie Hancock to George Benson and Roberta Flack. Take a listen to this—" he said as he worked the iPhone for a moment, finding what he was searching for and handing Nona the earbuds. "Because you won't hear this on radio—not anytime soon. But it's pure genius. The groove is . . ." He turned to her, scanning her cocoa-butter-smooth face as he searched for the right words, dropping his voice to a near whisper, "I don't know—passionate—if a melody can be passionate, then this is aural passion . . ."

Nona took a listen. Closed her eyes for a moment. Inhaled a whiff of his cologne as he sat back, shoulders brushing against hers—the scent of something she couldn't place—but it struck her almost as much as the music, this fragrance that evoked, along with the music, something strong yet soothing, black/white, yin/yang, darkness/light. Opening her eyes, she caught Brehan watching her. She was moving her head to the slow beat, nodding along with the passionate melody and this man that caused the pulse within her to spike— the music—infectious, like the artist's blue eyes and his engaging smile.

Returning the earbuds to him, Nona said, "I see I'm gonna need to be schooled." She said this with a gleam in her eye, and a seductive smile.

The moment was not lost at all on Brehan.

16

It was close to half past three when they left the coffee house. Nona and Brehan had sat side-by-side on the low couch, sipping coffee and Chai, conversing, sharing a Mediterranean salad and a still-warm baguette between them.

They made small talk at first: the gallery opening, his artwork, but then he shifted the conversation by asking a question that caught her off guard.

"Enough of me, Nona," he said, his shoulder brushing against hers as he forked the last of the Kalamata olives and red onions. "I'm trying to get to know *you*."

She nodded, enjoying the closeness, the warmth. "Tell me something that you've never shared with anyone else!" His eyes pierced through hers like a knife slicing through freshly baked bread.

Nona paused, taking a long sip of Chai. Brehan went to refresh their drinks, and she took the moment to watch him, his walk, a slow-motion groove whose rhythm she could *feel*; never in a hurry—not with his words nor with where he was going.

What to say? How do I truthfully answer the question that was posed to me? Should I say what's really on my mind?

And so, when he returned, sitting back down, handing her a fresh spiced apple Chai, fingers lingering over hers for a moment longer than necessary, she told him . . .

"It was a mistake to get married," she said softly, barely above a whisper. Nona said this without blinking, hands in her lap, stare locked onto his.

Brehan nodded, remaining silent.

She continued. And told him everything.

Brehan wasn't judgmental. He listened. Let her pour out this thing that had been locked away for far too long.

"I loved Malik when we first met—I was so tired of these men who thought that they could conquer you because of their looks, the car they drive, the amount of money in the bank. Especially black men—can I say that? I was so sick of bruthas stepping to me talking about how they were going to make me their queen!"

Brehan smiled. "Go on."

"Malik was different. He wasn't into material things. He was into spirituality, philosophy, culture, even though he'd never been to college—one of those people who is just intelligent, and can talk intelligently about things— I dug that!

"He's a hard worker. Works well with his hands! I used to love having him come over after a day on some construction site uptown, his jeans and work shirt tattered and worn, covered with white silt, his boots damp with mud. I'd make him remove all of his clothes at the door, and have him parade upstairs to the shower where I'd wash him down myself!" Nona smiled at the remembrance.

Ummmm . . . back in the day . . . those were carefree days . . .

"Back then, we grooved together, you know? Same beat . . . same drum. Our hopes, our dreams were in sync. I was fresh out of Bronx Community College when we met; was eager to apply to NYU— always wanted to go there . . . from the first time I stepped foot onto Washington Square Park soil—I was like, ohmygod, I so belong here!"

"What happened?"

Nona took a moment to sip at her tea and contemplate the answer to Brehan's question. What had happened? She mashed her lips together in thought.

"We got married. A way-too-quick rush to judgment, but it felt so right at the time. He seemed . . . I don't know . . . *perfect* isn't the word, but so very different than the guys I had dated previously. He and I connected, and I felt safe when I was with him. Does that make sense?"

Brehan nodded.

"But, at a fundamental level, we are, and always have been, two different people—with different ways of looking at things. If I had given our relationship time, I would have seen that early on— but I was in love . . . and nobody could tell me nothing!"

"And now?"

"Everything's changed. I'm no longer myself. I can't be. Because my husband won't let me."

"How so?"

"School, for example—he won't let me go back— uses the excuse that it's too dangerous for a woman to be traveling the subway alone after dark. I had a job—lost it—found another one, but the hours required that I work in the evenings. He flipped out. Made me quit after four days! At first I was rebellious, like 'negro, who the hell are you to tell me what to do?' But now, I just capitulate. It's easier that way. And far less stressful."

Nona drew silent. Sipping at her tea, Brehan watched her, his fingers steepled as he considered her words. After a moment, he said, "I'm sorry, Nona."

She rewarded him with a half-smile.

"What can I do?" he added.

Nona laughed.

"Something on your mind?"

"That's okay. It's best I keep my thoughts to myself."

She ran her palms flat against her thighs and down both legs, stretching out her chest in the process. Brehan's hand found her shoulder. Nona turned, watching his eyes that followed the curves of her torso. He wasn't shy with his eyes; not afraid to take in her features, her perky breasts, the outline of her nipples when pressed against cotton, and the cleft where her thighs met—yet he did this in a way that was non-threatening and non-sexist. Brehan didn't leer. He merely observed her.

His eyes made her feel special.

Desirable.

And beautiful.

Brehan took both of her hands in his. Her skin felt warm to the touch— rubbing the flesh of her palms with his thumbs, he could feel her begin to heat up.

"I want you with me, Nona, spending time in my studio. Helping me execute my vision. Assisting me in taking my art to another level." He let the weight of that sink in before continuing. "As an artist I'm known in this city—but what I need to do next is to take my show on the road. Expand. Let black people and white people alike see what I'm made of—what I'm capable of achieving as an artist."

Nona had no words.

"I know you're sitting there asking yourself, 'why me?' The answer is simple—because I believe in you—I see something in you that many do not—the passion, the *lust*, for lack of a better word—for a zesty life. You, Nona, are cut from the same cloth as me. I recognized this the moment I saw you. I could see it in your eyes. You are passionate about many things— am I right?"

Nona's stare was riveted to him as she nodded.

"It is not about me trying in a convoluted way to get with you. You are a beautiful woman, and I won't lie—I am attracted to both the physical and the passion in you that lies just below the surface. But I saw your wedding band when you came to Masquerade—and unlike many people out here today, I take the sanctity of marriage seriously. If you and your husband are meant to succeed as a couple, then I will not be the one to break you apart."

His eyes were clear. Nona stared into them, her own eyes panning over his smooth caramel skin, dreads draping down his back, linen shirt open wide, exposing his flesh—his well developed pecs; and Nona finding her breathing arrested as she considered his words, allowing them to flow inside of her, vibrating and colliding against her chest wall like protons and electrons.

"I don't know what to say," Nona responded after sighing heavily. "I'm flattered beyond words that you'd consider me—especially since you basically know nothing about me."

"I know enough. I know that I want to help you—and that you can help me as well."

"How? What can I do? I don't know the art world . . ."

"You have a way with people—you're personable, I can see that. And I detect a certain sense about you that I find refreshing—I can use that—I need to surround myself with people that can speak their mind—give honest, critical feedback regarding my work and its direction."

"Okay."

"You want to go back to school. Well, I have contacts at NYU. I can get you part-time work as a model—trust me, that won't be an issue. I might even be able to talk a friend of a friend into getting you a stipend for your studies."

"Ohmygod, Brehan, I don't know what to say!" Nona felt her dark face flush. Her cheeks were growing hot, so she pressed her palms against them, drawing away the heat.

"Do you have a computer?" Brehan asked.

"Ummmn, no. I don't have mail on my phone because I don't want my husband checking up on me."

Brehan held up a hand. "Not a problem. But you're gonna need one. Let me see what I can do. Okay," he said, glancing around, searching for a clock. "Brehan picked up his iPhone to check the time."

Nona smiled as she told him: "Five after three. I should be going as well."

She readied her things.

Brehan said, "I want you to do me a favor and think about the things we've discussed today. Please give them serious consideration, Nona. I meant everything I've said—I want you with me."

Nona stood. "I promise I will. How should I get in touch with you? I have a cell phone but I'm not sure if it's a good idea for me to be receiving calls—"

"You have my number, so call me in a day or two. In the meantime, I'm going to talk to people—get ready to swing into action once you give me the go-ahead. All right?" He flashed his smile and Nona knew that she was about to embark on a fresh new chapter in her life. The thought both frightened and excited her simultaneously.

He walked her to the door—holding it open as she stepped into the brilliant sunshine.

"One thing, if I may," she said, turning to face him once they were outdoors.

"Yes?"

"The woman with you at Masquerade—Angeliqué. I'm not trying to pry, but I don't want . . ." Nona searched for the right set of words, "our *relationship* to get in the way of anything you have with her. I just figured I'd mention it up front . . ."

"Understood. Angeliqué and I do have a relationship—but it's one that is not easily defined." He wiped a thick dread away from his forehead before continuing. "One thing you are going to learn about me is that I'm unconventional—my take on many things seems to challenge the basic premise of what we were taught, the way we were raised. I'm by no means a rebel. But I question things— why do things have to be a certain way? Is it simply because our fathers, mothers, and our forefathers and mothers did it that way? If so, then I find that unacceptable."

Nona was staring at him.

"I believe in a wide spectrum of alternatives when it comes to loving someone—most people see two extremes: dating and marriage, with little to nothing in between. I, on the other hand, see an infinite spectrum of possibilities, and it is these possibilities that excite me to my core—it's what drives me to paint—to create. You feel me?"

Nona nodded, pondering his words. She saw Brehan as an extremely complex creature. One that intrigued her, stimulating her mind as well as her body. She felt her nipples tense. Muscles in her loins began to contract as well.

"Yeah, Brehan, I feel you," she responded. "I really do."

They said their goodbyes with a hug; an embrace. Another kiss that lingered a bit longer than the one the night at Masquerade.

As Nona sat on the subway heading to Brooklyn there were a million thoughts running through her head. She felt excitement. Arousal. Angst.

Brehan was in her head.

So was Malik.

And Michael.

And Angeliqué. Her caramel face and unkempt hair kept returning to the forefront of her brain.

Nona knew that the artist's relationship with Angeliqué, whatever form it took, would spell trouble for her.

That was human nature.

Nona knew how women could be.

She had recognized that look in Angeliqués eyes.

She would have to tread carefully, if and when she decided to give this *thing* a go . . .

And she would give it a go.

She'd be crazy not to.

Regardless of what her husband said.

She was going to do this—because it felt right.

Brehan was right—there *was* passion within her, lying just below the surface.

Nona grinned wide.

Passion about to be unleashed . . .

17

Emerald eyes.
Steady and focused, blinking occasionally—the only indication that it was alive. Scanning the room—head unmoving, but those brilliant, unreal eyes missing nothing, switching from left to right like a digital circuit running at one gigahertz. The bell rang, and the head finally moved toward the door; soft green feathers ruffling at the nape of the neck.

Chantal peered through the small pane and frowned. A man stood on the other side patiently waiting for her to open the door. She cracked the door a few inches, sticking her nose out into the morning air.

"Can I help you?" she asked cautiously, pressing her left foot against the heavy wooden door.

"Yes, hello, my name is David Sands," he responded with a smile. "I live the next block over from you on Park Place." Chantal nodded silently. She had recognized him as soon as she had spotted him through the glass. Sands continued: "I was wondering if I might have a word with you."

"Is something wrong?" she asked in a hesitant tone, thinking to herself, what the hell could he want with me?

"No, I just wanted to talk with you regarding a mutual friend. It's very important that I speak with you." Chantal saw the pleading in his eyes, which confused her even more.

"What mutual friend are you referring to, Mr. Sands? I don't even know you." The door remained cracked, Chantal making no move to open it further. Sands was losing patience, but tried to remain calm and keep his composure. He spotted her searching his face for clues—and part of him couldn't blame her—he was a total stranger to her. On the other hand—the past week had been a nightmare—searching aimlessly for a seductress who may not even exist, a woman who may have died years ago.

He found himself wanting to push the door down, barge inside, squeezing answers out of her as if she were an overripe banana in the hands of a hungry gorilla—but that wouldn't solve anything.

"Nona," he said finally, exhaling slowly and dropping his stare to the ground.

"Come in," Chantal said, stepping aside, amazed at the speed with which she ushered him inside her home.

Sands, following Chantal through the hallway into the large parlor, marveled at the decor. A beau-

tiful exotic bird sat in a huge cage by the window,
following Sands as he traversed the room around
the white piano to the sofa. He sat down on the
plush leather, admiring the prints and statues that
decorated the place. The woman had taste, Sands
had to admit. She had money, too, that much was
obvious.

"Nona," Chantal repeated slowly. "Now that's a
name I haven't spoken in a long, long time."

"The two of you were friends," Sands mentioned,
making a statement more than asking a question.
Chantal looked at Sands silently. "Friends," he repeated, watching the bird by the window.

"Tea, coffee?" Chantal asked suddenly. Sands
shook his head politely.

"That's a beautiful bird you have," he remarked.

"Yes he is. He's a rare Hispaniolan from the
Amazon. My brother's an avid bird collector and
obtained him for me while on expedition in Brazil
several years ago."

"A collector, you say? That must be interesting
stuff. Is he serious about it?"

"Yes, quite. He collects all kinds of exotic birds
and raises them not far from here. It's a very lucra-
tive business. People are willing to pay top dollar
for exotic animals."

"I'm sure. Anyway, if we could get back to
Nona . . ."

"How do you know her?" Chantal asked.

Sands paused to consider her question. Considered lying outright, but thought better of it. "We
met . . . briefly." Half-truth.

Chantal eyed him. "She never mentioned you to me, and I'm certain she told me about all of her friends."

Sands nodded. "Well, I'm not sure what to say." He took a breath and said, "I was hoping you might be able to shed some light on the circumstances surrounding her death."

"Her death?"

"Yes. I understand she died several years ago. Isn't that correct?" Sands' stare was locked with Chantal's.

"I'm sorry," she said, "but what exactly is your relationship to her?"

"Forgive me," Sands responded, "I know how painful this must be for you, but I really need some answers."

"Answers to what?" Chantal asked, sitting up straight.

"I . . . don't know how to explain this," he said, fidgeting with his hands like a child.

"Try, because otherwise I can't help you."

"Well," Sands began, "I need to know what really happened to Nona," he said, wiping a hand across his sweaty forehead, "because . . . I . . . something transpired between us—something special—something that doesn't make sense given what happened to her—I need to understand exactly what occurred—I need to know the details." Chantal was silent for a moment. She looked to the bird silhouetted in front of a dazzling sun, then back at Sands.

"You talk in terms of the present as if you just lost her." Sands hesitated.

"I have," he said.

"But that can't be, Mr. Sands."

"Can't it?" he asked, staring straight at her and letting the question dangle like a rope.

Chantal shook her head in disbelief.

Sands was saying: "I know this is hard to fathom, trust me, I understand that. All I know is that I just spent several evenings admiring a very beautiful ghost."

"Just what in God's name are you talking about? You come into my house, attempting to pry information from me about my best friend, and now you tell me that you're having an affair with a married woman, one who allegedly died several years ago? Come on, Mr. Sands! What do you take me for?"

"Wait . . ."

"No, you wait. You're obviously a very sick man. I think you need to seek professional help. I'm sorry, but I can't help you."

"Listen, hear me out! I'm not asking you to explain what has happened. You don't know me—you think I'm crazy—you think I'm nuts—okay, I accept that. But I tell you, I'm as sane as you or anyone else. All I know is that several weeks ago I fell for a beautiful woman, and I need to find her. Call me crazy, but I know what I saw. I know what I felt."

Chantal stood up abruptly and went to the window.

"Just what did you see, Mr. Sands?" Chantal asked, turning to face him.

"I saw a beautiful young woman from my window. She was in her house, down the street," he said, pointing. "Third floor. I saw her, as sure as I'm standing here looking at you now."

"Impossible, that house is vacant. Besides . . ."

"Then she came to me. My apartment." Sands stood. "She was standing in my living room. Talking to me, no further than you are standing from me now." Sands wiped the sweat from his forehead and frowned.

"A dream," Chantal countered. "Very real and explicit, but nonetheless a dream," Chantal shot back, pointing a finger in Sands' direction.

"We made love," he whispered. "Did I imagine that?" Sands shook his head. "I doubt it. A man does not imagine making love to a woman the way we made love to each other. No, not like that. I know what I felt. That was real."

Chantal sighed heavily. "Mr. Sands," she said, "I'm sorry, but this conversation is over. I can't help you. No matter what you say, I can't or won't be swayed. Nor will I divulge personal information on someone whom you obviously have no right to get access to. Now kindly leave my house!" Chantal's heels echoed on the hardwood floor as she headed for the hallway.

"Wait!" Sands followed behind her. "Just tell me one thing. Did they ever find Nona's body? Did the police ever close the case?"

"Goodbye, Mr. Sands."

"Tell me? Don't you lay awake at night wondering what happened to her body? Don't you?"

"I feel sorry for you, Mr. Sands, I truly do. Now get out of my house before I call the police!" Sands brushed past Chantal and made it to the door before turning around. Chantal stood at the other end of the hallway, purposely keeping her distance, afraid he might lash out at her.

"Think about it tonight when you're lying all alone. I'm no lunatic. Ask yourself how come the case was never solved."

"Goodbye, Mr. Sands!" Chantal said coolly. Sands nodded once and smiled as he slid into the cool air, momentarily glancing back at Chantal who stood with her mouth closed, mind racing, replaying his words over and over in her mind.

18

Nona was downstairs when she heard the front door open.

She glanced at the wall clock.

5:55 p.m.

She dried her hands on the dishcloth, feeling the anxiety rise like bile in her throat. Malik worked a new development in northeast Queens, so it took him a while to get home. She checked the pasta sauce simmering on the stove; tasted a bit of it using a wooden spoon. She heard his footfalls as he took to the stairs, heading upstairs to their bedroom. He hadn't called out to her, hadn't announced his arrival.

He used to. She used to be waiting for him.

Just not anymore.

Nona frowned. Glanced around. Nervous energy wound its way up her spine, settling in her temples. She massaged them with her fingers, before sighing and leaving the kitchen. Walking up the stairs to the parlor floor, she could hear the shower running. He'd be a few minutes more, she knew.

She was flipping through the latest *O* magazine when he came down.

"Hey." This from him.

"Hi."

Malik wore a pair of khaki-colored cargo shorts, tight navy tee shirt that hugged his dark sinewy muscles like a glove, and a pair of old flip-flops. He collapsed onto the sofa across from her, a portion of his hair still glistening from the shower. Nona stared at her husband for a moment, his gaze absorbed on some magazine in front of him.

No kiss.

The affection that used to accompany their greetings was no more.

She remembered with certain angst how different things used to be.

How much affection used to flow from those dark lips of his.

How Malik used to come in, put his lunch pail down and kiss her, swooping her up in his powerful arms, lifting her off her feet. Placing her back down on solid ground before spinning her around, resting a thick forearm across her chest, drawing her back into his personal space.

Kissing that sweet spot at the apex of her neck— that sweet spot of flesh that made her legs weak.

Malik would kiss that spot, suckle it, lick it as he grabbed at her hair, pulling her head back—not

hard, but with just enough force to excite her—
exposing more of her tender flesh to his waiting
mouth. She'd cackle with delight, feeling herself
growing wet.

Moving into him, grinding against his pelvis
with her ass—hard; letting her husband know just
how much he was arousing her.

Back then, they fucked like rabbits! Operative
words being fuck . . . because that's what they used
to do.

Day in . . .

Day out . . .

Nona remembered when they closed on this
brownstone—Malik carried her across the threshold as if they were newlyweds, laying her down gingerly on the parquet floor, moving quickly on top
of her, arms and limbs flexing as they shed their
clothes, Malik spreading her thighs wide as sunlight blazed in warming their dark skin, neither of
them caring who saw their frenzied activity, not
being able to see past the moment—the passion
that spread like an avalanche to their limbs, Malik
rushing inside her without fanfare, fucking her
with uncontrolled fury, with unrestrained power—
and Nona remembered just how hard she'd come
that day, Malik pummeling against her womb until
he collapsed in a heap on top of her, feeling his
seed mix deliciously with her own.

"Dinner ready?"

Nona glanced up, the memory interrupted.
Malik stared at her—devoid of a smile, but without
a frown either.

"Yes."

They ate in the eat-in kitchen, in silence, for the most part; Malik, head down as he held his fork in his closed hand—something Nona always hated, as if he were a child; a source of great tension between them, but that was the way he was raised—and so, that was the end of that—forking his spaghetti into his mouth, chewing slowly, almost methodically before swallowing it down, reaching for another mouthful.

"I got a job."

She said this voice-steady, glancing across the round table at him as she spoke, eyes unblinking so as to not have him witness her mounting fear. Malik was in the midst of raising a cold Red Stripe to his lips, something he consumed every night with his meal—he heard the words, processed them, and didn't flinch, didn't slow down his movement in the slightest. If he heard her, he made no move to telegraph that fact back to Nona. Malik took his time swallowing, putting the bottle back on the table before looking up.

"Say again?" he asked, voice matching Nona's.

"I got a job." She paused for a moment, then added, "Starting tomorrow." Her lips pressed together, a move she did when nervous. Recognizing it, Nona opened her mouth, let her tongue flick against her lower lip, wiping the fullness of it, feeling her own warm flesh.

"Where? And when did this happen?" Malik had straightened up, sat taller—a move he did when he felt threatened, which was paradoxical, given his size.

Nona tried to look as nonchalant as possible. "I was offered the job two days ago. Called them back today to accept—"

"Where?" he repeated, a bit more forceful this time.

"Malik, I'm getting to that. I don't like it when you interrupt me." She was looking at him, her stare matching his. Not backing down. Not this time.

Malik was silent.

"An art gallery. Actually, I'll be working for an artist in the Village." She had rehearsed this part a million times—began playing this scene over and over in her head as soon as she and Brehan parted company . . . had decided relatively early on that honesty would be the best policy—that lying; telling half-truths would, in the end, be that much worse—because you never knew what Malik was capable of doing—following you to your job— waiting for you to finish work or school, whatever.

"Ummm-hmmmn," Malik responded in an even-toned manner, which was uncharacteristic of him, given the situation. He paused to fork another mouthful of spaghetti, chewed slowly as he glared at her. Nona met his gaze with her own, sipped at her glass of Chardonnay, which was a godsend, because it helped her relax. "So, how does this work?" Malik asked, resuming his thin-lipped inquisition. "What? You just happen to meet an artist who hires you to do what exactly?"

"Actually yes. I was in the Village a few days ago and I stopped at this gallery—I met this artist who—"

"Male or female?" he asked, interrupting again. Nona sighed.

"I met this very talented *male* artist who—"

"Black, white, or what?" Malik had lowered his fork. It hovered just above his plate, not moving.

Nona sighed. She began to open her mouth but then shut it quickly. She rose instead, taking her glass with her.

"You can clean up, Malik," were her words, trailing behind as she exited the room.

"Hold up!" he bellowed.

Nona froze. She turned from the hallway, glaring in his direction. "What?" she bellowed back. Took another sip of the Chardonnay to hide her apprehension.

His seat scraped against the floor as he rose. "So I see how things are . . ." he said, leering in her direction. "It's like you all grown-up now; on your own for the first time, no mammy and papi to hold your hand—making decisions and *shit*, without your husband. I see how things are . . ."

"Malik, please. I decided to take this job *today*. I'm telling you about it *today*. If I had told you about my offer you would have tried to talk me out of it—Lord knows you want me locked up in this house . . ."

"Whoa—" Malik responded, hands in the air, palms out in surrender, "is that so damn bad? Having a man who takes care of his woman—providing for her so she doesn't have to work—so she can stay home—I thought that's what we wanted?"

"Excuse me?" Nona asked incredulously, moving back into the kitchen. She placed her glass down on the table before continuing. "*We*, Malik? Since when did *we* want to stay home?" She didn't wait for him to respond. " 'Cause last time I checked, I've been trying to get the hell out of here and find a job; been feenin' to go back to school for what seems like *forever*!

"I found an opportunity, Malik, and seized it. It's not about providing for me. It's about me feeling like I am a productive member of society—I'm able to work—I'm able, thank goodness, to use my mind, instead of just sitting around here and watching dust balls grow."

"I work hard enough for the two of us . . ."

Nona cut in with a wave of her hand.

"Malik, you know what? This cave man thing with you is such bullshit and played out—you know that? We live in a two-income society, man—we're getting by—and I mean, just barely by. You may think you're providing—but we are scraping by. We're not saving . . . we have zero disposable income! We need the money my job can bring. Besides, there's more to it than a husband providing for his wife. And," Nona took a breath to still her spiking pulse, "this job gives me an opportunity to finally enroll at NYU and go back to—"

"Absolutely not!" Malik had been chugging the last of his beer when he heard this; he slammed the bottle down, causing Nona to flinch.

But she refused to back down—not this time.

Not with this opportunity presented to her.

She had spoken to her girl Chantal about it. Even asked her new neighbor, Michael for his thoughts and counsel—as another artist—and someone who was neutral, objective. Michael told her to go for it! To not look back—a wonderful opportunity—one that could open doors, given the right circumstances—a steppingstone to something greater—even more exciting!

"No, Malik—I do not need to consult with you— I do not need your permission. I am going back to school—it's in motion—I'm going to NYU, where I've always wanted to be. You will not stop me. You will not deny me this opportunity!"

Nona's hand was shaking as she lifted the wine stem to her trembling lips. Malik watched her, this look of complete disbelief painted on his face. She observed his mouth transform into a sneer.

Witnessed his fists tighten for a split-second before relaxing.

She felt her fear lodge in her throat—making it impossible to breathe.

Yet she stood there, refusing to give in.

Refusing to budge.

"Think you all grown now and shit? Like I don't exist?" he hissed, voice low, but his words crystal clear. "We'll see, Nona . . . we will see."

With that Malik shouldered past her, up the stairs that groaned with his weight.

Nona held her breath, waiting for him to return.

It would take thirty seconds more before she heard the upstairs door open followed by a sickening-thud shut.

Only then did she let out a deep sigh, heart rate returning, albeit slowly, to some sense of normalcy.

Round one—over.

She had won this one.

This fight.

Yet Nona knew the war was far from over . . .

19

Chantal ushered Nona into the white room without a sound. Her facial lines were drawn tight, expressing pain and displeasure. Nona sat down on the sofa and waited. She had been very busy the last few days and hadn't spoken to or seen Chantal. She assumed her best friend was a little pissed, but so many things had happened in rapid-fire succession: first, seeing the painting, "Red Leather Bitch"; then the gallery opening; meeting Brehan; finally, the job offer; and Michael, the other painter, moving in across from her.

Chantal smiled weakly. Why had she summoned Nona here anyway? Nona had things to do. She had spent the past three days with Brehan, averaging four to six hours a day; as a result her daily house chores had been relegated to back-burner activities. Malik had commented on more than one occasion about the house looking like shit. He was aware that as soon as he left for work, Nona headed to the Village to Brehan's studio. So far her husband had been silent on the job issue. She had been telling herself to spend at least a full day attending to domestic issues, cleaning and other much needed housekeeping.

Perhaps next week.

"So," Chantal said, "I see we have been quite the busy bee lately."

"Yeah, kind of. Listen, I'm sorry for not stopping by earlier, but things have been mad hectic."

"I can imagine." Chantal sat down next to Nona and patted her lap, smiling. Nona suddenly felt uncomfortable. She never got used to dealing with Chantal's mood swings, and sometimes became nervous around her. She couldn't put a finger on her discomfort; she just knew that Chantal could make her feel uneasy.

"Malik's been calling," Chantal said with a snicker that made Nona angry.

"What? When was this?"

"Oh, a few times. He called from work wanting to know where you were." Chantal played with her fingers nervously and flattened her jeans.

"What did you tell him, Chantal? I mean, he knows I've started working with Brehan, so why is he tripping?" Nona exclaimed. She was facing Chantal, a look of anger on her face. Her friend continued her blank stare, oblivious to Nona's anger.

"Probably because he couldn't reach you on your cell." She paused to let that sink in. "Malik's not one to fuck with. If he finds out what you've been up to, he'll hurt you real bad." Chantal smiled.

"What do you mean, what have I been up to?

I've got a job! Hello!" Nona shouted, forehead creasing.

"Okay," Chantal said, patting Nona's knee again. "But you and I know that there's more to painter-dude than just a j.o.b. You may be fooling your husband, but you ain't fooling me!"

Nona rose, going to the window. She stared across the street for a minute before spinning on her heels to face her friend.

Chantal held up a hand.

"Hold it. Don't go there—I'm not trying to start something with you— just stating a fact."

"You're wrong," Nona said, but the words lacked power. Lacked conviction.

"I think it's about time you and I get some things straight," Chantal said, continuing. Nona stared at her dubiously, wondering where this conversation was heading. "I've been covering for you every day, telling lies and fabricating stories, so you can go off and play model with your new-found painter friend. I think it's time for paybacks, don't you?"

For the first time a peculiar smile adorned Chantal's face. It was one Nona had never seen before on her friend. For a split second her thoughts went back to the leather shop and its proprietor, Jake the snake. Her first reaction was to go off. Instead she sucked in a breath, held it for a few seconds before exhaling slowly.

Perhaps this was about ReyShawn?

Every so often Chantal had these bi-polar mood-swings—where she'd get as foul as that Iranian chick in their kickboxing class—the one who would sweat her ass off for an hour, then towel off and head back to work, sans a shower!—nasty bitch! Ninety-eight percent of the time Chantal's foul mood concerned men. And these episodes would last for days—sometimes even weeks. Had he been calling, that trifling-ass ReyShawn? Tired of his white woman? Thinking again about the dark side? You know what they say, the darker the berry, the sweeter the juice . . .

"Listen, Chantal," Nona said, returning to the couch, taking her friend's hands in hers, "I really appreciate all that you've done for me, girl, you know that. Without you, I'd be lost. But I don't like this talk of payback. Friends shouldn't do each other like that."

"Yeah, I know. I'm just wondering when you're gonna do something for me."

Nona cocked her head to the side, eyeing her friend curiously. She said, "What's up, Chantal? Is something bothering you? You in a bad mood—that time of the month? What? Seriously . . ."

Chantal said nothing. Instead, she stood up and walked into the hallway. She emerged a second later holding the red leather suit.

Nona's suit.

Nona glared at her friend, opening her mouth to speak. Chantal held up a hand, silencing her. "Why don't you model something for me?"

"What's going on here?" Nona asked, rising from the couch to face her friend, anger on her face. "I thought we agreed you wouldn't touch my stuff!"

"Calm down, girl. I won't hurt it. And I certainly can't fit into it, not with this big ass. But I want you to model something for me. You're modeling for everyone else, why can't you model for me?"

Nona stood still for a moment, trying to contain her mounting rage. Was this a joke? Chantal's query appeared quite serious. Nona had heard her friend say some stupid things, but this was the most ridiculous yet. Why would she want Nona to do this? Was she kidding or what?

"I've been working on some new designs, based in part on this outfit," Chantal said. "You might say that night at Masquerade inspired me . . ."

"Oh. Okay." Nona's mind raced. She had tried on Chantal's designs before, many times actually— but it had never been like this, never forced— never as a condition for something else.

"Chantal," Nona said slowly, "I don't want to model that for you."

Chantal laughed. "Girl, stop trippin'. I'm not asking you to model *this* outfit. But I do have *something* I want you to try on . . ."

Nona stared at her friend. "Still don't want to." She said the words slowly, purposefully.

"Think you should reconsider."

"And if I refuse?" Nona asked, hands folded across her chest, deciding she's had enough, preparing herself to leave.

"Don't refuse me, Nona. I'm your friend. And now, I need your help." She paused for a second, then added, "With these designs. More importantly, if you want me to keep covering for you, you'll do it," Chantal remarked flatly.

Nona walked over to Chantal, her heels clanking on the parquet hardwood, staring into those dark silent eyes, searching desperately for some proof that Chantal was kidding.

She found none.

Nona lashed out, grabbing the outfit from Chantal's hand. Chantal convulsed, her entire body rippling backwards. Nona was marching down the corridor to the front door. When she reached for the handle and turned it, Chantal cleared her throat.

"Upstairs." Soft, almost whisper-like.

Nona froze.

Turned to glance back from the front door. "What?" Nona asked.

"The outfits are upstairs. Why don't you change in my sewing room. I'll be right up." Chantal had spoken the sentence with such kindness that Nona had trouble believing it had come from her friend.

One thing was clear. Something was wrong. This was a new side to Chantal, one Nona had never witnessed before. She had no idea what Chantal would do if she wasn't cooperative. What would she tell Malik, especially if he continued to call? Her friend could fabricate anything to get back at her. Did she wish to jeopardize everything she had worked so hard to achieve?

No, definitely not.

Her hand slid away from the handle and came to rest by her side. Chantal had already turned to walk back into the white room, leaving Nona alone in the hallway. Her head throbbed. Way too much to do and now this. Shit!

Nona climbed the steps to the third floor slowly, her entire body woozy from the sudden pain, anger, and escalating trepidation.

The boyish-looking salesman smiled when Nona approached the counter.

"May I help you?"

"Yes, could you show me one of these?" Nona asked, pointing to the collection of telescopes under glass. "A present for my nephew," she added. Nona had been browsing in Target for more than forty minutes. The telescopes caught her eye. God knows I don't need one, she mused, but what the hell! Besides, I'm working now . . .

"Yeah. My mom bought one of these for me a few years ago." He scratched at a pimple on his forehead, while Nona waited patiently. The salesman handed her a narrow black one with a short tripod.

"This is a good one," he said. "Inexpensive and pretty powerful."

Nona peered through the lens, focusing on a fluorescent light hanging above the automotive department thirty yards away.

"How about something more powerful?" she asked.

"Sure."

The boy handed her a larger white model, this one heavier and longer than the last. Nona placed her eye to this one and focused once more. The image faded in and out of focus, the tiny shake in her hands magnified by the scope's powerful lens.

"Here, extend the tripod legs," the boy said. "You can see a lot better without it shaking."

"Thanks."

Yes, the boy was indeed right. With the tripod extended, Nona was able to focus the instrument to get a razor sharp image. Even in the store's artificial light, she found herself being able to focus on small objects around the store, their detail surprisingly clear.

"And if you turn this knob, you'll zoom in even closer."

Nona followed the boy's instructions.

"Damn!" she exclaimed, as she zoomed in on the back of a shopper's windbreaker. The "A" in "Adidas" filled the lens. She looked up from the scope, noticing that the woman by the checkout counter was at least a hundred yards away.

"I'll take it," Nona told the salesman. "And wrap it for me, if you don't mind. It's a present," she declared with a smirk.

20

David Sands stood in front of the large floor-to-ceiling windows watching the heavy rain as he sipped from a tall glass of Jamaican rum. A small fire hissed in the corner throwing up shades of firelight onto his many canvases. Large raindrops fell on the panes and streaked down the glass, meandering down past his feet. The sky was completely cloud covered. No moon shone down tonight; no light bathing the buildings or backyards as far as the eye could see. Dark facades of stone stood defiantly in the evening showers, most of their windows dark and lifeless. Reflected blue from an occasional television set poured its feeble light out to darkness—it was no comfort. Sounds from the stereo invaded Sands' ears. Soft jazz: Boney James blew haunting riffs from his sax that seemed to mellow Sands but not make him forget.

It had been three long and uneventful weeks.

The days had passed slowly—his classes at P.S.

9—each painful, sluggish hour seeming to take forever. The evenings, worse.

Sands was depressed.

The conversation with Chantal had not appeased him. He had hoped for and expected to hear good news. But now, standing in his loft, his eyes glued to the dark house facing his, he knew it had all been a dream.

David tilted his head back and drank down a long gulp of the strong liquid. It felt nice and warm, a total contrast to the dank coldness spread before him. The rain seemed alien tonight. Harsh and unfriendly. Sands was grateful for the warmth of his drink.

Three weeks.

No sign of her anywhere.

He had watched the house faithfully for three long weeks. His work in the evening kept him indoors by the windows, searching for a glimpse of her, a simple movement behind the shade, any sign that she was there. Night after night, he stood by his easel, drink in hand, the glow of late-night television reflecting off his smooth face, waiting for the seductive ghost to reappear.

Waiting for the woman that *moved* him . . . a woman he hardly knew… waiting patiently for her to return to his life.

She never showed, not even once. Neither did he observe any activity at the house. It was as if he had scared her away for good. Or perhaps she just did not exist.

Perhaps Chantal had been right.

Perhaps it had been a terrible dream, one so lifelike, so intense, that he had become mesmerized, wrapped up in its eroticism so deeply that he couldn't tell the difference between the dream and his waking reality.

He felt angry, empty, and used.

She, whoever she was, had done this to him—whisked in and out of his life so fast it made his head spin—and to what end? Pretending he was special when in actuality he was nothing more to her than a quick fuck?

Even if it had been all a dream, it had been one hell of a vivid fantasy. Look at him—his mind was messing with him, leading a perfectly sane man to think insane thoughts—believing such foolishness.

If she had been real, he reasoned, if Sands meant half as much to Nona as she meant to him, then she'd come back, at least one more time, and explain everything.

Perhaps she was afraid, scared of what radiated from within both of them—frightening her with its intensity.

But at least she could give him a chance, he thought to himself as he stared out through the heavy raindrops that plummeted to earth.

She owed him that.

Where, then, was she?

Why was she doing this to him?

How long would the loneliness continue?

This was crazy—Sands reasoned—why on earth was he consumed with a woman who did not even exist?

Because she did exist—or Sands believed she did.

He'd bet anything on it . . .

The end to the CD broke the spell.

The sudden rush of silence sliced through his concentration like a knife. Sands quickly left his spot by the window and went to the phone, his breathing ragged, forehead moist as he lifted the receiver, staring at it, glancing once more out the window. He had dialed the number numerous times lately—except each time he'd quickly hung up the phone, not having the guts to see it through. This time, he again dialed the number from memory; this time, he let it ring and ring. Sands clenched his fist and counted the seconds it took for the phone to be answered, grateful for the familiar voice at the other end. Suddenly, he realized he didn't even know what to say. Seconds of dead silence slid past, but the person on the other end was no stranger to this game. She held on for a moment, let the seconds drag on before she said in that voice that always stirred, always comforted: "Rain makes me think of sweeter times, too."

Sands smiled. He waited a moment, fighting the rise of emotion that abruptly choked him.

"Can you, I mean, would you—"

Thankfully, she didn't let him finish.

Sands was grateful when he hung up, glancing over to the window quickly, almost scornfully, as he downed the last of his drink, daring the ghost behind the shade to watch the scene that was about to unfold . . .

21

The front door slammed shut with a wallop. Nona, dozing, awakened suddenly and was frightened.

She glanced up from the couch, disoriented.

Stealing a quick glance at her watch.

6:18 p.m. Oh shit . . . She'd fallen asleep on the couch—neglected her chores—hadn't prepared dinner. Malik would be pissed.

An understatement.

Nona had had good intentions this day since Brehan was busy with Angeliqué—so she had planned on cleaning around the house, running some much needed errands—but the day and its distractions had a way of stealing her time away . . .

She had gone out to pick up some items from the supermarket, but then found herself in the new Target on Atlantic Avenue. Spent over an hour in the store futzing around; purchased the telescope—an impulse decision all right—Nona had no need for a damn telescope, no interest whatsoever in studying the heavens, her interests were more *earth-bound*—but she just wanted it . . . thought for a minute about what Malik would say— felt the rising fear—then pushed it back down. The new Nona—no longer bullied—no longer a slave to her husband, gonna stand up for herself and what she wanted—each and every time from now on!

Right after she made it home, Brehan had called her on her cell— something about a package being delivered; was she home?

An hour later—some guy, an NYU student, she presumed, shows up at her door . . . with a computer.

A computer!

OMG!

Not a new one, mind you, but still, a desktop computer and a printer—in excellent condition. He set it up for her in the top-floor room facing the street—Nona deciding that was where she would make her office—Brehan had been talking to her about the "marketing" aspects to this job— and that he was anxious for her to get started on soliciting magazines, newspapers, and galleries outside of New York on his behalf—Chicago, Atlanta, Washington, D.C., Oakland, to name a few.

The computer had erased whatever funk she had been in since this thing with Chantal the day before—modeling outfits for her as she made minor adjustments to her designs, Nona's mind going numb—blocking out the discomfort she felt— weird, because she had never felt this way around her friend before—but this time, it was as if Chantal was looking at her differently, for the first time noting the curves to Nona's smooth dark flesh, the sharp rise to her bosom, the deep cleft to her plump ass.

Then Brehan came through—lifting the fog, restoring sunlight as he did each time she gazed upon his sweet face—listening to his unhurried words and the philosophy behind them; watching the way his dreads swung as he moved his head to his self-powered beat—this time with a simple phone call.

"You gonna be home in the next hour? Got a package that needs delivering . . ."

The uncertainness of this thing; the air of secrecy surrounding it excited her.

She had spent the rest of the afternoon on her computer. Nona liked the way that sounded—*her* computer—feeling utter delight, a kid in a candy store—getting to know the machine, familiarizing herself with its applications, getting online, checking her mail, setting up an IM account; contacting her friends, surfing the web . . . other mundane stuff.

By four she was physically drained but emotionally exhilarated; couldn't wait to begin work in earnest. Brehan had done so much for her in a short amount of time—he had come through. Not one of these bruthas out here who talked shit—he delivered . . .

It was time she did the same . . .

Lie down, Nona commanded herself around four—lie down for a minute, catch your breath and then straighten up—start dinner so it will be ready when Malik gets home . . .

But then, as she was powering off the desktop, she spied Michael, her neighbor, outside; cup of coffee in one hand, folded newspaper in the other. So, she ran downstairs and out the door—spent the next hour chatting with him—sharing her good news! Michael was so easygoing—so easy to talk to. Nona became lost in his sincerity—his way of listening— like a long-term friend, and not someone whom she had just met. They talked about computers, her new job, the Brooklyn Museum, school . . . Nona smiling at Michael as they talked and talked, forgetting every little thing that had nagged her or brought her down—this was what it was all about— engaging someone in delightful conversation— someone who understood you—who vibed to the same rhythm, the same beat as you . . . along with this aura of sexual tension that hung in the air like smoke—Michael eyeing her—she eyeing him, but both keeping things neutral—just under the surface, where it was safe—yeah, this was what living was all about, Nona mused!

By the time she had come inside it was after five o'clock.

She had lain down on the couch—the plan was to close her eyes for just a moment before starting dinner. But then she had fallen asleep!

And now it was after six—and her husband had just come home . . .

"Malik?" she asked cautiously.

"Yeah," he responded, a shortness to his tone that she knew all too well.

Malik fumbled by the coat closet, cursed under his breath, and took the stairs two at a time without showing his face. Nona ran a hand through her hair, then rubbed her face. Was something wrong?

Her heart began to race.

The computer—she needed to tell him about the computer.

And there was her purchase.

She could hear him upstairs. Fumbling with his clothes—running the shower—same routine every day.

Nona rose from the couch, went to the stairs, tipping her head upstairs. "Malik?" she said.

He didn't answer.

She walked down the hallway, into the parlor room and peered out at the garden. It was getting late, the remnants of another beautiful day receding away. For a moment she thought about Michael as she glanced across to the building facing hers. She had a micro-fantasy about being single—living alone—meeting him at the fence-edge at dusk, a night just like this one, a bottle of chilled wine in one hand, glasses in another. Wearing one of Chantal's new designs as his eyes roamed over her dark skin—desire in his eyes, heat in his loins—fast-forward to Brehan—the two of them alone in his studio—his feet bare, shirt off—the way it was the other day as he stood in front of his easel, sunlight blazing in, Nona feeling herself flush from the heat—Angeliqué nowhere to be found. Brehan telling her about jazz, about art, Nona consuming all of his words as if they were a meal—a supper—taking it all in, feasting on his wisdom. Feeling the desire course through her body—making her sex

pulse—on fire—fingers going to her blouse, playing
with the buttons, desperately wanting to reveal herself to him—bosom heaving, breathing arrested,
nipples distended.

Paint this, Brehan, she says, as her blouse slips
off, floating to the floor in slow motion; Brehan
licking his lips, wiping his brow, abandoning the
work in progress; instead coming to her, but not
touching instead, observing her curves for what
seems like hours, silently; moving around her as if
she were a statue, studying her methodically before dipping his brush into his paint, beginning a
stroke on fresh new canvas.

The thought was alluring, and fleeting. The
water upstairs shut off, and Nona returned to the
present.

Pressing her palms to her jeans, Nona sighed,
headed for the kitchen downstairs.

Malik joined her ten minutes later.

"I told you not to leave the lounge chair out in
the middle of the yard," he said without preamble.
"I hate the way that looks!"

Nona was frying chicken in a cast-iron frying
pan. The oil splattered her tee-shirt, causing her
to wince.

"I'm sorry," Nona responded softly turning to
him. "I kind of forgot; things were mad hectic
today."

"Bullshit!" Malik shouted, grabbing the refrigerator handle and pulling the door open. He grabbed
a beer and spun around. "I'm fucking sick and tired
of hearing about how goddamned busy you are
lately. Like this new *job* suddenly exempts you from

your responsibilities. You sit on your ass all day while I work my tail off, and you have the nerve to tell me how fucking busy you are?"

"Wait one damned minute!" Nona growled. "What crawled up your ass and died? If you had a bad day I'm sorry, but don't come home and take it out on me!" Nona's face had turned red with anger. She faced Malik now, breathing heavily, the chicken frying behind her forgotten.

"What did you say?"

He approached Nona who instinctively backed into the stove, suddenly frightened.

"I told you about talking back to me. Whatever shit I decide to bring home, you better just sit there and take it, understand?" Malik quickened his pace and suddenly lunged at her, reaching for Nona's arm. She instinctively jerked it backwards, a convulsive move that caused it to smash into the frying pan.

Nona screamed.

"I don't give a shit how busy your day was!" he yelled, ignoring her pain. "Fuck you and your busy day!"

Malik backed away.

"I am sick and tired of you and your lame-ass excuses. The house has gone to hell because you're too busy. Well, I'm here to tell you this shit is gonna stop!"

Nona had dropped to her knees, sobbing, holding her bruised arm in her other hand as if it were lifeless, eyes the size of quarters as she cowered beneath her husband. Malik took a wild swig of his beer, moved closer, standing over her.

Nothing like this had ever happened before.

It happened to other people—but not her.

The room spun on its axis.

Her mind raced.

Nona couldn't even think. Her mind had shut itself down.

Shut itself down cold.

Malik had tried to grab her; he had almost put his hands on her—in all the years—he had never done *that* . . .

Her arm was on fire. Glancing downward she saw the skin on her forearm was bruised . . . it looked foreign to her—she floated for a split-second—left her cowering form to float above the room—to the ceiling where she could look down, the chicken continuing to fry; the hot oil continuing to spit and spatter over the stove surface and onto the floor. She looked so small and cramped on the floor; legs folded underneath her, rocking back and forth, hugging herself, almost fetal-like position— her husband glaring down at her, Red Stripe quivering in his hand. She would call the police— yeah—no, yeah, in a moment—she couldn't think straight—no, she would—yes, nobody would be allowed to do that—lunge at her, reaching out—almost grabbing her—it was he who had caused her to burn herself. Him, Malik; all of this spinning around her cortex like one of those firework sparklers—in a moment, she told herself, she'd finish thinking this through—her heart was racing so fast she thought that if she moved she'd cause the organ to rupture—have a heart-attack right then and there— on the cold kitchen floor—and die as her husband sipped at his beer, watching her body convulse and shudder . . .

Nona returned to herself and glanced upward, Malik breathing fire as he glared at her.

He went to the door and spun around, glaring at his wife on the floor. *He could help me,* she thought—*he could reach out his hand and help me to my feet, make sure I'm all right . . . but he doesn't . . . he won't . . . just stands there and stares . . .*

"Yep, the shit stops now! Today! End of story! End of conversation!" Malik turned on his heels and left the room, his footsteps echoing down the hall and up the stairs toward the bedroom.

22

Nona rubbed a thick cube of ice on her arm. The tears, which had streamed down her face, had ceased. So had the heave to her breasts. Rubbing her forearm incessantly back and forth with the ice cube made her feel better— if just for a few moments.

What had just transpired?

What, Nona wondered, had happened in that instant to make her husband snap?

Why was this happening to her? First Chantal and now Malik.

Nona did not deserve this.

She had seen her husband angry with her before, but usually his actions gave her some advanced warning.

Occasionally Malik was like this.

Once in a while he came home and vented his anger at her.

It was his nature; she knew he didn't mean to hurt her, but that did not ease the pain.

This time, however, he had hurt her, both physically and emotionally. Along with the scene at Chantal's yesterday, it was going to take a very long time to heal.

"NONA!"

Malik shouted from the top floor, shocking Nona with his force and intensity. She instinctively jumped back from the refrigerator, shivering like a wet dog. Her fear pinched at her nerves and caused her heart to thump in her throat.

"NONA! You have five seconds to get your ass up here NOW!"

Nona held her arm gingerly in front of her as she took to the stairs, the bellow in Malik's voice ringing in her ears. Her mind raced, but it was dead to any form of analysis—to rational thought. She had not considered just remaining in the kitchen—ignoring his yells. In the few moments that it took to reach the top floor, she couldn't for the life of her decipher what was wrong now.

When she reached the landing she turned toward their bedroom, but immediately stopped. She could hear him rustling about in the front room facing the street. She entered the room cautiously, still very much scared by Malik's irrational behavior. This whole thing was beyond ridiculous. He sounded like he might hurt her for real.

"Malik, honey," she began, her words spoken slowly, almost whisper-like to keep things from escalating out of control, "let me explain about this computer." He stood, arms at his sides, by the table that she had taken from the basement—the table the computer was sitting on. She moved towards him, scanning his face and the dark eyes for a clue as to his sudden schizophrenia. "It's from my new job—they wanted me to have it—the artist, Brehan, needs me to begin contacting art galleries so that . . ."

Malik wasn't paying attention. His fingers were gliding over the keyboard; going to the color screen. Touching the mouse briefly.

"Awfully nice guy, this artist, setting you up with your own computer—at home no less . . ."

Nona gulped.

"Yeah, well, he thought it would come in handy for my school-work as well . . ." Nona immediately regretted her words, so she added quickly, "But the main reason is so I can contact various places; begin setting up interviews and shows."

Malik smiled. "Wow—this guy, I mean, imagine that—an artist who hardly even knows you, going to all this trouble . . ."

Nona tried to smile, but it came out flat.

"It's not what you think, Malik," she responded, standing taller, squaring her shoulders. Malik brushed past her without a sound. She held her breath—let it exhale slowly. He returned momentarily with the telescope in his hand.

Nona had left it on the bed—still in its gift-box—and yet, Malik had seen it, opened it, without having the decency to ask her—

"What the fuck is this, bitch?" he bellowed, pointing at the telescope.

Nona backed up, ignoring the words that stung in her face.

"It's a . . ."

"Don't play fucking games with me; I know what it is! Where did you get it?"

"I bought it. With my own money." She paused. Took in a lungful of air, then held her hand out so he would give it to her. She moved towards him. "And you have no right to go through my stuff."

Malik allowed Nona to get within arm's reach before raising his hand, and slapping her hard, his large palm connecting with soft flesh, knocking her to the ground.

What happened next dissolved into a kaleidoscope of fast-moving images.

She heard herself say, "I bought it today. Didn't think you'd mind, baby. I'll take it back, tomorrow, first thing, I swear!" Nona winced at her words; so subservient, so slave-like. Nona hated herself for speaking like this, splayed on the ground, cowering in fear like an animal, but it was about survival, and right now, survival was key.

"You think we have money to just throw away on fucking toys like this," he yelled, swinging the telescope down in her direction.

"I'm sorry, baby," Nona whispered, the tears meandering down her face, her body quietly convulsing with fear. Had he just slapped her? It was all a blur—everything running in slow-motion—one second she was standing there, the next moment. . . .

"Sorry's not good enough. What the fuck were you looking at anyway? The stars? The moon?" Malik glared down at Nona, who on her back flattened herself with every forceful word. "Or perhaps it was that new guy that just moved in across the way?" Malik bent down, the barrel of the scope inches from Nona's bruised face.

"WELL?"

"No, honest, it's not him," Nona pleaded. She pushed herself up on one elbow, wiping the tears away with her free hand. "Honest, baby, I would never . . ."

"BULLSHIT!" Malik bellowed, arcing the scope in his tightened grip and flinging it against the wall. It shattered on impact, the cool white metal buckling, the white-washed wall denting and scuffing. Nona instinctively flinched as the instrument exploded, thousands of tiny lens fragments suddenly raining down upon her like a waterfall, punishing her for daring to bring this object into his home—without his express permission. The sound of shattering glass lingered in her ears long after Malik marched out of the room.

Again, Nona floated free of her physical being— floating to the ceiling so she could glance downward at her shivering form.

What she observed there made her ill.

Nona saw herself, lying there without movement on the floor for a great while, not daring to get up, or even touch her bruised face.

Later, the sound of the television could be heard coming from the second floor; sounds of sitcom laughter that made Nona want to cry. She observed herself gather her strength and get up, circumventing the mess of glass and steel like it was a huge water bug, slowly going to the bathroom where she gingerly washed her face, avoiding the reflection that stared back at her. Nona knew she should call the police—couldn't let her husband get away with this—no, this time, he had gone way too far—actually willed herself into the bedroom and to pick up her iPhone.

But the weight of the smartphone in her hands was too heavy.

Besides, what Nona needed right this moment, what she desperately wished for above all else was deep resounding sleep, an escape from all the disillusionment and pain she had experienced. She tried to think happy thoughts: Brehan in his studio; Michael and his contagious smile, but her head began to pound and the pain was too deep to bear.

Still floating, Nona watched herself in a detached sort of way extinguishing the lights, crawling under the covers.

Her mind opined—Malik had had a hard day.

Perhaps his boss had yelled at him or one of his coworkers had said something he didn't like.

Whatever the reason, her husband had come home, taken it out on his wife.

Nona knew that as sure as her cheek and eyelid would be a sickening blue-black color tomorrow, Malik would forget the whole thing, chalking it up to no big deal.

A kiss, a hug, and it would be over.

Life would go on—that's the way he was.

This time, though, Malik would prove her wrong.

Her husband would come to her, late into the evening, almost into the next morning, awakening her with his confession of his wrongdoings. He

would ask her—no, beg her—for her forgiveness—
for another chance—a chance to make things right.

Nona's spirit had yet to return to her body—she
was still floating when Malik awoke her, still watching, still observing, and it sickened her to watch
herself consider Malik's words instead of calling
the police right then and there. But he loved her,
he said. She was his life, he told her. He became
insane with jealousy because of the thought of
losing the one thing he loved more than life himself. Her . . .

Nona watched herself give in to her husband.
Watched the two of them make love—no, it wasn't
love, Nona told herself from the ceiling by the
window, it was what animals do—it was fucking, a
few minutes of make-up sex, done because Nona
didn't know what else to do . . .

The next day her husband would surprise her
with a brand-new telescope when he returned
home from work, all wrapped up with a pretty blue
bow.

One bigger and more powerful than the one
she had bought.

He would tell her that he had decided that attending NYU and taking this job was a really good
thing—he had decided!

Nona would display a diminutive smile; thank
her husband while keeping her distance, fearful of
anything, anything that would set her husband off
again.

Regardless of how he tried to satisfy his wife that
night or the next, no matter how close he'd hold

her body next to his as they slept, Nona would forever be changed . . .

It no longer mattered how much he said he cared, no matter how many times he uttered the words, "Baby, I'm so sorry for hurting you," Nona would never feel safe again.

The best course of action would be to leave now.

Because next time, Nona might not be this lucky.

Next time, Nona might not get a second chance . . .

23

Two dozen blue crab.

Two dozen! And a bottle of Yellow Tail Shiraz. Sands couldn't believe it.

Eleven o'clock on a Friday night, and she'd brought two dozen live blue crabs.

"Where on earth did you find these?" Sands exclaimed to Lisa as she ran into the bathroom to deposit her dripping umbrella.

"South Street," she yelled back as she patted her hair. "I had the cab stop for a moment. Hope you don't mind, Sands." She returned to the living room looking refreshed, a renewed amount of bright lip gloss covering her full lips. Sands looked up from the bag of crabs and smiled. Five-five, rich, mocha brown complexion, slender build, hair to her shoulders and cut in a style that he hadn't seen before, thin glasses resting atop a sculpted nose. Tight jeans, brown boots, a thin sweater that accentuated her curves.

"You always know what to do, Lisa. Always." He

smiled and added, "Love the hair—it really looks good!" What he didn't say was: *baby, you're a sight for sore eyes . . .*

"What can I say, other than thanks? You sounded like you could use a little pick me up." She winked seductively and wiggled her ass as she crossed the floor to the counter top.

"I still can't believe it. Crabs on a Friday night!"

"Sure, and I hope you got some beer, because I plan on making some of the best steamed blue crab you've ever tasted."

"Beer?" he asked.

"Yup, it's the Maryland shore way. You'll love it." Lisa went to his cabinets like she owned the place, pulling out utensils and pots, starting a fire, and waiting for the water to boil. Sands grabbed several Coronas and poured two tall ones, toasting Lisa silently, immensely appreciative for her friendship on a night like this.

The crabs were ready in a half-hour. Sands and Lisa ate on the living room floor in the comfort of the rug. The beer flowed into tall stems of crystal, because he didn't own beer mugs, and the salad that David fixed up was a perfect complement to their evening meal.

"You look good," Lisa started, after she was half-way through. Sands smiled sheepishly. "Really, Sands, you're looking good these days—much better than I remembered."

"I knew it was coming," he responded, nudging her thigh with his glass.

"No no, now is not the time to bring up the fact that a sistah hasn't heard from you in, let me see, three, no four months!" Lisa laughed but Sands knew this was her way of letting him have it. "Let's not bring up the fact that you moved and I didn't even know your new number—damn, what's a sistah to do? Stalk a brutha?"

"My bad, Lisa! I'm sorry for not calling you, but I've had a lot on my mind lately. Besides, I figured you were probably far too busy with that gym teacher—what's his name? Tyrone—brutha was sweating you bad! Figured his muscles and his fade were too much for you to bother with a two-bit painter like me."

"Yeah, right! Please! He didn't do anything for me then—and he certainly ain't doing anything for me now. Besides, I'm tired of these knuckleheads talking trash to me like I was born yesterday!"

"Damn, sorry to touch a sore spot," Sands said, pouring another beer.

"It's all good—at least I got to see your new place—I dig the digs, Sands— very nice—you are moving on up!" She giggled and reached for another crab leg. "Seriously, the loft is off the hook—it fits you to a tee." Her stare found his and she gave him a smile. "And I'm glad you *finally* called, Sands. Better late than never, I always say . . ."

Sands nodded. "Me too. I'm just sorry I took so long. Forgive me, Lis?"

"We'll see, Sands, we shall see."

He reached over, taking her hand in his, fingers interlocking as he moved over, reaching up, head in his hands, leaning in, kissing her on her lips.

His mouth lingered on hers for a moment before he felt her leaning back—and so he moved along with her—to the rug, where she stretched her legs out, Sands climbing over her as her arms went around his face and neck, pulling him closer. Crab legs, salad, and beers forgotten, they longed for one another—Sands hadn't realized just how much he had missed her until now. For Lisa, it was their lips touching that created the spark that ignited the flame. Lips gave way to tongues savoring each other, the aftertaste of crab legs and beer mixing with their own saliva. In minutes, Lisa lay prone on the rug, her breasts bare to the firelight, dark bosom rising and falling to the beat of her short and sporadic breathing; Sands' tongue bathing her skin; teasing her nipples as his own bare torso flexed in the half-light.

"You know what I like," she whispered, eyes closed, glasses removed.

Sands lay beside her, playing with her breasts, softly caressing her erect nipples with his wet tongue. Sands let his hand glide up her leg, squeezing and feeling the denim until he reached her hip, crossing over to her zipper, tugging at it gently, unbuttoning them, fingers settling on a pair of panties, hand moving down, first over the cotton, teasing her with his fingers, lightly rubbing the wet spot between her thighs, then slipping off her jeans, and running his hand from her belly to the crack of her ass. He tantalized her, Lisa moaning to his touch, as she reached for him, her hand finding his hardness beneath his own jeans, giving him a seductive squeeze, before tugging on his zipper, begging him to undress. Sands pushed her hand away with a grin.

She lay back and sighed, her hands groping along the cool floor for something to feel. She found his knee, ran a finger up his leg to the bulge in his jeans again, massaging his growing member with an expert hand, rubbing her palm against the length that stretched the denim to an insane tightness.

"Damn, you feel good—I've needed some of this . . ." he whispered into her ear.

"Should have called, Sands," she replied, her hand snaking inside jeans and boxer shorts, grasping his shaft in a firm grip. He glanced down at her—Lisa's eyes were glazed—a seductive smirk adorned her lips as she took him between fingers, jerking slowly, his meat inches from her lips.

The rain had weakened and the window became clearer. The lights from the kitchen were off, living room track lighting on, bulbs resembling far away suns in a very distant sky. The coals in the fireplace produced very little light, but were comforting nonetheless. Sounds wafting upwards, *Best of Fourplay*, Bob James stroking piano keys in the same the way that Sands stroked her thighs; Lee Ritenour plucking guitar strings in the same way that Sands plucked the inside of Lisa's thighs.

Lisa coaxed Sands out of his jeans, slipping his dick out from the confines of his boxers. It stood straight up and thick just like she remembered. She expertly stroked him, closing her hand around it until she could feel his blood course through him, its pulse rapid and strong. Sands slipped Lisa's panties off and spread her legs wide. His hand found her bush and rubbed lightly, spreading her lips and covering his fingers with sticky juice. Lisa moaned with pleasure when he slipped inside of her, his fingers massaging her walls; his thumb rubbing against her engorged clit.

"Oh God!" Lisa exclaimed, sucking in a short breath, squirming on the rug, her mocha skin a stark contrast to the color beneath her.

"Please eat me," she moaned and Sands complied, replacing his fingers with his mouth. His hot breath on her wet skin caused her to flinch and she reached for his dick, tugging on it fiercely. Sands licked her slowly and methodically, bathing her as if she were an ice cream cone. Her sweet taste was reassuring, the scent of her sex forcing him to lose himself in this act with this woman— forgetting the other woman who loomed outside of his window. Lisa's hips bucked in time to his stabbing tongue, a miniature phallus that fucked her rhythmically. Bathing her with juices and saliva, Sands' finger slipped inside her effortlessly as he took her clit inside of his mouth and bit down. Lisa half-screamed, convulsing with pleasure and pain. She spread her legs wider, pushed his head down farther into the depths of her thighs, offering her flesh to him, allowing him to swallow her up. Sands drank her juice as she bucked her hips feverishly and came, grunting, thrashing about as Sands kept her clit firmly between his teeth, distending her sex, refused to let up, making sure she would remember this night.

"Oh shit!" she cried when it was over, body slowing to a shudder. "Never, Sands, never did you do it to a sistah like that!" She paused to catch her breath, rolled over, squeezed her legs together, gritting her teeth as she ran a hand over his bare chest. "Damn, brutha, what's come over you?"

Sands was silent on his side, stare riveted to the widow and what lay beyond. "Needed to see you cum . . ."

Lisa considered his words as she eyed him. "You're sweet." She tried to control her breathing but to no avail. Sands laughed at her aborted attempt. "Come here," she whispered, "your turn, baby . . ."

Lisa spun around until she was facing Sands. She tugged at his shoulders, guiding him until he knelt in front of her, his dick swaying in front of her face. She took it slowly into her mouth, wetting its full length until it was shiny with saliva. She moaned softly as she sucked him, his dick seeming to expand in her mouth, filling her throat with a bit of pre-cum. Sands had his head back, eyes closed as his hand rested on her shoulder, his brain flat-lined like a malfunctioning EEG, mindless, concentrating on the pleasure that he was receiving. Lisa sucked him just the way he liked—long full strokes that took her mouth from the tip of his cock all the way to the base of it, just the right pressure and suction, always the right amount of wetness to make him slide inside her mouth effortlessly. Lisa knew he wouldn't be able to stand this too much longer, knew Sands would soon grab her head and emit a low animal groan, the way he used to when she sucked him in her bed, his signal that he was about to cum. She increased the rhythm of her sucking, pumping the shaft with her wet hand. Cum, she pleaded with her eyes, cum in me, long and hard . . . I can see you need your release.

Sands pulled out of her mouth suddenly, leaving a trail of saliva that arced toward the floor. Lisa was momentarily frightened because of the intensity of the action. Before she could question him, Sands grabbed Lisa by the arm and silently pulled her over to the window. She went to lie down, but Sands pulled her back up, positioning her on all fours with her body parallel to the glass. He rubbed her ass with both hands before spreading her cheeks, marveling at her lovely, seductive form.

"Don't move," he commanded. When he returned a moment later, sheathed and engorged, she hadn't moved a muscle. Head cocked to the side, she followed his movements with glazed eyes.

Sands maneuvered behind her, plunging deep inside of her with a quick satisfying stroke.

He fucked her with a passion that she hadn't witnessed before. He was like an animal—the rhythm unbridled, rampant, body convulsing like in a seizure. Filling her swiftly; frenzied; pulling out abruptly, head of his dick breaching the lips of her pussy for an instant before plunging back in, pipe filling her shaft, rocking her to the core with his pump-action, like a shotgun cocked.

This night, the pulse feeding into her was unwavering; the pounding was steady, a digging machine. She moaned in time to his thrusting, their rhythms synced. Palm to the window, other splayed across her lower back, fingers extended, thumb nestled in the crevice of her sweat-glazed ass, Lisa lifted her head as Sands rocked her, glancing back, staring into his expressionless face; marveling at his form that tensed as he moved—his entire being like a tide, push/pull/push/pull/push/pull inside of her, pussy swallowing him up, only to spit him back out a moment later; Lisa observing all of this, her eyes traveling upward, finding him staring blankly out the window. Pumping her like a well-oiled engine, but staring blankly out the window . . .

Lisa blinked, wiped the sweat from her eyelids with a quick gesture. Head back down, eyes closed, reaching back, between her own legs to his legs, palm up, fingers splayed, letting her hand connect with the underside of his balls. He responded by pinching a nipple, tugging on it hard for a moment before leaving it to sway and dangle in space. One hand braced against the window as he fucked her, the other massaging the left cheek of her ass.

Minutes went by.

Lisa, astounded that he could last this long, hung on, riding out the storm that seemed to be brewing. Her insides began to ache, but she wasn't ready to shut things down. Not yet.

As quickly as he had begun Sands suddenly pulled out, tearing off the condom in one fell swoop. Lisa, still on her knees, sunk down on her elbows, sticking her ass high as she cocked her head sideways, eyes darting back towards him. Gasping for breath, head toward the ceiling, Sands jerked as he came, painting a portrait on her dark ass with globs of white-hot semen. Dipping his brush back into the paint as he smeared his ink around, moaning, groaning, teeth-gritting as his pulse slowed to a dull roar.

For a minute he seemed to moan aimlessly, squeezing the last of his sap from his softening appendage. When he was finally through, his hands went to her ass cheeks and settled there, leaning in, the warmth of his pelvis against her flushed skin, pushing her gingerly to the floor. Lisa panting like a sun-whipped dog; Sands collapsing onto her for a moment before rolling onto the floor, a stream of unintelligible gibberish spewing from his lips. For what seemed like an eternity, Sands lay there in Lisa's arms, his cum drying on her naked ass, his stare riveted to the rain-streaked window pane. As if reciting an ancient ritual from a now-dead language, David Sands repeated one name over and over again until he finally fell softly asleep.

24

Hot, dripping summer.

One-hundred-degree days made one wish for winter months, like December.

A river of rain cascaded down a single arching window, meandering through fields of glass like a lost child at a night-time carnival. The nonstop tap against the panes faded into white noise that was soothing.

Brehan's body hugged the crescent-shaped window, his hands pressed against the glass, willing the silvery raindrops to yield around his fingers. An unlit joint hung from his mouth. The moistly heated air drained his strength to light it. He stared out the window, silently glancing through the haze and fog of the storm. The rain afforded little panorama. The backyard of the apartment building on the lower East Side was narrow and dull. A towering mass of brick in front, faceless save for an occasional fire escape, blocked what little light reached his loft. Black tendrils of iron clung to the building like an oversized insect, dripping and creaking in the early afternoon shower.

Nona stood off to his left in a relaxed pose; completely nude, her body was covered with a layer of perspiration that Brehan found invigorating. She flexed her calves, working the muscles that had cramped from an hour on the low futon. Her full breasts jiggled, stomach creasing. The painting was taking shape. Brehan was pleased, and this in turn pleased Nona.

The joint was lit, its smoke trailing upward for a moment before becoming caught in the crosscurrent of a ceiling fan. It was whipped away and out of sight in a moment, the memory quickly lost.

Rain was soothing. It was therapeutic to these long sessions. Nona could concentrate on the sound, allowing the dull drumming to massage her temples. Brehan always had his iPod going while he worked, its output going to a pair of Bose speakers on the shelf. Soft melodic stuff today— piano and acoustic guitars—Keith Jarrett and Jeff Lorber, Acoustic Alchemy and Pat Metheny, to go along with the rain. It helped to get him in the mood to paint.

Nona placed her hands over her head and stretched. Brehan looked away from the window and toward her, taking in the way her breasts rose up when she stretched. Her upper arms were strong but not bulky, just enough to be deemed sexy. Nona's body was not overbearing—she was not a bodybuilder—but Brehan had to marvel at the way she kept herself in shape. Every appendage, every muscle was lean, shapely, and solid. It excited him the way her ass was perfectly round and smooth. Sometimes, he would stare at her richly brown bottom for hours, pretending he was painting, instead focusing his attention on her smooth skin, the way it undulated when it moved, round crescents of flesh that ached to be touched and licked. Nona had become his most prized model. She had shed her inhibitions weeks ago. Now, she posed for him however he wished. Brehan placed her in the most erotic positions imaginable and captured her sensuality on canvas, all the while his desire for her was building—the tension growing, true pleasure unfulfilled, ready to burst, soon to explode.

"I love watching you move," he said, breaking the long silence that had ensued since their break.

"Hmmn . . ." she mumbled, almost unaware of his presence. His loft had practically become her home. In the few short months that they had known one another, a friendship had developed that satisfied both of them immensely. Brehan allowed Nona to live out her fantasies on canvas without fear, and Nona, with her naive innocence and sensuality, sparked Brehan's creativity like no other woman before.

Nona moved slowly across the expanse of floor, her feet sliding across the hardwood like a dancer's. The balls of her feet tested each plank, applying pressure and moving on. She exaggerated the movement for Brehan's sake, her thighs flexing and extending, muscles contracting, then expanding, the perspiration glistening off her back and sides as she moved. Her hair was worn in thin cornrows today, flowing over her neck and shoulders as she moved her head, extending it back and allowing the ceiling fan to anoint her with fresh cool air.

Nona was particularly aware of Brehan's stare. He watched her as she moved, never growing tired of her stance. This excited Nona, for she enjoyed being the object of his desire. Although there was a fine line between good friends and lovers, Nona had to be cautious that she didn't pull him over the edge.

"I feel so safe here" she said at last. "This is like a second home to me. I feel totally secure and relaxed when I'm around you. Isn't that strange?"

"Not really." Her innocence made him cringe. Brehan fought the rising urge to reach for Nona and impale her soft flesh with his hardening sex. It would be over in an instant, he knew, but the thought of slipping inside of her was so overpowering that he almost fainted.

"I've never felt so comfortable with anyone before. I'm so glad that I have you as my friend," she said. Brehan smiled weakly. "With you I can be myself, uninhibited and uncaring. God, I can't even do that with my husband—sorry," she said, sensing the change in expression without glancing back. "I didn't mean to, you know," she said, turning toward him. "I just want you to know how very special you make me feel," she remarked, traversing the space until she stood beside him. Her shoulder rubbed against the coolness of the glass. She flinched involuntarily, then settled back, enjoying the refreshing feeling. Brehan's hot breath tickled her nose and mouth, his eyes dropping to her pert breasts that rested only inches from his own bare chest. He passed the joint to her; she took a long drag, letting the smoke invade her lungs, filling her chest before exhaling through her lips. Brehan was silent. "You're a good friend, Brehan," Nona said, reaching for his arm and rubbing it. "A true friend. I just want you to know that." An electric current drove through him like a freight train. It surged and crested, riding higher and higher, dangerously close to peaking and making him commit to something that he'd later regret.

"Don't have to say another word, Nona," he managed to say. "You know how I feel," he said, smiling back, the waves of desire being wrestled down. "Besides, look how much I've accomplished in just a few months." Brehan spread his arms wide. "All of this, because of you." After Nona had come into his life, an entirely new line of paintings littered the walls of his loft. Already he had sold three of them for prices ranging between four and seven thousand dollars apiece.

He bent forward and kissed her cheek, his lips catching the edge of hers, mouths brushing lightly against each other's moistness. He found himself almost totally consumed with passion, practically lunging at her, wanting to take her down to the floor with him. Brehan quickly turned away, embarrassed by the erection that was evident in his pants.

It is indeed true, Nona thought as she flopped back onto the futon and spread her legs, massaging her calves. *Look around,* she thought. *Before me, you were good, very good—but this new stuff would take you to a new level.* She had inspired him to create some wonderful things. *I helped him accomplish this,* she mused.

"I almost forgot," Brehan said, walking by Nona and tapping her on the head. He crossed the room to an oak dresser by the bed. He picked up a white envelope and light blue box and returned to the center of the room. He handed her the envelope without fanfare.

"What is it?" she asked.

"Open it," he replied. Nona tore the paper carefully and pulled out a card, opened it and discarded the torn envelope by her side. A folded piece of something with sequins and sparkles fell into her lap. She turned her attention to the card—an invitation. Her name was embossed in gold lettering. A sexy masquerade ball. Held at this trendy new club uptown called aural. Party starts at midnight. By invitation only. Four days from this evening.

> *Ms. Nona Scott-Walker*
> *is invited to be our guest at a*
> *Masquerade Ball*
> *4 Sexy Grown Folks*
> *Midnight until . . .*
> *aural*
> *2525 West 5th Street*
> *By invitation only*

Nona's jaws relaxed, her mouth forming a wide grin. "Damn, is this what I think it is?"

"Only the hottest party in the City! What? You thought you weren't VIP? Please. You're with me!"

"Damn, boy, you are blowing the hell up!" Nona reached for the item in her lap and unfolded it. It was a thin mask made of blue, green, and gold sequins. She held it in her fingers, rubbing her palm against the elaborate pattern that ran from one edge to the other. Nona laughed, placing it to her eyes and glancing at Brehan.

"Ohmygod, this is gonna be off the hook!"

"No question. They pulled all stops when planning an event like this. Everyone who is anybody's gonna be there. All the usual high-profile party people plus some influential art buyers and critics. It's gonna be mad crazy— best part—yours truly is showcasing his latest works up in that space!"

"Are you for real?" She jumped up and embraced him, pressing her bare body to his. His bare chest felt the contact and shuddered. "That's wonderful! Congrats!"

"This is exactly the kind of publicity that I was referring to—taking things to a whole new level— getting my art into mainstream hands. We need to work on some press releases and make sure we do some follow-up interviews with all the local rags—I want everyone to know my name!"

"Ohmygod!" Nona exclaimed again. "Am I really on the guest list?"

"Please! They know better than to not invite you. Hell, you were the main attraction last time. I'm sure the word is out that you will be attending this event." Brehan relaxed his smile and handed her the box. "Just in case you have nothing to wear," he mused. Nona grabbed the box and flung open the top, her hand rummaging through the white tissue paper on top. She pulled out a black lace camisole, thong and matching garter belt with stockings. A weave of intricate design adorned the lace, a haunting pattern that in and of itself was strikingly sensual.

"I love it!" Nona replied, reaching for Brehan and kissing him quickly on the lips. "Where on earth did you find it?" she asked, running her fingers over the soft material.

"Uptown," he replied, and Nona fought to keep her composure.

"I love it, really. Thanks a bunch."

"Put it on, will you?" Brehan asked, his eyes watering, begging for her to don the outfit.

"Sure," she said, patting his arm affectionately. Brehan watched Nona slip the camisole over her head, pulling the thin translucent material over her large breasts. It fit her well, the spider web artwork expertly covering her nipples ever so slightly, creating an illusion. Nona slipped the garter onto her hips and slowly began the job of rolling the nylons up her thighs. She stood up and did each one in turn, her bare foot on the glass coffee table as Brehan's eyes followed her long fingers rolling the nylons toward her thighs. When she was finished, she hooked them to the garter and slipped her feet into shiny black pumps. She stood up and moved away from the futon, allowing Brehan an unobstructed view of her lace-clad body.

"Unbelievable," he said, "Nona, I swear no one can wear it like you can. You're incredibly sensual—

and beyond that, incredibly beautiful." Nona blushed and ran to him, wrapping her arms around his waist and jutting her face up into his.

"You spoil me, Brehan," she said with a smile, squeezing him with her affection. Her uncovered sex brushed against his jeans, the heat and perspiration making her pubic hair damp. Her smell, a combination of musky sweat and sweet perfume permeated his senses and drove him wild. *So close,* he thought, looking down at her smooth skin that beckoned for his touch. Hot breath on her cheeks, yet she didn't pull away. A growing pain, a rising slab of rock-hard flesh. He couldn't stand it.

Brehan reached for Nona's face and pressed his mouth against hers, exhaling forcefully and grinding his erection into her pelvis. His hands found her breasts and squeezed the soft mounds before descending to the half crescents of her ass and drawing her into his hardness.

"No, Brehan!" she whispered, half-wrestling against his grip. His tongue invaded her mouth, finding her tongue and tasting her insides. Nona struggled for a moment before settling into the kiss, tasting him, reaching for his head, his dreads, fingers tightening against the thick hair, her body and his moving backwards together in unison until they reached the window, the shock of instant cool painful against the exposed flesh of her arms and ass. She could feel him grinding against her. She knew she should stop—hands went to his chest, felt the muscle there, fingers glazing over his hardened nipples as he sucked at her tongue before pushing him away.

"Brehan, we shouldn't—"

A sound behind them stabbed through her words. Brehan spun toward the noise, his mind racing, eyes unfocused, taking a half-second to make out Angelequé's form in front of him. He instinctively backed away from Nona, the erection poking through his pants clearly evident.

The same glazed eyes, frizzy brown, unkempt hair, damp from the downpour. Black nylon raincoat, tied at the waist; sharp, pointy black sculpted knee-high boots. She glared at them for a moment; Brehan was silent, his body tense. Angelequé shrugged and walked into the room, hand on hip before issuing a smirk.

"Can a sistah get some?" she asked real cool-like, eyes dripping seduction.

Brehan cleared his throat, hand by his swollen cargo pants. "Baby . . ."

Angelequé interrupted. "No, not you, lover, I mean her—damn she looks absolutely delectable . . ."

Nona stuttered, "I was just getting ready to go," gathering her clothes by the edge of the futon. "We've done enough for today, don't you think?" Nona rolled her things into a bundle and headed for the bathroom.

"Don't leave on my account, girlfriend," Angelequé said. "Looks like the party's just getting started . . ."

Brehan was speechless, but glared at Angelequé as soon as Nona had left the room. Angelequé stood defiantly in the center of the loft for a moment, one hand remaining on her hip, the other running along her hair as she stared back at Brehan. She went to him silently, placed her mouth on his as she reached down. Gripping him through the loose fabric of his pants, tugging at the rising phallus of flesh that met her touch.

Minutes later Nona slipped out of the bathroom fully clothed. She came into the room and stopped dead in her tracks—Angeliqué, her rain coat and clothes thrown to the ground—sat on the low futon, naked except for the knee-high boots, her smallish breasts pert, nipples taut. Brehan stood before her fully nude, Angeliqué's head in his crotch as he stared towards Nona, eyes unfocused.

"Come join us," he uttered, barely above a whisper. Nona was frozen in place, unable to move. Angeliqué was fellating Brehan—Nona saw her hand was gripping his thick, long cock—it was fully hard, extending straight towards her, brushing against her cheek. His ass was delicious—brown and tanned, round and tight; not an ounce of fat to his thighs nor hips. Nona swallowed hard, willing her legs to move. They wouldn't budge. The sight of Brehan, fully unclothed; his manhood, unsheathed, in all of its glory made her wet.

Brehan walked silently over to her, his swollen cock undulating in front of him. His abs seemed to ripple as he moved, and Nona found her breath and pulse arrested. Stopping inches from her, placing a hand gingerly on her shoulder, Brehan said, "Don't leave. Stay, please?" Angeliqué had risen and joined them. She stood beside Brehan, one hand looped casually around his waist. Nona stared at her—she was beautiful. Both of them were. They made quite a pair.

The incessant rain drumming outside the window was therapeutic; the air inside of the loft, hot, stuffy; the smell of sex hanging like fog in the room, naked flesh, mere inches from her body that flushed all over—all of this conspiring against her, making her dizzy.

"Rainy afternoons," Angeliqué said, reaching out to stroke Nona's cheek, "make me horny. Come play," she whispered. Nona observed Angeliqué's hand snake down her stomach to touch herself.

Nona managed a quick shake of her head.

"Another time."

Grabbing her purse by the door she quickly let herself out, not glancing backwards.

The door shut with the finality of a deep thud, lock settling into place.

Brehan and Angeliqué stood for a moment, he inhaling the scent of Nona's departed essence. He licked his lips while closing his eyes for a moment, savoring the feeling from moments before, his mouth on hers, hands on her breasts, pressing himself into her lovely fissures, their tongues wrestling each other like playful children.

Angeliqué had dropped to her knees to take him into her mouth. The rain drummed to a beat that both found mesmerizing. Brehan glanced down, stroking her face as his thoughts drifted to Nona. Her sensual innocence drove him to create new art. Raw sensuality, a beauty, an appeal that consumed him even when she was not around . . .

Angeliqué increased her sucking, making sloppy noises that drove Brehan wild. He grabbed her head, directing himself deeper into her mouth, reached down with his other hand, grabbing her left nipple, twisting it hard, just the way she liked, hearing her groan, feeling the adrenaline rushing and rising.

Conjuring up Nona's chocolately smooth form in his mind's eye, heart-shaped ass, curvy hips, heavy breasts, delectable inner thighs. He pondered the taste of Nona's lovely mouth as Angeliqué fucked him with hers.

Angeliqué always knew just what to do.

Always knew just how to deliver.

Guaranteed to get him off . . .

But Nona—Jesus . . .

He groaned when he came—toes curling off the floor, muscles contracting and flexing as he filled the back of Angeliqué's mouth with his seed; thrusting his cock deeper down her throat as she gripped his balls between slippery fingers—Brehan almost screaming out her name . . . Nona.

Jesus!

Angeliqué and Nona.

Nona and Angeliqué.

Together, they formed two halves that made up a whole.

The perfect woman.

Two crescent moons that together drew a perfect circle.

25

She felt it at first, the thump in her chest as she took the narrow stairs; the deep rumble of bass, the cadence of a dozen subwoofers pounding out stone-cold funk tunes. As she neared the large black man, neck the size of a Hummer, headset on like he was Secret Service, guarding the front of the gleaming aluminum door, the rhythm became perceptible. She handed the man her invitation as the quick groove caused her foot to tap. He inspected it carefully, checked the name against his tablet, and nodded approvingly at her delicious figure. Whispered into his headset and the door swung effortlessly open.

Nona wore the camisole and garter that Brehan had given her, along with a short leather mini and matching pumps. Her hair was cornrowed in thick rows tonight—better to keep it off her face and neck as she moved. Nona strolled in as the music enveloped her senses, permeating her to the bone.

The place was enormous and unbelievably crowded. The size of a high school gymnasium with oversized ceilings, the abandoned warehouse had been renovated for the club's use. An array of concert-style lighting hung from the ceiling—colorful neon, spots and strobe lights radiated their energy on the crowd below. Everyone was dressed sharp—trendy, chic. Some wore costumes. But everyone wore a mask. Different styles and colors, some frilly and feathery, others plain, yet everyone had one.

A masquerade ball—mask a prerequisite for attending.

Nona fit hers over her eyes and walked around the room, accepting a cold glass of champagne from a waiter in a mask and tails. She gulped the liquid down quickly and reached for a refill before setting out across the room. People turned and nodded as she walked past. Men dressed in well-tailored yet fashionable suits, D&G, Sean John, Kenneth Cole, Armani; women in jeans, short skirts and tops by Bebe, Diesel, FCUK, Prada. Nona noted some of the more bizarre costumes she passed: a gray spider (or octopus) with eight lanky tendrils bouncing up and down, a sailor in drag, a man dressed like a hard-boiled egg. Nona nodded to each one approvingly, suppressing a laugh. These people had balls, she had to admit.

A score of paintings and photographs hung from the walls: a collection from various art galleries. Nona glanced up and down the long expanse of walls searching for Brehan's work. She spotted his at the far end by the bar. "Red Leather

Bitch" hung in a corner, well lit from above. She blushed when she arrived at the portrait. It didn't matter how many times she viewed the painting, it always moved her beyond words.

The floor was littered with dancers, pounding and grinding to an up-tempo house beat. A deejay spun records from an elevated booth across from the bar. Soft red light from their equipment reflected on his sweaty face as he smiled to the cheering crowd. Nona leaned against the wall taking in the sights and sounds. Several blond women in holey tank tops battled it out on the dance floor. Men stood around watching them and gawked as they shook their tits and ass, parading around for all to see. A few bystanders tried to converse with Nona. She politely smiled and moved on, not terribly interested in talking quite yet, more interested in watching the scene unfolding before her.

She thought about Malik—how he hadn't said a word when she told him she was going out this evening. Malik hadn't said much of anything after their fight a few weeks ago—he knew just how badly he had messed up— knew that Nona only had to pick up the phone and dial the police—that he, his job, his marriage would be finished. She hung this over him like a scythe—waiting for just the right timing to swoop down and cut his head off clean at the neck.

A cloud of blue smoke hung in the air. The lasers and strobes cut through it like a knife, waving at the crowd like a wand. The bass rumbled in her chest, but by now she had grown accustomed to the feeling. Nona tapped her fingers against the crystal of the champagne glass, wishing someone would ask her to dance.

Several minutes later, someone did. A hand seemed to reach out from the middle of the crowd and gently pull her onto the dance floor. Nona took a wild swig of her drink and left the glass on the floor, following the hand into the mass of people. She didn't know the man who was pulling her; the sound level was sufficiently high to drown out all low-level conversation. She could see him smile when she faced him and she smiled back. A good song was on, one she liked. *Great timing*, she thought, and began to dance.

Nona's partner was a good dancer. He had strong arms and shoulders, she could tell, even through his dark suit. He moved well, in time to the music. He enjoyed the rhythm, his body taking in the melody and swaying with the beat. She found the groove easily herself, moving in sync with her partner. Nona searched his face for clues as to his identity, but finally gave up. He was a faceless man in a sea of party people. It was far more exciting to not know, she finally surmised; let the fantasy evolve. He could be anyone: a schoolteacher, priest, or a paroled rapist, for that matter. Who knows? And he might be masterminding his crime right now. Nona watched the sweat as it formed on his brow and ran down his cheek. Nona began to sweat, too, a film of perspiration forming on her arms and chest. She fanned herself to keep cool, pulling the camisole away from her heavy breasts for a moment to allow them to breathe. The man saw this and smiled; Nona grinned back.

They danced for five songs. Three cuts so expertly blended together that she didn't even know when one song ended and another one began. She felt wonderful. Nona hadn't danced like that in a long while. She was tired though. The end of this song would be her last for a while. A chance to cool off, get a drink and a bite to eat. She had noticed a bunch of waiters walking around with trays of finger foods—smoked salmon, gourmet cheeses, deviled eggs, jerk chicken. Plus, there were two more levels above her. She wanted to explore the rest of aural and see if she recognized anyone.

Brehan would certainly be here. She felt bad about what had happened four days ago—uncomfortable with the way she had reacted, the way she had left in a panic—overreacting. She felt foolish, like a schoolgirl on her first date. Nona understood Brehan's feelings. She wasn't that naive. His feelings for her had been building since he had laid eyes on her. She had become accustomed to having him around and feeling so carefree in his presence. Nona had allowed her inhibitions to go free and lose herself in his world. Perhaps that had been a mistake. She loved Brehan, for his art, for his intelligence, but not the way he was feeling her. There was an incredibly strong attraction between them. That was part of the problem. Nona was partly to blame for letting things continue, to grow until it got out of control. Problem was Nona felt divided. Part of her wanted all that Brehan was willing to give without the sexual asking price. Yet, the other part wanted him as badly as he wanted her. Especially with things being what they were between her and her husband, Nona felt invincible, in control for the first time in her married life. Malik couldn't tell her shit! Nona felt wonderful. She knew it was a matter of time before she would abandon her fears and go to Brehan the way he most wanted—freely and armed with a fiery desire.

Another few minutes on the dance floor made Nona's legs heavy. She vowed to leave the floor in a moment whether the song was over or not. Her camisole was damp with sweat, the leather miniskirt becoming hot and uncomfortable. She wore no panties this evening, so her thighs were hot and sticky. She smiled at her partner and fanned herself off. He nodded understandably and whispered something which was lost to the music. He reached for her hand and Nona took his, the two moving toward the edge of the floor. Suddenly, the tempo of the music changed: a familiar beginning. Snoop, Justin Timberlake, Pharrell, a jam she absolutely adored.

"Oooh, this is my song!" Nona yelled. The man frowned before shrugging his shoulders, turning, and heading back to the middle of the dance floor. Nona suddenly felt revitalized, invigorated, and ready to go another round. The slight pain that had been building in her chest from the nonstop dancing had subsided. Nona's dance partner seemed amazed. He was visibly exhausted and worn-out. But he hung on throughout the song. The crowd's enthusiasm shifted into high gear for the Snoop cut. Yelling, fingers popping, hands to the ceiling as they stamped the floor with renewed energy. This was their night and their song. When it was over, a large crowd left the floor exhausted, ready for a drink and a breath of fresh air.

Nona took a long gulp of cold champagne while resting her frame against a dark wall. She fanned herself frequently, wishing the sweat to instantly dry up. A few waiters passed her by with trays of hors d'oeuvres; Nona snatched up handfuls, suddenly feeling very ravenous. Her bladder was also close to bursting—she needed to find the ladies room.

Nona climbed the steps to the second floor admiring the multitudes of costumes, hairstyles, and outfits. At the top she turned right, glancing at the wide expanse of hall that served as a second dance floor. Off to the right were the rest rooms. She walked toward them, aware of an elegantly dressed black couple that stood by the entrance deep in conversation. The woman wore an exceptional dress— chic, and incredibly bold—back plunging all the way to her cleft of her curvy full ass, front just as deep, barely containing surgeon-enhanced breasts. The man (probably her husband from the way he held onto her waist) was dressed in a smart black tux. His hair was shortly cropped and graying at the edges, a feature Nona found grandly sexy. Nona watched the couple for a short while. The woman was in a relaxed pose against the wall, her knee drawn up and one hand resting behind her. She carried an air about her, not one of royalty, but one of authority; a woman who was perfectly at home in social setting like this. Nona became fascinated with the woman. A younger gentleman stood off to the side, his back to the adjoining wall, drink in hand, casually taking an occasionally swig from his glass, his mask-covered stare never straying far from the alluring woman. The husband's back was to the younger man as he conversed with his wife, oblivious that another man was seducing his wife with lust-filled eyes. The woman wore a painted smile, but Nona caught the woman's eyes straying to the younger man. She gave the man a sexy beam when her husband wasn't watching. Occasionally, the husband would turn around and stare out at the crowd, and when he did, the wife's head would turn in the direction of the man. He, in turn, would tip his glass toward her in a toast. Nona was fascinated with the exchange between these two. Here was a woman who was controlling both husband and potential lover with mind-blowing ease. And the grace at which she was accomplishing the feat! Nona envied the woman. She possessed courage and guts. Nona wished for the strength to command men like that.

Just then, Nona watched the younger man drain his glass and push away from the wall like a swimmer. He walked toward the couple with an air of confidence. He reached the couple and tapped the husband's elbow, the woman grinning and enjoying the show that was about to unfold.

"Excuse me," the younger man began, "I hate to interrupt, but I felt compelled to come over and speak with you. I just needed to tell you that I think you are a very lucky man." He glanced at the woman and smiled, who remained against the wall innocently sipping her drink. "I believe this woman," he continued, "is about the most beautiful I have ever seen." The woman blushed, while the husband stood there wondering whether to grin at the man in front of him or punch him.

"Thank you," the woman said, staring into the younger man's eyes.

"Just telling the truth. You're a very beautiful woman. Treat her right," he said, tapping the husband jokingly on the shoulder, "or someone else will." The younger man winked and walked away, leaving the husband speechless. The woman's eyes followed the younger man's exit before returning to her husband's and pursing her lips.

"Damn, boldness up in here!" she said, watching the husband's stare scan for the younger man who lost himself among the throng of partygoers.

The tempo changed from fast to slow creating a mass exodus from the dance floor. This left a small number of couples remaining to dance close and slow. The lights dimmed; Nona noticed that several men took advantage of the low light by getting extra close to their dates. Nona finished her champagne and looked for a place to set the glass down. The black couple was still in the same place as before, and Nona walked past them to the ladies room, smiling at them as she went by. The rest rooms were lavishly decorated and Nona took her time staring at herself in the tall mirrors before leaving. She wiped her forehead and cheeks lightly and applied a small amount of makeup and lip gloss. Nona was satisfied with her appearance tonight.

She looked sophisticated while still keeping her sensuous appeal. She liked that. Very few women she knew could do both.

Nona left the restroom and was surprised to see the beautiful black woman standing outside the ladies room. The younger man was beside her, grasping her hand very lightly. The woman was glancing around nervously, as if expecting her husband to appear at any moment. Nona slowed her pace, wishing to try and catch a part of their conversation.

"You have at best two minutes," Nona heard the woman say, "So state your business and jet."

"K—I couldn't leave without telling you just how lovely you are," the young man responded. Nona leaned against the wall about five feet from the couple. There were lots of other people around, so Nona didn't appear out of place.

"Give me your cell and I'll text you later," the woman said.

"Not a problem, but I want to hear from you. This conversation is far from over—just beginning, you feel me?" She nodded while he took out a business card and placed it in her palm, closing his fingers around hers. "Don't lose it."

"Don't give me a reason to . . ." the woman replied.

"Whatever you say," he responded. Nona observed him stroke her back suggestively before walking away.

"Make it worth my while, playa," she whispered, leaving him with a seductive grin.

Nona returned her attention to the black woman. She remained by the restroom entrance, her back to the wall, a look of satisfaction written all over her face as she glanced at the card before placing it in her purse. Nona had to smile in admiration. She was intrigued by the conversation that had just transpired. Nona was determined to make her relationships work like that. She wished to be able to command someone who yearns for her the way that woman had so casually.

It was all about control.

Nona's thoughts whisked back to Brehan—their time in his studio. She had been nervous, unsure as to how to flaunt her raw sexuality without coming off as a whore. As a result she held back—letting Brehan take the lead.

It was all about control.

Nona decided that she would handle Brehan and her husband the way the woman had. With a mere glance—a mere stare.

Command them, never losing control.

Tonight was the perfect time to start. Nona suddenly yearned to find him. She hoped she'd run into him and his sidekick, Angeliqué, soon. She'd show Malik and them the new and improved Nona, the one who would blow their fucking minds.

26

"Hi, sugar," a male voice announced. Nona spun around and looked up into the dark eyes of a mask. "Gosh, you look so good. They could serve you up on a cracker and I'd eat you right the hell up!" Familiar voice, something to the way he moved.

"Jai?"

"Me, bay-bee!"

"Thought that was you," Nona exclaimed. "How Ya Livin', man?" She had moved to the east corner of the second floor, where the lights were dimmer, making it difficult for her to see.

"Large, but forget me, look at you? Damn, shorty!" Jai gushed, kissing Nona on the cheek. Nona smiled, but recoiled slightly from his wet lips. The smell of perspiration made him undesirable, but Nona stood her ground, determined to chat for a moment with the man before asking him where she could find Brehan.

"So, you feeling this party?" she asked.

"Oh yeah, loving it. Have you had a drink?"

"Yes, thanks."

"You sure?" Jai grabbed two champagne glasses from a passing waiter and thrust one haphazardly in Nona's direction. She had already consumed about five or six glasses—enough to make her legs rubbery. She took the glass regardless, not wanting to have to explain her concern to Jai.

"Cheers," she said.

"Cheers." He downed his in several gulps.

"Have you seen Brehan?" she asked, hoping she didn't appear too forward. Brehan might have told Jai about the night before. Then again, he probably kept his personal life to himself.

"Yeah, he's here. Last time I saw him he was upstairs in one of the private VIP rooms."

"Oh yeah? Haven't run into him yet. I need to holla. Wanna come?" Jai stood motionless, deep in thought. He rubbed his nose several times in rapid succession. Nona patted his arm and left him there to contemplate his immediate future.

The top floor of the hall was a maze of smaller rooms separated by a collection of dimly lit hallways. Nona began checking rooms randomly, sometimes disturbing a couple engrossed in talk or foreplay. Fifteen minutes later she found Brehan. He and Angeliqué were lounging on a leather couch; she in the midst of snorting a line of cocaine that was spread before them on a glass coffee table. A crowd of about nine others were huddled around them, some deep in conversation, others merely staring off into space, waiting for their turn to take a hit.

Brehan, clad in a pair of dark baggy jeans, camouflage vest, and Timbs, waved Nona over. His mask had feathers that sprouted like hair and a beard.

"Come in, love. Join us, won't you?" Nona stood hesitantly at the door. Angeliqué looked up briefly, smiled, then dropped her head back to the table. A man to her left stood in the corner massaging the bare breasts of a dark-skinned sistah. Her head was tilted back, eyes closed behind her black mask, a joint dangling from her lips, blouse opened to her navel, the man's hands tugging and squeezing at the exposed flesh.

"Come now and don't let in the draft!" A few chuckles could be heard from around the room. Nona hesitated, then walked in. Nona joined Brehan by the table, nodded to Angeliqué, who patted a space between them. Brehan reached over and kissed her fully on the mouth.

"Lovely," he said, "As usual."

"Listen, Brehan, about what happened several days ago—"

"Everyting irie, baby girl. Right now we're here to party. So relax, let your hair down, enjoy the fruits of our labor—yours and mine!" Brehan grinned widely, adjusting the mask over his face. He licked his lips, snorted once before lowering his jaw to the glass. Inches away, he exposed one nostril snorting up a single line of coke.

Brehan was silent as he wiped his nose with his

wrist. Out of the near darkness, someone handed Nona a roach with a glowing tip. She contemplated it for a moment before gripping it between her fingernails, taking a hit, sitting back, mask-covered eyes closing as the chronic hit its mark.

Time in that dim room melted away like a Dali painting. No one was aware of the passage of time; no one seemed to care.

The coke had been consumed hours ago.

All that remained was the bluish-gray haze that hovered over their heads like a shroud.

3:30 a.m.

Not that anyone in the room was keeping track. No one gave a fuck. For them, this was the after-party, and the after-party lasted till dawn.

Nona, like the other party goers, was leaning back on the low couch, her jaw agape, eyes closed, her mind a cerebral cesspool. Images and thoughts bobbed like floating trash down a ghetto alley, ultimately lost and forgotten. She was dead tired, drunk and stoned. She lay there with her head resting on Brehan's shoulder, the opposite holding up Angeliqué's.

I should gather myself together and go, Nona told herself.

Yup, in a minute, she mused.

Much later, Nona opened her eyes with a snap and sat up, suddenly ravenous, craving munchies, feeling so fucking good, words were useless. Her hand lashed out across the glass top of the coffee table raking the remnants of Bolivian flake that were left. She played with these between her fingertips, chuckling to herself, wondering how all of this must look to an outsider.

She nudged Brehan who answered her with a low groan. He was fine when he just laid there, eyes opened and semi-alert, scanning the room with a cold robot's eye. But when he moved, look out! His nerves felt like fishing line stretched to the limit by one big-assed Marlin! Sit tight was his philosophy right now. Sit tight and wait for the sunrise, soon to come. Nona commanded all of her strength and stood, utilizing Brehan's head and shoulders for support.

"Come on," she said, words coming to her slowly, half-speed, tugging on Brehan's vest, "We gotta talk." She giggled, legs wobbly, practically losing her balance. "Come on, man!" she said, louder this time, "Don't got all night!"

Nona paused to consider her own words. Then added: "Shit, maybe we do!" This elicited laughs from several of the folks. "I gotta pee!" she uttered suddenly, the last syllable awkwardly exaggerated. She laughed heartily, squeezing her legs tightly together.

"I'm coming," Brehan managed to say in between groans. Angeliqué lay on his left like a lifeless doll, her head thrown back in a seemingly uncomfortable position. Nona rubbed her eyes and adjusted her mask. She made it to the door and opened it, managed to negotiate the turns in the hallways, found the bathroom, and relieved

herself. When she was finished, she splashed some
cold water on her face, which accomplished nothing but to cause her to shiver momentarily. Nona
left the bathroom after applying an uneven amount
of gloss to her lips. She met a waiter halfway back
who pushed a glass of champagne into her hands.
Nona accepted it, not wishing to argue with the
man. She had a hard time finding her way back.
All of the rooms looked the same at this point:
dark, lifeless. Every huddle of unmoving forms appeared the same to her. Junkies, every last one of
them. Nona giggled. *God, I'm glad I'm not like that,*
she thought.

A slightly ajar door beckoned Nona in. The
room was darker than the rest, the ceiling light extinguished; an empty champagne bottle that Nona
almost tripped over when she entered; she regained her balance and continued moving. A thin
window was cut into the far wall. An old radiator
under the shellacked window sill housed the remains of a few wine glasses. Nona focused her eyes
out the window and across the street. A huge
building with "Hotel" in red neon, the last three letters dark, provided the soothing light. That got her
giggling again—a neon signing proclaiming "HO!"

It took a moment for her eyes to adjust to the
near darkness. Had there been a window before?
She didn't remember. And she didn't care.

A movement off to the side caught her eye. A
figure swam into focus, a man whose features
Nona couldn't distinguish, regardless of what little
the mask hid. Nona smiled, showing her teeth.

"About time, I thought you'd gotten lost."

"Me?" the man responded.

"Yeah. Man, I had to go so damn bad!"

"Everything okay now?" he asked. He led her to the window and brushed off the radiator so Nona could sit down. He watched her and shook his head in disbelief. Beautiful, dressed out of some dream—fantasy, a goddess, a princess—too good to be true. And yet . . .

"Everyting irie now!" She giggled before continuing. "Listen, about the other day." Nona took his hand. "I just want to clear the air between us." She paused to sip her drink, spilled some down her chin, laughed uncontrollably for a minute before continuing.

"You straight?"

"For sure!" Nona waved the thought away. "Look. You and I have been playing games—" she said, rubbing his arm, "and I think it's time we ceased the drama, you feel me?"

"Drama?"

"Yeah, let's put a stop to it right now, okay?" Nona pulled him nearer. She tipped her head back and downed the rest of her champagne, then tossed the glass aside. It crashed to the floor shattering. Nona nor the man paid it any mind.

Instead, she reached for him, drawing him near. Kissed him longingly on the lips. He responded to her kiss and touch by draping his arms around her frame. His tongue invaded her mouth easily. They tasted each other hungrily, all of his guilt falling away like icicles on a wind-blown day.

Nona was thinking: this man has made me so

happy, with everything he's done for me, allowing me to grow—to shed my old outer layer, and grow into my thicker skin. He has freed me to be who I've always dreamed of becoming. Someone independent. Someone free.

Nona's hands massaged his back and ass. "So very happy," is all she said. One hand snaked down his chest to his stomach, finding his thighs and reaching between his legs. She grabbed his balls and squeezed lightly, licking his ear and neck. He moaned softly and she tilted her head back and laughed. "Time to make your day."

He moaned softly, nervously looking around the dim room for vacant stares. Nona had lain back on the radiator and hiked up her skirt, inviting him to play with her inner thighs. His hands lay still on her silky legs; she spread them wider, teasing him.

"Your turn, baby," she whispered, nibbling on his ear and kissing his face and neck. The skirt was rising, thighs spreading wider. Thinking about Malik—those feelings that were now gone. The thought left her as quickly as it had come.

His rock-hard dick stretched against his briefs. He could feel the pulse of blood through the veins; he swore he could almost hear its pounding. She unzipped his pants and freed him, rubbing it between her moist hands. Her legs open fully, the skirt wrinkled up by her stomach. He pulled one hand away and cautiously brushed the insides of her thighs, feeling for her panties. He found none, instead rubbing against bare wet flesh.

"You have a condom?" she whispered, thinking

about the woman she had seen earlier, the woman who commanded others with a mere glance. A look that said it all . . .

Her hands jerked his cock along the ridge of her throbbing pussy, squeezing the flesh as he palmed her breasts. Mouth over hers, his breath rushing fast, harried.

He groaned as he tweaked her nipples, felt the fullness of her ass. When she whispered softly, her lips grazing his ear, "Put it on, please, so you can fuck me," he just about died.

Separating from her, fumbling for just a moment, he located the wrapper in his wallet, tore the foil off and slipped it on. Moving back to her, she guided him into her effortlessly, letting out a soft moan as he breached her opening. The feeling was fantastic, sliding in and out slowly, her pussy wet from the anticipation, just the right amount of tension and squeeze to set him off. Nona reached behind and grabbed his ass with both hands, pulling him fully inside her. He grabbed at her camisole, pushed it upwards until her breasts were bare, and immediately sucked at each tit until they were wet with saliva, nipples taut as he attacked them voraciously.

Nona wanted to yell—so wanted to scream, "Take me, Brehan, fuck this pussy—it's yours!" But the lady who commanded men with a mere glance wouldn't be yelling—wouldn't be screaming at the top of her lungs.

No, she wouldn't have to.

Instead, Nona licked at his earlobe, grunted as he increased his pumping, her ass lifting off the radiator to meet his thrusts with her own, jutting out her pelvis, tongue forking out from between her teeth as she watched him work his magic down there—sweat dripping from his forehead, disappearing beneath the mask.

Fuck me, Brehan, she thought—*fuck me with that beautiful mocha-colored cock; give me all that you have to give . . . and then, baby, give me even* more . . .

He groaned and exploded, cumming several minutes after being guided into her. He pulled out so quickly and backed away, his chest heaving with a shortness of breath that she felt herself chilling. Nona lay back against the cool glass and suddenly she found herself weeping. This intimate act, over so suddenly, had sobered her up in an instant. She glanced around the room, taking in her spent lover in a darkened corner. She gathered her camisole down, mind racing as she struggled to straighten her skirt. Her silent lover seemed to shrivel away into the darkness.

How could this be?

It was not as she had imagined.

Brehan had failed her. He hadn't brought her to new heights. He hadn't infused her with anything delightful. It had all been a mistake.

Nona shook her head, eyes growing wide as the man moved closer, light from the window bringing his features in focus.

The mask was gone, and the horror of what she saw struck deep, a blow that almost knocked her off her feet.

The man standing in front of her was not Brehan.

He was just some stranger—some guy. A man she had never laid eyes on before.

Face illuminated by the half-light from the window, holding out his hands, grin painted on *thick*, whispering, "My name's David, by the way . . ."

Nona wept harder, then ran.

27

Forty minutes later, the taxi deposited Nona in front of Chantal's home. The ride seemed to take forever, regardless of the non-existent traffic at the early-morning hour. Her demeanor had morphed from frenzy to breakdown.

Asking the cabbie the time, her voice croaking; she shrieked when he told her: 4 a.m.

Paying the driver by haphazardly tossing a twenty at him, Nona raced from the cab and up the stairs. She pounded the door and was relieved when she saw her friend's familiar face. Chantal ushered her inside without a word, and Nona finally begun to calm down when an all-too-familiar voice bellowed from the next room: "WHERE'S THAT BITCH!"

Nona's blood froze that instant.

The voice was Malik's . . .

28

Short flecks of warm firelight danced off David Sands' dark body. A small fire burned softly as he painted, his mind engrossed in the fantasy of his art. The painting, tentatively called "Gray Matter," adequately portrayed his present feelings. The meter-by-meter canvas showed a weary traveler sitting alone in a deserted train station. On the other side of a barred window, the snow fell. The outside filled the interior of the station with thick gray light. The traveler's depressed look meshed with the dull interior to form a dismal scene. The painting was done in shades of gray and black. Sands had been working on it for a little more than two weeks now. The idea had come to him when he had returned home from Manhattan late one night and had seen a woman sitting on a bench in a dimly lit subway station. She was not sleeping, but sitting there, her eyes fixed in space, neither moving nor uttering a sound. Sands had begun to work on the painting the next day. Each twenty-four hours that passed thereafter had caused him to sink deeper and deeper into depression. He spent long hours in front of the easel, overcompensating for the way he felt. The work was indeed a good one, probably one of his best. The detail was extraordinary. It was just that he had nothing else to do but sit and concentrate on his work.

Nona was gone. That much was fact now. It had been what—thirty or forty days—since he had last seen her. The images of her sweet face were rapidly fading from the confines of his mind. All that was left was a tattered photograph whose likeness was beginning to fade as well. The finality of the situation was sobering indeed. It was a final gesture, the end of a fleeting fantasy that had caused him a great deal of joy, and a great deal of pain.

Nona represented something that only came around once in life—a dream that became reality for a few fleeting moments. For this, Sands was grateful. But the naked truth was that the fantasy was over. Was it a dream? Had those things actually happened? Sands had trouble remembering now. Perhaps it was all a dream. A vivid, yet powerful dream.

It was time to forget and press on. The last few weeks, although not at all easy, were beginning to erase the images from his head. Sands was thinking about other things now, though it was hard not to let thoughts of Nona invade his mind every few hours or so. There were more important things to do. Sands felt as if it was time to move on. A phase of his life was over. Period. Time to move on. Press on.

Painting helped. When nothing else would soothe the pain he was feeling, immersing himself in his art was a sure-fire way to make him forget. Actually Sands never really forgot, but painting, the concentration it required, the abstraction of ideas, the details in the strokes of his brush forced him to turn the pain into useful energy. All artists needed a source of inspiration—a cup from which the creativity would flow. For now, Nona was that cup, and Sands painted with a fever that had never been matched.

Gray Matter.

The name said it all.

A sense of everything gray—a blend of images, life experiences, senses, odors—all intermixed into a shower of gray. Lately, everything took on a shade of gray. Maybe it was the coolness of autumn; the loss of summer always made Sands feel down. Summer was upbeat and full of fun; autumn was a time for slowing down, for somber moments, for reflection. At least the painting was a good one. Sands hated to feel down and not be productive.

One good thing—he was back in school with his kids. They always made him smile—these young, energetic minds, full of life, anxious to test the limits of their creativity. At least he had them— during daylight hours, he was focused on his students; there wasn't much time for thoughts of Nona to creep back in . . .

The fire had burned down to near coals—not enough light to paint by. Sands decided to quit for the night, storing his paints and brushes away. He knelt by the fireplace, preferring not to turn on any lights and spoil the scene. This was one of his favorite times, when the light of day was fading, colors subsiding, and a dull gray haze seemed to fill the air. The small fire that he kindled each night was in defiance to this twilight gray, his way of keeping the light of day alive. The warm firelight cuddled and soothed, and brought back the color to his cheeks and forehead. Sitting close to the fire, as he did now, Sands felt good. The warmth from the coals nuzzled his skin and he shivered as he looked out across the expanse of space. The confines of the home were comforting and the dance of firelight mesmerizing. The building across from him—the one he now knew all too well—remained dark and drab in the twilight. Thoughts of seeing Nona for the first time invaded his head. Sands smiled as he remembered her rhythmic form moving in the nighttime air, her hips swinging to a silent beat. The shock of her wild hair, alive as it bounced along to the melody; her cheekbones strong, high, and shapely; the gold chain gently lapping at her half-exposed breasts, sparkling as she moved. The vision, for one singular moment, was crystal clear. Then it faded as fast as it had appeared, and all that was left was a dark-brown face of stone. A building facade. Lifeless like the wind.

Why him? This was the question that taunted him night after night. Sometimes, when he was unable to sleep he would toss and turn for hours, those two words nicking at his brain over and over. Why him? Nona could have had any man on earth. So why had she shared herself with him; why had she even paid him the slightest bit of attention? Sure, Sands was good looking, but Nona was a goddess! It didn't make any sense. These thoughts bothered Sands most of all. In time, he knew he would get over her. Time had a way of making things seem unimportant in the overall scheme of things. Nona would be fleeting history one day, but these fundamental questions, if never answered, would haunt him for the rest of his life.

Life was cruel. Had this been a sick joke played on him? As he tossed this idea around in his head, he became angry. It wasn't fair. Teasing him with someone so beautiful as Nona and then snatching her from his very grasp was grossly unfair. Perhaps it was something he had done. No, that could not have been it. One thing was clear. Sands was determined to stop all of the self-pity and get on with his life. But, if she ever did appear again, even for a moment, Sands would not let her go ever again. This, he swore before God.

Light sprung from the third floor of the vacant brownstone building. Perhaps the fact that Sands did not recognize it immediately was indeed proof that he was well on his way to overcoming Nona. But finally, after a period of minutes, the stab of light seemed to reach out and tug on his sleeve, waking him from his sleep, causing his heart to flutter.

Could it be Nona?

Sands was afraid to move.

In the near darkness, his prone form lay stiff as a board, not wanting to be fooled again. His hand went to his face and rubbed his tired eyes.

No, this is not a dream, he told himself, *this is real.*

12:30 p.m. He climbed slowly out of bed, his nakedness ignored as he clamored over to the large window and pressed his face against the coolness of the glass. An image swam in and out of focus against a yellowing shade. Unconsciously, he held his breath as if exhaling would shatter the image-fantasy that was unfolding. The form moved rhythmically in and out, here a moment, then gone. Was it Nona? The shade rolled up in an instant, and his question was quickly answered.

Nona's beautiful body moved to a groove Sands could not hear, but instantly the pulse of his soul found her rhythm. His heart pounded against his chest wall with an intensity that he was sure would kill him. Nona moved and Sands' eyes followed her every movement. Every thrust of her hip from one side to the other was captured on his retinas. Atop high cheekbones rested dark sunglasses. Sands smiled. A defiance to the night, like his firelight. God, was she beautiful. Sands felt the desire for her swell. The intensity of what he felt was overpowering, and Sands had to grasp the cold glass for support. His fingers slipped through the sheen of condensation and slid down to the floor, leaving a trail of parallel streams in the glass. On the floor, he exhaled heavily and closed his eyes for a moment. When he opened and focused them on the building's third floor, Nona was gone.

Sands erupted from the floor like a rabbit. He ran to the side of his bed and grabbed his clothes: worn Levis and a dark tee shirt. He slipped on a pair of sandals and raced to the door.

His hair was a mess. His hand tried in vain to tame back his curly hair, but to no avail. Sands flung open the door and raced down the stairs. This time, he would not lose her. He swore before God!

Sands yanked open the door and ran outside. He stopped at the bottom of the steps for a second to take stock of his situation. For a moment he considered sprinting around the block to the vacant building, breaking the large slab of wood that covered the door, and running up to the bedroom to scoop Nona up in his arms and away. But something inside made him pause and reflect on what he was about to do. He sat down on the cool stone stoop and gritted his teeth. *I've been down this road before,* he told himself. His eyes scanned up and down the block. Dead calm. On impulse, he got up and went back inside, climbing the steps to his apartment and opening the door. Sands went to the large window and stared out at the dark house. For a long while he just stood there, taking in the expanse of dark stone. No movement, no lights. No sign of Nona. Nothing.

Sands expected as much.

That night David Sands dreamt about windows: tall ones of thick dark glass and a wide stretch of opaque, silent windows. Then Nona appeared and the fantasy began.

A woman in a window.

A woman clad in dark sunglasses atop high cheekbones with long, unkempt funky hair. Seductive, sensuous—a fantasy come to life.

So many windows, Sands thought. All of those windows cut into dark building faces, the miles and miles of cold glass that served as portals into the house—lives of the masses. A magical looking glass. For Sands, he had managed to be in the right place at the right time.

Nona was a fantasy that had come to life. And for the duration of that fantasy, she had been his.

That alone made him smile . . .

29

The automobile glided from one intersection to the next as if in slow motion, a dream in which sound was non-existent. It was like the seconds before an accident, where everything is peaceful, quiet, and so deadly.

Malik hadn't said a word, and this caused Nona the greatest concern. She sat crowded in the corner of the passenger seat, silent and frightened, not daring to utter a word, lest Malik lash out and strike her.

Where is he taking me? Nona's head barely moved, not wanting to draw attention to herself. Her eyes scanned the street signs searching for a hint to their destination. Malik's dark hands firmly gripped the wheel of the '78 Chevrolet Impala, his baby, stare unwavering, breathing loud and forced.

Malik was hot.

No, that was not an adequate description.

Nona had never seen him like this. From the

moment she had stepped foot in Chantal's home, he had remained quiet, but in his eyes sparked the fire of a madman.

"Let's go," was the first and only phrase he had uttered before gripping Nona's elbow and directing her down the steps, into the car. He had thrust her inside, not showing the slightest bit of emotion when she was thrown against the passenger door frame.

Nona's makeup was running and pasting, and the tracks of dried tears meandered down her cheeks; she sat there quietly, hoping their silence would dissipate the furor that was brewing. Little did she realize it was just beginning.

Mind spinning...head throbbing. Should she say something? Threaten him with the cops if things escalate?

No, better not say that just yet. She gripped her cell in her hand, fingers rubbing the keys, ready to dial 911. As if that would do any good right now.

The car slowed to a stop and Malik backed into an open space behind a parked van. It was still dark—not even five in the morning yet. Nona looked up, did not recognize the place—a dark block somewhere in Brooklyn—and put her head back down.

"Malik?" she whispered, her scratchy voice barely audible.

"Shut the fuck up. Don't say another fucking word!"

"But . . ."

"BITCH!" Malik lashed out, his balled fist crashing into her cheekbone. Her face smashed into the window with a thud, the pain so unbearable she blanked out for a moment—a short time—enough for Malik to get out of the car, come around to the other side, and drag her hurting body out.

Nona screamed.

"Quiet!" Malik hissed. He brought his face level with her blackening cheek, his eyes narrowed and on fire.

"You listen to me. If you make one fucking sound, I swear I'll kill you right here, you understand me? Don't fuck with me; keep quiet and live."

The words, lightning harsh, almost too unbelievable to believe, but crystal fucking clear, seeped into Nona's head and chilled her to the bone. This time, she knew that he would do what he said, killing her if necessary.

Malik dragged Nona down the block to a tall brownstone by the corner. Her flimsy outfit, the top ripped away in a coke-induced haze, flapped in the morning breeze. Her right hand clutched her chest trying in vain to keep herself from shivering. She eyed the ground around her like a madman—her cell phone was gone. Malik ignored her exposed breasts and rattling teeth. He dragged her onward, up the steps to the second-floor landing, pushed her against the door, and rang the bell. Nona wiped her hair away from her bruised face and glanced up at the nameplate above the brass bell.

Dr. Jose Melendez—Internal Medicine.

A pain shot from the base of her spine to her

neck. What were they doing here, Nona wondered? Why Dr. Melendez? Why this time of morning?

Malik punched the bell furiously, soon becoming impatient and pounding on the glass. A top-floor light came on and several minutes later the tired face of a man emerged from behind the curtains. His eyes focused on Malik and then Nona before a wave of recognition passed over him. He opened the door while a hand went to straightening his hair.

"Mr. and Mrs. Scott-Walker, is something wrong?" the doctor asked.

"Open up, Doc! We've got to see you," Malik responded.

"Can't this wait? It's not even light out!"

"No, damn it; now get out of the way." Malik barreled his way in, the doctor easily giving way to Malik's weight. Nona entered last, propelled by Malik's firm grip. Dr. Melendez switched on the foyer light and tightened his robe. He stood in the hallway and spread out his hands.

"What is the meaning of this, Malik? This is my house!"

"Look, Doc, I need you to do this. Now. Check her! Tell me if she's slept with anyone else but me."

"Now listen here, Mr. Scott-Walker, I . . ."

"No, you listen. You're going to go into your examination room and check my wife. And then you're going to tell me if she's had sex earlier tonight!" Nona closed her eyes and wept, her back pressed against the door, wishing to be engulfed by the house walls and disappear. Suddenly, all the talk, all of the emergent feelings of finally being in control—a new woman—evaporated.

"This is ridiculous!" Melendez said. "I won't be treated like this. I won't allow you or anyone else to barge into my house and make idiotic requests or threats like this. I won't have it!" He quickly glanced at Nona, taking in her torn outfit and bruised face. "Are you okay? Who did this to you?" he asked, gingerly taking her chin in his hand. "Did you do this to your wife, Malik? Did you? My God! I will be forced to call the police if you don't leave my home at once!" The doctor made a step toward the door, but Malik intercepted him. Grabbing the elderly man by the arm, he spun him around toward the stairway, pushing him into the banister. As the doctor recovered from the recoil and turned around angrily, a flash of metal arced from Malik's waistband to the doctor's head. Nona screamed, the doctor staggering backward into a wall, hitting it with a sickening thud.

Malik, holding a gun, snickered.

Smith and Wesson.

Thirty-eight caliber, Gleaming steel.

The barrel of the pistol level with the doctor's temple.

With a steady hand, Malik pulled back the hammer.

"No!" Nona screamed.

She pushed off from the wall, but Malik's hand

caught her and slapped her backwards. The doctor remained motionless, beads of sweat forming on his brow. Nona began to cry uncontrollably. This situation was beyond out of hand. Why couldn't the doctor live with a house full of people? His kids, as she remembered were off at college, and his wife, Nona had heard, had divorced him a number of years ago. He was rumored to be gay and had taken a lover. Nona looked into the doctor's eyes and saw pain, desperation, and pity. She looked back reassuringly, more for her sake than for his.

"Now, everybody is gonna shut up and do what I say!" Malik said a bit too controlled. That scared Nona more than anything else. He was being too methodical.

Too in control.

"Doc, one more time, 'cause I don't think you understood me the first time. We're going to go in there, the three of us. Nona here, the slut-bitch, will lay down for you, her legs wide," he sneered. "That shouldn't be too hard, should it, baby?" Malik ignored Nona's pained eyes. "Then you'll examine her for signs of sexual intercourse. Any questions? All routine, right Doc? Now, do I make myself clear?" The gun pressed into the doctor's temple, the metal barrel deathly cold. The doctor swallowed once. Nodded.

"Perfectly clear," he managed to say.

The white, sterile room frightened Nona. She had come here a hundred times. Perhaps a thousand. She had met Dr. Melendez when she had first come over—that was over a decade and a half ago—he had watched her grow, blossom from a pug-nosed kid to a mature, beautiful woman. This morning, though, none of that mattered. Her life was falling apart, tearing at the seams, about to be unraveled by a jealous husband who had come unglued. Malik had gone postal!

She had ceased her crying by this time. She willed herself to calm down, her whimpers silenced by what was transpiring around her. She was incredibly frightened, but determined to keep her dignity. Malik was going to force this no matter what. She might as well bear it to the end and keep her head up, showing him he couldn't break her despite his abuse.

Doctor Melendez led Nona to his examination table and handed her a cotton robe. Malik snatched it from his hands and threw it on the floor.

"Stop stalling!" he yelled. "Get on with this shit!"

Silently, the doctor picked up the robe and placed it on a chair, shaking his head slowly as Nona lay down. She fought back the tears and hiked up her skirt, spreading her legs for the doctor in front. Melendez looked at Nona and turned away embarrassed.

"Gynecology is not my specialty you know," he told Malik. "I won't be able to give you a definitive answer."

"You don't have to be a specialist, doc, to tell whether someone's been fucking or not. Even I know that." Malik kept the gun trained on the doctor who shrugged his shoulders while donning a pair of latex gloves. He dragged a stool over by the table and sat down, grasping Nona's legs and positioning them on either side of the examination table. He shook his head again and began to probe.

A few minutes later, Dr. Melendez sat back, peeling off the latex gloves and throwing them on the table beside Nona. Nona sat up and covered herself without a word.

"What do you want from me, Mr. Scott-Walker? My examination is inconclusive. She's not a virgin, that much is obvious. But whether she had sex in the last few hours is unknown. I see no swelling or reddening—so she did not have forced sex, I feel confident about that. But I'd have to run some tests, swab for semen to be certain." The doctor shrugged his shoulders. "Why don't you just go home and forget this nonsense? And please, put that gun down before someone gets hurt!"

"Bullshit. You're a doctor. You're telling me you can't tell whether someone has had sex?" Malik walked over, gripping the pistol tighter in his hand. "Is that what you're telling me, doc?"

"I'm sorry, but . . ."

"Shut up!" Malik yelled, smashing the steel barrel of the gun into the back of the doctor's head. He fell sideways onto the floor and Nona cringed, her hands flying to her face. "Get back over here!" Malik yelled, pulling Nona's legs back into position. He forced her legs apart and thrust a finger into her vagina without concern, pulling it out and looking at it carefully. He poised his finger by his

nose and sniffed, suddenly groaning, swinging his
fist wildly.

"Get up!" he bellowed, practically pulling Nona
off the table and onto the floor. Nona complied
without a word. Malik hunched down by the doctor who lay sprawled on the floor, dazed but conscious, holding his bruised head in his hand.
"Listen, old man. You don't have to be a fucking
M.D. to recognize this," Malik hissed, wiping his
finger on the doctor's nose. "Cum, you asshole!
The answer to my fucking question." The doctor
remained silent, watching the gun waving in front
of his face. "You make one fucking move to pick
up that phone to call anyone, especially the police,
and I swear as God is my witness I'll come back and
hunt your ass down!"

Malik stood up and grabbed Nona by the arm,
shoving her out of the room and into the hallway.

"Let's go, slut! You and I got a few things to dis-
cuss," Malik hissed. He shoved the thirty-eight into
his pants and pushed Nona out the door, down the
steps. Her mind had shut down—she was unable
to speak. Words would not come.

Dr. Melendez remained on the floor alone for a
while, scared to move even a single muscle, wondering if what had just transpired was real, or just a
horrid dream?

Malik unlocked the door to the brownstone
quickly, shoving Nona inside. It was a few minutes
before six a.m. She was beyond exhausted.

Her entire body hurt.

The only thing she was aware of was the pain.

He shut the door behind him, slammed the deadbolt into place, and twisted the second lock. Nona rubbed her bruised face and wrist (now red from Malik's firm grip), and stood still in the foyer, waiting for Malik to speak. He was cold and silent, leaving her to contemplate her fate as he went down the stairs to the kitchen. She went up to the third-floor bathroom and sponged off her face and neck, her cheek stinging from the water. Her tears were renewed when she saw her face in the mirror. Her features showed a worn and bruised woman, nothing like what she had been just a few hours ago at the masquerade ball.

That seemed like another time. It was an event that she had trouble remembering now. Images swam in and out of focus, the detail, like the memories of a long-ago childhood, lost forever. What would happen now, Nona wondered? Malik was acting like a madman, beyond irrational. She kicked herself a thousand times for not calling the police a few weeks ago. That was her biggest mistake—she had had the power to shut this down—to end this before it ever began. But she hadn't. Why? Because Nona was frightened of the unknown. What would happen to her if her husband was locked up? What would happen to her when he got out? Who would pay the bills in the meantime?

So many unanswered questions. And who do you

talk to about this? Chantal? Brehan? Michael—her neighbor?

No. There was no one who could truly understand what she felt. Better to just shut up and wait out this storm.

She wondered how much worse it was going to get. Body shuddering, convulsing with fear at the answers that nudged inside her head . . .

Nona met Malik on the second-floor landing as he returned from the kitchen holding a bottle of Red Stripe. He took wild swigs from the brown bottle, spilling a generous amount on his tank top. Nona watched him in silence, fearing him, wishing he would put the bottle down and speak to her.

"Are you going to talk to me, Malik?"

"Shut up," Malik responded simply, neither shouting nor whispering, merely speaking in an even tone that cut Nona to the bone.

"I can't remain quiet, Malik," she responded. "You've been dragging me around for hours. When is this going to stop? You haven't even heard my side of the story—didn't even bother to ask. Instead you drag me to the doctor's like I'm some dog . . ."

"Your side of the story?" Malik asked incredulously. "There is no *your* side of the story. You've been unfaithful—you've fucked around on your husband—"

"You don't know that!" Nona yelled, testing the waters.

"The fuck I don't! You think I'm stupid? Think

I'm just one of these dumb mutha fuckas who can't see what's staring him dead in the face?" Malik asked, pausing to take another swig of the beer. "Don't play me, 'cause I'm past playing games. I will fuck you up for real—I don't even give a shit anymore."

"Look, Malik, let me explain to you what is happening. I'm still your wife—let me tell you my side, so you can understand just how wrong you have been." Nona smiled weakly, hating herself this very instant as she walked over slowly to Malik, sensing the rage inside him was subsiding inside him, that it was all about survival. Minute-by-minute survival.

"Things between you and me haven't been right for some time now," she said, reaching out to stroke his face—thought better of it, and at the last second touched his elbow instead. "Regardless of what has gone down between you and me, you are still my husband. And I still love you, Malik." Left her hand on his forearm for a moment. "Need to know that I would never—"

"Cut the shit!" he yelled, arcing the bottle up toward her head. Nona ducked, the bottle missing her temple by mere inches. "Fuck you and your stories. I'm done—through with this shit!" He stomped up the stairs to the third floor, leaving Nona dazed from the near collision. She remained in the hallway for a moment, contemplating her next move.

The wall phone was six feet away.

Go to it, she commanded herself silently.

Dial 911. Don't even think—just do it!
The man is an animal!
He's beat the shit out of his wife; pistol whipped an-other human being!
Insanity!
What's next? What can possibly happen next?

The rage inside her began to boil, simmering over the top.

Nona checked her other options: sit tight, wait out this storm—perhaps; confront Malik now, tell him he was wrong—no, a non-starter—that shit would get her killed. The image of the gleaming gun stuck in her mind. Where had it come from? Where had Malik gotten a gun?

Would he actually use it on her?

Nona rubbed her temples as she contemplated the question. Her mind raced. Had Malik ever shown himself to be violent? Did he possess what-ever it is one needed to take a life?

Nona didn't think so . . .

The rage mounted. She desperately wanted to hurt Malik—show him how wrong he had been, treating his wife like an animal. Man-handling her, forcing her to submit to some stupid-ass exam, legs spread as if she were a whore! Thoughts of what she did a few hours ago didn't even enter her psy-che at this juncture.

It would be a gamble, she knew, to confront him, but what other option did she really have? Call the police? She'd be dead before she replaced the receiver . . .

Run? To where?

Talk to him—it was the only option she had left.
One she had to take. Now. Nona would put her
foot down and show Malik that he could not walk
all over her. She was a woman, a human being with
feelings; she was his wife, and she would not let
herself be trampled. The last few weeks had taught
her plenty. She had learned a great deal about herself, about the woman who had been trapped
under glass for so long. Finally, that woman was free,
and Nona was determined not to have her caged
ever again.

With a renewed sense of courage, Nona climbed
the steps to the bedroom, knowing fully well that
this decision could prove fatal. But the conse-
quences of not confronting Malik were far worse.

If he hit her once, he would do it again.

It would never stop.

Nona had always said she'd be damned if she allowed herself to become one of those women—an
abused wife.

And yet, as she glanced around at her surroundings, one eye misting from the onset of tears—the
other puffy and half-closed from Malik's clenched
fist—she realized that that's exactly what she had
become. A piece of meat— a punching bag for the
man she had once loved.

Nona mused over the woman from the party.

She remembered how she had felt after witnessing her in action.

She recalled the admiration she had felt then.

Nona, too, could have that strength.

It was all up to her . . . as long as she remained

strong. She could come out triumphant. A winner. Or she could be dead.

But remaining here, in this place and space was not an alternative. Not anymore.

Sacrifice was inevitable. The road uphill not yet paved . . .

Her next move would be her life's greatest gamble.

The outcome unknown.

This frightened Nona most of all . . .

30

A blanket of fresh mist huddled against the street curb. David Sands walked slowly down the brownstone steps, stopping at the bottom to light a cigarette. He had recently begun smoking again. He had quit for a long time: four or five years. But recent events had caused him to take up the habit again. He really didn't like smoking; the air hung in his nostrils and throat and worst of all, in his clothes—making him wrinkle up his nose and cough. And yet, he lit one this gray evening. He twirled the cigarette between his fingers, running them along the edge of the white paper, feeling the roundness of the thing, finding comfort.

Sands was dressed in a light gray suit, double-breasted, with a starched white shirt underneath and a dark tie. *Probably overdressed,* he thought. But then again, he was going out; he didn't want to appear casual. He wanted to look and feel good.

His fingers reached into his coat pocket for the keys to his car, but as he approached the automobile he decided to head for the subway instead. He felt like walking. The air would do him good. He started down the street, concentrating on the sound that his shoes made—taps against the cold, wet ground. He checked his watch—eleven-thirty. It would take him approximately forty-five minutes to get into the city. That was okay. He needed the time to relax, time to not concentrate on anything too cerebral. Walking gave him a sense of not belonging to anything; he was able to let his mind go free and wander. He stared at the brownstones as he walked by—their colors, their textures, the roughness or smoothness of the faces of the stones.

A light rain began. Sands turned up his collar and cursed himself for not bringing an umbrella. He thought about turning back, but the idea of returning to the empty apartment drew him onward. Some of the gas lights in front stoops were on, others burnt out. He observed the still automobiles, the light patter of rain drumming against the windshields and metal bodies. Some thoughts came to mind—images for new works, paintings that he would later create. Suddenly, warmth flowed into him, the rain notwithstanding. Sands felt good tonight. The adrenaline began to flow within him.

Sands waited at the corner for the light to change. Red light from a traffic light bathed the corner asphalt. It reflected onto the wet pavement before shifting to green. Sands concentrated on the changing colors. He was also struck by the fresh scent of rain. The mixture of wet foliage and stone gave off an interesting aroma. No matter where you went, whether into the countryside or the steel and glass jungle of Manhattan, the scent of fresh rain always remained the same. It was wonderful to fill your lungs with the fresh precipitation. Rainy days cleansed the earth and made things whole again.

Sands continued to walk. Past row houses, brownstones dark, their occupants fast asleep. A few lights remained on, a few blue hues from television sets, a few low-wattage yellow bulbs burning in the corner by a window. His thoughts went to the occupants inside these homes, warm and content, probably curled up tight against a loved one, reading the paper or a good book, watching a movie, catching the last of the evening's late news. They weren't like him—a man alone—a man seemingly obsessed with a dream.

He came to the subway and took the steps down, fished a MetroCard from his pants pocket and slotted it into the turnstile. Sands waited on the platform for a train to take him into the city.

The ride was uneventful. The subway cars were sparsely populated with a few people: several couples; a lone teenager with spiked hair and tattoos; a woman with reading glasses huddled down, a book inches from her face, seemingly too scared to glance up. This was New York; at night, on the subway, anything could happen . . .

Sands decided to stand, not sit. He stood against the door of the subway car, watching his reflection in the glass, and thought about her.

He felt the need for another cigarette but fought the temptation. Was he feeling anxious?

Yes.

Sands wished that he had close friends, people

he could really count on and talk to. But then they would never fully understand him. And he would never be able to fully explain just how he was feeling right now. Would he even want to tell another person about the attraction he felt for this fantasy woman? Maybe they would understand. But probably not. They would write him off as a lunatic, a crackpot, an artist with crazy visions. So Sands kept to himself—kept his thoughts, dreams, and secrets to himself.

It was better off that way . . .

Sands got off at Eighteenth Street on a whim and began walking north. Ten minutes later he turned onto a side street and noticed the bright neon of a tavern sign: The Oyster Shell Lounge. The large red neon lettering coaxed him nearer. In the window, signs for Budweiser and live girls helped Sands quickly decide that he could use a drink.

The brass knob to the heavy oak door seemed threatening. He grasped the handle, feeling the metal cold to his touch. He glanced to the left, then to the right. The street was dark and desolate. He was alone. He pulled the door open and went in.

The size of the place was deceiving. From the outside, it had looked like a small little tavern, one bar jutted between two buildings made of brick. Once inside he noticed that the place went back quite a ways. There were two bars: one by the door where Sands stood, and another diagonally across the floor by the rest rooms. Dead center was a raised stage. It was a small thing, about four feet square, and stood three feet off the ground. A thin nude woman danced there, her body highlighted by a number of spotlights. The music emanated from a small jukebox across from the stage by the wall. A leggy blonde stood in front of the machine, pressing buttons, feeding in quarters, waiting for her turn to entertain.

He noticed the colors first. Deep reds: imitation leather chairs; high-back bar stools; small, circular glass-top tables; the walls that seemed to glitter with a satin finish. Rich browns: thin wooden floor-boards, a low drop ceiling. A few photographs graced the walls of The Oyster Shell Lounge: dancers too numerous to name, faces that once adorned the small, center stage—now only memories.

The place was not crowded this evening. One couple, the rest white males, a few in suits sat off to the sides in the shadows away from the activity on the stage. Several tables were placed around the stage. They contained men drinking beer and watching the woman dance to R&B tunes. Sands walked up to the bar, pushed his collar down and pulled out his wallet.

"What'll it be?" the bartender, a young woman with dyed blond hair and fake eyelashes, asked.

"A tall glass of rum with lots of ice, to start." Sands grabbed his drink and walked over to one of the tables. He didn't get too close to the stage. Too close and the dancers would stare at you, parade their wares in your direction, make you feel obligated to stuff a dollar bill or two in their garters.

Sands wasn't into that, so he found a seat about eight feet from the stage, took a sip of the icy rum, and watched the woman dance.

The dancer was a thin Japanese woman with small, pert breasts, nice ass, and a lean, lithe body. She moved well considering the four-inch-high stiletto heels that adorned her feet. Sands looked up at her; she returned his gaze for a moment and smiled. He felt himself blush, took another sip of the drink and looked around, trying not to seem conspicuous.

Sands counted four waitresses serving the customers. All were dressed in scantily clad outfits: short miniskirts that left nothing to the imagination, fishnet nylons, and shiny black pumps. Low-cut blouses revealed mounds of breast whenever they bent down to give you a drink. Sands glanced around the room. Atmosphere wasn't an issue here. Nothing fancy was needed for a go-go bar like The Oyster Shell Lounge. Although it was a simple, quaint place, it didn't have much class. The patrons came for the dancers, not the decor. They came to lose themselves among the shadows of deep reds and rich browns. They came for booze and for the women. They came to lose themselves in their erotic moves.

Sands focused his attention on the dancer. She moved her body well and appeared carefree, as if she belonged on stage. She seemed unaware or unconcerned that men were watching her, as if she were alone, dancing in her own living room. She moved from one corner to the next, not remaining in one place, swaying her hips seductively, sending her hands over her head, causing her breasts to rise, throwing her long, dark hair back. A twinge of excitement shot through his body. He felt himself growing hard. *This wasn't such a bad idea,* he thought. *I needed to get out, get some fresh air, and be among new faces, new sights; hear new sounds.* A change of scenery was just what the doctor ordered.

The woman smiled at him again. He looked around. Most of the other patrons were locked onto her rhythmic movements. A large number of the men seemed dazed—perhaps drunk; some hunkered down here until closing time, men with nowhere to go.

Was Sands like these men?

Perhaps, and the thought was indeed sobering.

A younger man sat at the bar. Because he was well-dressed, Sands had singled him out of the crowd. He wore a nicely cut suit with a white scarf around his neck. The man left his seat and walked over to the Japanese girl. She moved to the edge of the stage and danced in front of him. He reached into his pocket and pulled out a bill—just how much, Sands could not tell from where he sat. The man folded it in half length-wise and waved it in front of his nose. The dancer smiled at him and they played their little game. He pushed the money toward her; she backed away. As she moved in front of him, the thin patch of dark hair between her legs revealed the flesh of her sex. The man concentrated his stare on it. He didn't move. He seemed to be inhaling her womanly scent. Then he laughed and she tilted her head back, laughing along as well. He slipped the bill inside the elastic of her garter as she bent down, pressing her small breasts together and kissing the man on his cheek.

Several minutes later the dance was over. Scattered applause sounded as the lights faded to black for a moment. Another woman came on stage. This one was a little heavier, darker skinned, yet equally as lovely as the one before. Sands watched her attentively. A new set of songs sang out from the jukebox—a heavier beat, something he could relate to. One of the waitresses came by and asked if he'd like another. Sands nodded slowly. She returned momentarily with a fresh glass and a bowl of beer nuts. He paid her silently, nodding but not taking the time to converse with her. She took the money and sauntered away.

Halfway through the black girl's dance, he felt a tap at his shoulder. He turned around and stared up at a woman. She was wearing the same flimsy outfit as the rest of the waitresses, but he hadn't noticed her before. She bent down toward him, let her smile linger a moment longer than necessary. Sands' eyes traveled to her low-cut blouse and her oversized breasts that pressed against the thin, almost translucent, material.

"May I sit down?" she asked.

Sands shrugged. "Sure." The fingers of her left hand curled around a tall glass of white wine. She took a small sip, tilted her head back, and let it drain down her throat. She licked her lips seductively.

"Looking for anything special?" she asked. Sands smiled.

"No, not really. I just came for the entertainment. I enjoy watching girls dance. It's good for the soul."

"Yeah, sure," she said. "I understand."

"Is there anyone else that you might be interested in?"

"No, thanks anyway." He lowered his head, feeling suddenly embarrassed.

"Too bad. But if you change your mind, ask for Amber. I won't be far away." The woman rose and left.

31

Malik looked up from the bed when Nona walked in. He clutched the now-empty bottle of Red Stripe like a scared child holds his teddy bear. His clothes were in disarray; his wild-eyed stare told Nona he was still furious. She sat down slowly on the bed beside him, fighting the rising fear that welled up inside of her. *Take it slow,* she told herself; *slow and easy, and everything will be all right.*

"Malik, baby, listen to me, please," Nona pleaded, touching his arm. He pulled away quickly, as if her touch was infectious.

"Leave me alone. I have nothing more to say to you."

"You do," she replied matter-of-factly, but the words were barely above a whisper. "You can not treat me like an animal and expect me to just sit there obediently, dragging me here and there until you are finished throwing me around. And what about the doctor? Think he's just going to forget about you pistol-whipping him?"

"Don't fuck with me, Nona," he retorted, eyes red, finger outstretched in her direction. "You should be damn glad that you're still in one piece right about now," he hissed.

Nona stood abruptly. "And just what is that supposed to mean?"

She moved to the top-floor window. She felt a twinge of hope—a thin ray of light in otherwise utter darkness; sensing Malik was tiring, he was slowing; and she was gaining the upper hand, albeit slowly.

"It means just what it sounds like," Malik yelled, getting up from the bed and lashing out at Nona. She pulled back, safely out of reach.

"I'm sick and tired of you, Malik! You think you can treat me like this? Slapping me, pulling me around? I'm your wife, damn it, or have you forgotten?" Nona yelled, pointing her finger in his face. "What are you gonna do next—shoot your own fucking wife?"

Malik swung at her outstretched hand with his own, his body tipping slightly from the effects of the beer. It was obvious that Malik had been drinking for some time now.

"You're the one who's forgotten! I'm not the one fucking around here!" Malik reached for Nona as she recoiled backwards, his muscular arm catching her at the small of her back, hand rising upwards. His hand found her hair, yanking down hard, forcing her to scream in pain. Nona retaliated by kicking savagely about, connecting with his shin and knee. It was Malik's turn to yell out.

"Crazy bitch! You think this is a game?" he yelled, grabbing the bottle by the neck and raising it to shoulder height.

"Go ahead!" Nona yelled, her back to the window, her body boxed in by Malik's solid frame. "Do it, kill me. That's what you want, isn't it?" She paused for a split second as Malik's eyes darkened. "Look at where we are, Malik—you're standing over me, drunk as shit. You've beat your wife, beaten her—you hear me? You've assaulted another man— all because of what? I'll tell you—because you don't trust me—because you don't even know who I am anymore."

Malik backed off an inch. Then another.

"Our marriage is on the downslide, and all you care about is your macho pride, even more than you do about me!"

She pushed away from the window sill, into his space.

"You used to care about me—used to care about what I wanted. You used to tell me all you wanted to do is take care of me—to shield me from the bad things in this world. But look at you—you're holding a bottle—ready to hit me again."

Nona shook her head morosely.

"I don't know how things got to this point—but here we are. You're ready to beat your wife down— fuck her up so damn bad she no longer moves— as if that's the only way you'll know with absolute surety that she belongs to you and no one else. Well, I'm here to tell you—you've lost me, Malik—

not because of another man, but because of your actions . . ."

She moved forward, until inches separated them. She could feel his foul breath on her face. With little effort, he could strangle her from where he stood. It would be easy—the end to what he began. And yet, Nona was no longer afraid. Adrenaline coursed through her veins, making her strong. Giving her renewed strength.

"I don't love you no more, Malik—not because of some other man—but because of this—" She gestured to the bottle that now dangled limp from his fingers. "Because you're ready to smash a bottle against my skull. You're ready to fuck your wife up, and you didn't even bother to find out the truth."

Nona shook her head. Spied the .38 on the dresser.

"You are so ready to do this—" she said, pointing to the gun behind her, "ready to shoot your own wife?"

There were tears in her eyes. She turned back—leveled her gaze at her husband. She did not blink. She did not move. Instead, she held her ground, until Malik blinked and glanced down.

Her voice was near-whisper when she spoke next. "I will not let you abuse me anymore. I should have called the police weeks ago when you hurt me. But I didn't. Told myself what happened was a fluke—an aberration—made myself pretend it didn't exist. But this?" she said, touching her swollen eye and cheek, wincing in the process, "is no aberration—it's not make-believe. It's real. You did this, Malik—look at me—look closely at what you did to your used-to-be-beautiful wife."

Malik slowly raised his gaze, trained it on Nona's bruised face. His features were strained. The weight of what he had done began to settle on him.

His shoulders sagged. His eyes watered.

"This is what pimps do to their bitches . . ." Nona whispered.

"You're a pimp—treating me like your bitch . . ." Nona glanced down to the ground. Then back up. "But I'm nobody's bitch . . ."

Sucked in an audible sigh, the first deep breath since stepping out of the cab hours ago. Stepped back, out of her husband's range.

"Nobody's bitch, Malik—not some pimp's, not your bitch," she recited.

Raised her stare until it locked onto his.

"You feel me?"

Malik stared at his wife for a long time while Nona stood silently against the window, arms crossed over her chest. He raised the Red Stripe to his lips, letting the remnants drip down his throat, shaking his head, whether from her words or from the empty beer Nona would not know. He considered what she had said, weighing the bottle in his hand and they stared, eye to eye, fighters sizing each other up, the only sound their respective breathing— heavy burdened sighs.

Malik slowly transferred the beer bottle to his left hand.

Nona watched disinterestedly. Wondering what his next move would be.

Then, without warning, Malik punched Nona dead in her face.

32

After an hour and a half of watching women dance, after five or six glasses of Jamaican rum, David Sands lost track of the time. He lost track of the women and their moves as one woman's dance blended into another's. He was just another lonely face with a hard-on, sitting in a dimly lit go-go bar called The Oyster Shell Lounge with imitation red leather chairs, and a plastic jukebox that skipped when you hit it too hard. The Oyster Shell Lounge. What a fucked-up name for a go-go bar. He would have expected something far more catchy. Something a bit more risqué. He had no idea what time it was and couldn't find the strength to glance at his watch. Twelve, one? It really didn't matter. As long as the women were here, teasing the patrons with their bare tits and lovely asses, Sands could care less.

As the night wore on, the place seemed to grow darker. The lights seemed to grow colder. His head began to ache. Sands knew he had consumed too much alcohol. Each time he drained his glass he swore it would be his last, but when the waitress reappeared with a smile, he'd agreed to one more. He made countless trips to the men's room, almost losing his way back several times. He ordered Cokes, then just plain ice water. The waitresses brought them to him faithfully. They didn't care what he ordered, just that he ordered something and tipped. They charged him the same, and Sands didn't seem to take notice.

The crowd thinned. Sands forgot about the others. They seemed to blend into the surrounding red chairs and brown floor. It was then that only he and the dancers remained. They danced for him and no one else, or so he believed. Every so often a woman would come by, ask if he needed a refill, ask if he wanted to stretch his legs and go upstairs. He'd shake his head, and stare toward the stage. The heaving of bare breasts; tight, young, round asses; G-strings, camisoles, bras, and panties filled his vision. Naked flesh strutted up and down the length of stage. Strobes and spots highlighted the hedonistic moves of dancers.

Suddenly the lights blinked out and the entire bar was bathed in darkness. Sands focused on his fingers that touched the edge of his drained glass. The music had stopped. Was the dancer's set over? He hadn't noticed a woman leaving the stage or the short round of applause. Then the music began to play. The sound began so softly that he had to concentrate to hear it. The melody was haunting. It caused him to shiver and peer closely at the stage. It was dark and empty, as far as he could tell, and yet he could sense a presence on the stage. Sands continued to stare as the lights came up; he held his line of vision awaiting the movement that he knew would surely come. A pair of chocolate-colored legs swam into focus. First only the ankles and jet-black high heels were visible. He strained his eyes against the fog of smoke. The light crept upward, revealing more of her. Long strands of shapely muscle gave way to knees, then thighs. Sands sat up, the watery remains of his drink forgotten. He saw the high-waisted, black G-string disappearing into the shadows as the woman spun slowly on her heels, revealing a perfect heart-shaped ass. The strand of string disappeared and reappeared between the cheeks of her tanned bottom. Sands felt himself growing hard.

A single spotlight focused in front of where the woman stood. The woman remained still, hands on her hips, legs apart; then slowly, slowly she bent down until her large, ripe breasts were emblazoned in light. Held by a translucent bra that showed dark nipples growing erect. With one hand she reached behind her and unhooked the bra, letting it fall from her to the ground. Her fingers went to her nipples, teasing them slightly as she used one of her shoes to hook the bra with its point and toss it haphazardly into the crowd. It landed near Sands' chair. The spotlight whirled around her for a moment, then settled on her taut stomach. A film of sweat covered her lovely skin. The spot rode up her frame, past the valley of her breasts, to her slender neck. The light hadn't yet settled on her face, but traces of it lightly touched her lips, cheeks, and chin. Panning upwards, the light hit and reflected off of smooth, dark sunglasses, high cheekbones, and then to her hair: long and dark, flowing down her back almost to her ass. Sands felt his heart quicken as the music peaked. The lights winked out and Sands almost bolted from his chair. His chest was heaving. His water lay forgotten in front of him. Before he could move, the jukebox rumbled once and the lights kicked back on. A low bass sound coursed through the bar and the woman began her dance. Sands watched, mesmerized. The woman spun easily on her heels, her long, flowing hair following her ripe body. The lights kept the majority of her within the shadows. She played with the crowd, darting out into the brightness of the strobe light, only to recede into shadows and out of sight. It almost appeared that there were two women, each one working the light to add to the illusion. The dancer would go to the edge of the stage as if she was going to dive into the crowd, stand there gyrating her hips with her head tilted back, shaking it before moving on. Sands followed her every move. All he could think of was the first night in his new place when he had seen Nona dancing by the window. Her swaying hips matched this dancer's to a tee.

Was it Nona?

The resemblance, sans the hair was uncanny. He couldn't see clearly. It could be someone else. Of course it *was* someone else.

It had to be.

A waitress passed by his table, asked him if he needed a refill. Sands gestured her away, a quick flick of his wrist, as in, not now, not interested. His attention was on the dancer—her dance, the way she moved her body. It all reminded him of her . . . Nona.

He had had too much to drink. That was it. The dancer looked at him, then turned away. The conversation level in the bar had dropped to a hush. Even the waitresses were standing with their backs against the bar watching this woman's dance. They were impressed. It seemed all eyes were on the dancer, watching her every move. Sands felt jealous. He wished he were alone, this a private dance only for him.

Her long fingers grabbed the top of the G-string and expertly pulled it down. She arched her back and tightened her ass as it went down her thighs. She stopped when it was clear of her knees and spun around. Then she bent down and continued removing the G-string. There was loud applause from the crowd. This was some dance!

When the G-string was fully removed, she kicked it away from her and lay down on the stage. She lay on her side and opened her legs, rubbing the insides of her thighs before settling a finger by the entrance of her sex. She parted the lips to her pussy with one hand while she licked her forefinger and inserted it inside. The crowd went wild. She hung her head back, the dark sunglasses sparkling and reflecting the strobe lights overhead. She gyrated her hips on the stage and bucked up and down before continuing her dance. Turning over now, on all fours, she crawled to the stage edge as a rhythmic bass-line assaulted them. To Sands, it appeared that she was seemingly staring only at him. He could imagine their eyes locking; feel the recognition in her gaze. She smiled and danced for him. At that moment, the rest of the patrons melted away, the bar became empty again, and only this dancer and Sands remained. She danced in and out of the shadows, the lights playing tricks with his eyes. But all the while she danced for him, her stare appearing to never falter, never straying from his table, from his face.

All at once the music ended, and the dancer was gone. For a second the crowd was speechless. Then they erupted into a roar of applause. The lights came up, temporarily blinding everyone. Sands sat there, catching his breath, waiting for the hardness to go down. He heard the sound of running footsteps, the sound of heels on wood heading toward the back of the tavern. He caught a glimpse of a nude woman as she rounded a corner by the rest rooms. For a moment he played with his sleeves, downed the last of his drink, chewed on the ice to satisfy his urge to smoke. When he was convinced that the dancer wasn't returning, he got up and walked quickly toward the back of the lounge. Passed a few empty tables, past a bunch of old men with scruffy beards, past a few waitresses by the second bar who paid him no mind. Passed a set of rest rooms to a door marked "Private." The door was held slightly ajar. Sands knocked twice, then pushed the door open. It led to a long narrow hallway with a closed door at the other end. He walked its length slowly; a naked bulb hung from the ceiling. Autographed photographs of the dancers were affixed to either side of the wall. Eight-by-ten color and black-and-white glossies touted names like Porché, Starr, Alizé, and Wetness. Sands paused at the end of the hall. His fingers ran across the glass frames searching for the dancer's image. Her face was not among them.

The door at the end of the hall was closed. He knocked once, received no response, and placed his hand on the knob. He heard stirring behind the door.

"Hello!" he called, but heard no response. Sands walked in. He found himself in a dressing room devoid of people. Along one wall was a long mirror surrounded by small bright bulbs. A bouquet of flowers sat in one corner. Makeup was spilled haphazardly on the vanity surface. Behind four chairs that faced the mirror was a long rack of dancers' costumes. Judging from the large handle and metal plate at the far wall was a door that appeared to be an emergency exit. He went to it and pushed the cold handle. The door groaned and creaked as a gust of wind entered the room. Rain splashed against his face. Sands again heard rushing footsteps, the sound of heels clicking on stone. Suddenly, a shadowy movement caught his attention. He erupted into a run calling out to her as he went. The rain picked up, slapping against his suit and face. And yet he didn't let up.

He scanned right and left, frantically searching for the dancer as his legs and arms pumped furiously. Down the street he could hear footsteps. The rapid pace told him she was running . . . running away from him. But why?

Sands found himself in an alleyway behind the lounge. He passed trash cans overflowing with rotten garbage, waterlogged newspapers, and a soaked mattress, toward the opening to the alley. His suit was becoming drenched yet Sands didn't care. He would ruin a suit in pursuit of his dreams any day. He wiped the rain from his face as he ran. The woman ahead turned left onto the street. Sands followed, almost falling as he pivoted after her. It was then he saw the woman clearly in the light of an overhead street lamp. It was indeed the dancer. She was covered with a tan raincoat, but wore the dark sunglasses. She paused momentarily to hail a cab. For an instant, it appeared that their stares locked. A taxi sped past her, dousing her with water. She shook her hair and crossed the street rapidly without looking back.

Sands yelled: "Nona? Nona, it's me. Stop, please!" He darted into the street, oblivious of the traffic. His chest heaved as he ran. His clothes were soaked—weighing him down. The rain cascaded down his forehead and cheeks. Oblivious to everything going on around him, Sands yelled her name over and over.

"WAIT!" he screamed. "NONA!"

She continued running past a row of glass-front buildings, her steps drumming loudly in his ears.

The harder Sands ran, the farther he seemed to fall behind her. It was as if everything had slowed to a crawl: the traffic, the falling rain, his movements—everything but the dancer. He watched horrified as she faded from sight. Soon she was gone, and all that was left was the hypnotic drumming of her footsteps echoing in the rain-laden air.

33

Malik stared at the unresponsive body beneath him.

It was all a dream, he told himself.

Had to be.

Look at her—face covered in blood, barely recognizable from the blow; arms and legs splayed at ungodly angles, flesh limp, lifeless. A thousand razor-sharp shards of dark glass—bits and pieces from an empty Red Stripe littering the floor around her.

Did I do that, he mused?

God help me if I did, he told himself.

Malik turned his back on his wife, suddenly nauseous. He glanced back only once to ensure that she had not yet moved.

She had not.

Minutes dragged on.

The sound wafting overhead was of faint crying. Whimpering—it could have come from a child. Even an animal. Something, someone, deeply wounded.

It did not come from Nona.

She remained motionless.

Seemingly without life.

Malik stared at the crumpled form of his wife, his sobs barely audible. Without warning he wept like a baby. Hands and fingers clenched, unclenched. Willing her silently to move—praying that she would do so.

As usual, Nona didn't listen to a fucking word he uttered . . .

Malik called to her, softly at first, later yelling her name; all in vain. She was not going to wake up. He walked over to her, cringed at the sight of her face, her beauty gone, devoured, swept away by razor-sharp shards from a Red Stripe bottle.

Wait...

It wasn't the Red Stripe bottle that inflicted this violence, Malik reckoned.

It was me . . .

Never again would any man see her as beautiful; no way she would ever look the way she had before. He shook his head sorrowfully, quickly wiping away the tears, as if someone might see him, catch him in this unmanly state, crouched over his wife, weeping for a woman who no longer loved him.

The gleam from shiny gunmetal captured his attention. He sighed extra heavily.

No man would, from this day forward, look upon his wife.

Not that fucking artist, not that fucking neighbor.

Not even him. Her husband.

Damage done. Through. Finished.

This time, Malik knew, there was no turning back.

He went into the bathroom to splash water on his face. He stared at the mirror; for no longer than a few measly seconds—realizing with the cold slap of harsh reality that he didn't recognize the man staring back; Malik no longer recognized himself.

That's because he was no longer Malik—son of Job, sheet-metal laborer from Trinidad, no longer Nona's husband. No longer clear as to who he had become—morphing into something else—this *thing* staring back at him—a stranger. So he shook his head sadly and marched out.

Back to the bedroom again, glancing down— still she hadn't moved, blood congealing on her used-to-be-oh-so-beautiful face; arms and legs still at those morose angles that could only mean one thing; he sat down on the bed, looked to the bureau and the pistol, before turning quickly away.

Went back into the bathroom, returning with a pair of scissors.

Dropped them on the foot of the bed.

Sat down.

Rose again.

Restless.

Bending down, for a moment afraid to touch her, as if what was left of his wife was lying in wait for him like a beast, and as soon as he got close, she'd pounce, sucking him into some horrid vortex, and he'd scream, yet no one would hear his pain, because the vortex would imprison his cries as well as his soul.

That didn't happen, though.

She remained motionless. Malik, carefully, almost lovingly, placed his hands under her broken form, the way a child carefully picks up a shivering pigeon whose damaged wing means they can no longer fly; lifted her up, and carried her, like a bride over the threshold, to the bed they used to share.

34

5:42 p.m., the next day.
David Sands climbed the stairs to Chantal's home and wasted no time ringing the bell. When no one answered he began to pound on the door, rattling the glass in its frame. The events of the last few days had caused him to question Nona's existence. But a stabbing ache deep inside made him feel she was real. Every night, when he nuzzled against his pillows waiting for the answers to come, his thoughts turned to Chantal. The best friend. She would possess the answers. He had seen something on her face the day he had spoken to her. She had hidden something from him that day— that was for sure. Sands had reached a dead end. With no place to turn, he realized he had no choice but to confront Chantal and demand the answers that he searched for. If she refused, he would make her tell him the truth.

Sands banged again. Still no answer. He glanced

up and down the street. A few kids rode their bikes down the block. Across the street an elderly woman sat on her stoop, unaware of Sands. He alternately rang and pounded again and again. Still no answer.

A Spanish boy emerged from the next building and walked over to Sands.

"No one's home, Mister. I see them leave a while a go," he said.

"Who, how long?"

"The lady who lives here. I don't know, maybe two, three hours ago. I saw them."

Rage welled up inside and rapidly turned to raw fear. What was happening here? What was Chantal doing?

Sands looked up and down the block searching for answers, but finding none. He thought about breaking into Chantal's house. Get inside and search for clues to Nona's disappearance. Whatever the cost, he would find out just what in God's name was going on—there was no turning back now. He was going to find out—or die trying. He swore this!

8:10 p.m. The last of the day's light had faded. Sands, clad in a pair of jeans and a dark tee, checked the flashlight that he was carrying. Satisfied, he went out the door.

Prospect Place was dark when he reached Chantal's house. He glanced around to make sure no one was watching him. Satisfied, he climbed the steps to her house and rang the bell.

No answer. The windows were dark, no move-

ment behind the drapes. He rang the bell a few
more times. Still no answer, as expected.

Eight-thirty. When he was satisfied that no one
was home he backed away from the door and barreled into the wood with his left side. He crashed
through easily, the door and its lock no match for
his large frame. Sands was not concerned with the
sound of tearing wood and twisting metal. His
mind was ice-cold clear.

The house was dark. He arced the flashlight
about, searching for a light switch, his breathing
heavy, adrenaline shooting through his veins. He
switched on a light in the hallway and ran toward
the large white living room where he had spoken
with Chantal a month ago. The room was dark, but
he had managed to find a brass floor lamp. He
switched it on and cocked his head to the side as
the green bird began to shriek.

Sounds of pounding wood. Footsteps. A scream.

"Who the hell is that!" someone yelled. A woman's
voice. Chantal's. She entered the white room and
Sands spun around, the light in his hand held tight
like a weapon.

"What the fuck are you doing in here!" she
screamed, "Get out of my house!"

"Where is she?"

"Get out of here! I've called the police!" Chantal, clad in a sweat suit, ran back into the hallway.
Sands intercepted her, slamming the butt of the
flashlight into her side. She reeled back in pain
and fell to the floor.

"No more fucking around—just tell me where
Nona is!" Sands yelled. The words, spit out of his

mouth like a piece of bad food, shocked him deeply with their intensity. He had never done anything like this before. But the heaving of his chest and the gritting of his teeth told just how capable he was.

"What are you talking about?" Chantal responded.

"Where is she?" Sands bellowed. Chantal, an expression of terror drawn on her face, backed away, trying to put some distance between herself and Sands. Meanwhile, Sands searched frantically around the room for answers. A microsecond. No more. Distraction.

A thick 9mm pistol. Gunmetal blue gleaming, poised in Sands' direction. The calmness in the room caused him to turn. His face morphing to distortion when he saw it in her hands.

Unsteady fingers gripping the gun. A twitching finger coiled around the trigger, waiting . . .

"You get the fuck out of my house NOW!" Chantal roared.

Sands groaned as he lunged left into the white room, dropping to the floor like a rock thrown as the gun erupted in a deafening roar above him. He scurried sideways, kicking over the brass light as he went. The room plunged into total darkness. The bird screeched in the shadows.

Three . . . four seconds. One shot followed by another.

Blood splatter from open wounds.

Flesh tearing, ripped by an immense slug.

Body groaning, hitting the floor with a sickening thud.

Silence, eternal silence.

Then the bird began its screeching . . .

35

It took him over an hour to unbraid her hair. He did this unhurriedly, her head cradled in his lap, using the end of a comb as his assistant. While he performed this task, his thoughts went back to his homeland, Trinidad, and his father, with the hair-trigger temper. A man who had bequeathed his anger onto his son via his genes.

Malik had watched the way Job had beaten his mother. Over the years it was something he came to accept, but hated with fervor, vowing that when he grew up he'd never be like his father—never ever put his hands on another woman.

And yet, here he was . . .

Glancing downwards, eyes swollen shut, skin blue-black from the sickening impact of Malik's heavy fist, blood on his hands, his clothes; half-way done in this final task, anxious to finish this so that he could lie down and rest— so fucking tired, no, *tired* didn't do what he was feeling justice. It was *exhaustion*; Malik'd never been so fatigued in all of his life—so close to sheer over-the-edge collapse. Life, draining out of him—that's what this felt like—like he was bleeding, life leaking out of him; dying.

Snapping his head suddenly up, he realized how right Nona had been.

He was a pimp!

No better than some ghetto fabulous pimp, over-sized pants sagging to their knees, plenty of street smarts and little to no common sense.

He hadn't risen above his father.

He thought he had.

But he had been wrong.

Leaving the island of Trinidad, he vowed to be better than those before him—surely something more than a fucking sheet-metal laborer—making a few cents a day—what the fuck was that?

How could a person live on that? Raise a family? Make something of himself on that?

So he emigrated to the United States when he was nineteen, land of the free, home of the brave. He'd show Job and the rest of them who remained: unemployed, uneducated, dark-skinned fools—unwilling or unable (Malik no longer distinguished between the two) to lift themselves up, unable to break the cycle that had plagued his people for generations.

Yet, here he was.

A laborer like his father.

And an animal—a beast who violated his wife with his fist.

When he was done, where Nona's hair was back to its wild, unkempt form, Malik gripped the dark hair of her afro in one hand, the shiny, glinting blades of the scissors in the other, her head tipped forward in a sickening pose that made him want to gag; vision, his, swimming in and out of focus as he stared at the scarred bloating remains of her face. Minutes went by as he gazed, trying to remember the good times, trying to remember just what Nona had looked like back then, when things were all good. When all they cared about was each other—and their burgeoning love.

The images eluded him.

The memories were gone.

Malik gripped the scissors in his hand, its blade shimmering from the morning light. He slipped the blades between the strands of hair he held in his fingers and pressed down, severing her hair smartly from her head. It took him twenty minutes more to cut most of it off, until only about an inch remained; afro gone, haphazardly sheared by an animal, a madman, just like Job. The hair he had cut pooled by his legs and thighs, in his lap, on his forearms and clothes, on his wife's bruised face.

Malik didn't seem to notice.

No longer would any man lust after his wife, Malik thought.

No more. She was done; finished. He sat back on the bed, and then got up, restless, scared, confused, feeling empty. The images of their short life together receded away into a dark tunnel until what lay before him was a stranger.

A woman without a familiar face.

Done, finished.

The .38, its barrel gleaming, lay on its side, muzzle facing him. Malik picked it up, weighing the cold metal in his hands.

Done, finished.

No longer would any man lust after his wife.

He felt the anger and jealousy rise in his throat until it burned fierce. Nona lay there, head and face unrecognizable, hair sheared off; she couldn't see the damage she had inflicted.

She had done this—done this to both of them. If only she had listened— if only she had abided by her husband.

STOP IT!

That's exactly what Job used to say, Malik recalled, the same line of bullshit he used to spew as his wife, Malik's mother, lay on the cold earthen floor, arms hugging her beaten extremities, rocking herself back and forth, as if that would somehow heal her wounds.

Nona lay sleeping.

Oblivious to this madness.

No longer here to witness the final action of an animal—a madman, just like Job.

Nona, her face disfigured not by a Red Stripe bottle, but by the hands of her husband, lay motionless; seemingly lifeless. The river of dark blood had ceased to flow.

Done, finished.

As if signaling her own demise.

Her own ending.

Nona wasn't around to see what came next.

She never saw Malik pick up the gun and weigh it in his hand.

Never saw him rub the barrel along his tear-strewn face.

Against his forehead, then cheek.

Never saw Malik place the barrel of the gun against his forehead.

Never heard the ear splitting sound.

Never saw the body jerk backward.

Never felt the splatter of blood that exploded from his wound.

Never knew her husband ended this thing the same way his father had—with a bullet to his brain.

As Malik's mother would say years later, "Just as well."

Whether she was talking about her husband or her son one would never know.

Just as well . . .

36

He hid among the walls of the dead house. A thief among the shadows that hid the blood of insane murderers; thieves who stole lives came to such a place where they could be alone with their grief and misery. It was here—to the abandoned house—that Sands came to hide.

He had been shot.

The bullet had not lodged itself in the shoulder, but rather had grazed the skin, taking a fair amount of flesh with it. Sands attempted to remove his jacket but thought better of it when the pain caused him to yell out. The blood had stopped flowing, so it was better to keep the wound sealed than open it far from a doctor's office.

He imagined the heavy semi-automatic between his fingers, never leaving his hand. It brought him comfort. He held it tightly, squeezing, then relaxing his grip when he felt his palm sweat—the metal was cold no matter how many hours he cradled the imaginary thing. It would never warm to his touch. It was an alien thing, not made for his hands. But as he walked the vacant halls of the house, he felt safe only because he carried the weapon raised in front of him. It was his security blanket; his insurance for continued survival. Allegedly, a man and woman had died within these same walls. Their blood splattered on the surfaces and ran down, pooling in the cracked floorboards. The house groaned even when Sands didn't move. The ghosts flourished amidst the dusty walls. The 9mm was his deliverance—his calm before the storm.

It had been...what? Two, three hours? Days? Time meant nothing here. It had no value. Was there anything worth looking forward to? Something to constantly check a watch for?

No.

His rapid breathing was his timepiece. And there was no regularity to that.

He wandered from room to room like a zombie, unconsciously ensuring he was alone. The billowing whiteness of the drapes frightened him no more. But it was the groans rising from the bowels of the foundation that caused the hair to rise on the nape of his neck.

The events surrounding the shooting sped away in a blur of images. He remembered rushing madly down the stairs to the kitchen, blood oozing from between his fingers, dashing out to the backyard and scaling the low fence until he was safely in the shadows of Nona's house. He entered the house easily without being seen and returned to the attic where he stayed, waiting for the familiar sound of Nona's voice to come and set him free. Minutes turned to hours; Sands waited. And waited.

This was her home, her lair. Wherever she was, whatever she was, Nona would return. She had to come back . . .

The night grew darker. Sands began checking the windows more frequently, peeking out from the shades and boarded-up windows, searching for something—a movement, a sound—the police— where the hell were the police? Surely Chantal had called them—in fact, he was astounded that the entire S.W.A.T. team wasn't surrounding the vacant building this very instant— news choppers littering the air, emblazoning every inch with harsh white light, until Sands had no choice but to give up, exiting the dead house—hands held high above his head in defeat and surrender.

It was not meant to be.

Instead the night slowed to a crawl. The silence enveloped him until his gaze panned frantically outside, searching for *anything* to reassure him that he was indeed still alive.

But the world had ceased moving. He saw that now, vacant stare as his nose pressed against the glass, no longer even feeling the coolness. It was evident from the scene displayed before him. Everything had died; he was trapped within the sanctuary of his one-time lover.

And so, Sands would die.

It was inevitable, he told himself aloud. A husband had taken his life after destroying the one thing he had loved. Things had devolved from there. Sands should have seen it—should have run the other way after spying Nona in this very window. Yet what she offered was far too great to ignore. And now, Sands was paying the ultimate price. It was a natural selection—he would be next.

The house spoke to him. It groaned and creaked, the walls whispering secrets that only Sands could hear. The world might be dead outside, but life was brewing within these musty walls. The suspended particles of dust began to vibrate and dance into a feverish pitch as they arose from the wood. Sands had to blink twice to be sure he wasn't seeing blood flowing from those old walls. Nona's blood. The blood of his lover.

STOP IT!

Sands walked the halls of the deserted house, touching the walls, leaving a trail of dust behind his trembling fingertips.

A new thought coursed through his head. *I've never painted her portrait.* It pulsed almost to the point of causing pain. It would not go away no matter how hard he tried.

A portrait of Nona. He had never thought of that before. He had painted many of the scenes around him: the school yards of P.S. 9; the buildings in the neighborhood; a lone face among a crowd of strangers; a faceless lover from a masquerade ball; but never a portrait of *her*. There was the painting that he had begun after the first night that he had spotted her. That, however, wasn't a portrait. He needed to paint a picture that would do her justice.

An image of her. One that would portray her exactly as she had revealed herself to him. And one that would help him forget—because he had to get over this—stop obsessing and move on.

This new thought consumed much of his time.

Sands didn't notice the hours as they passed by. His stomach rumbled, the pain in his shoulder throbbed; his bladder filled and he relieved himself in a top-floor commode with a little more than a puddle of water within. His stubble sprouted and grew; he didn't care. The portrait consumed his thoughts.

How would he do it? Charcoal or paints? Abstract or details? Should he do it on a two meter by two meter canvas? The various options presented themselves to him. All the while he remained within the shadows of the house.

Had the police come and gone? When would it be safe to leave? The pulse of Prospect Place had regained its normal pace. People came and went— so did cars, traffic. Sands no longer concerned himself with anything other than her portrait. It was time to leave—get the shoulder looked at. Clean up, something to fill his stomach—a full night's sleep-and then, he'd tackle the painting. Then move on . . .

The sound of a door slamming turned his blood to stone.

Sands froze in his tracks, one foot poised above the next stair, suspended like the particles of dust, which floated lazily in the stale air. With his back pressed against the cold wall, he cocked his head to the side, all of his attention focused on that singular sound. The house groaned once, then fell silent again.

A nagging fear, a stabbing pain that erupted out of nowhere and ran up his spine to the base of his skull. His body spasmed, yet Sands turned slowly and glanced upward.

The third floor was bathed in shadows. Like an optical illusion, the walls seemed to disappear and reappear among the shadows. If he concentrated and focused really hard, the three closed doors leading to the bedrooms would remain in place. But let his stare wander and the motion would commence. Sands clenched the imaginary gun tight in his right hand and raised it in front of him.

The middle door held his attention—it seemed to rattle on its hinges. A gust of cold air blew from underneath and chilled his skin. He glanced down expecting the door to open on its own at any second. Perhaps Nona was behind that door, waiting for him to turn the knob. Perhaps it would be as simple as that—turn the handle and end his pain. Sands didn't dare think of what would be waiting for him on the other side if it were not her . . .

Light spilled from where the door met the cold floor. It was an eerie light—white, yet not bright. It appeared like moonlight, but that couldn't be right. Sands stepped up slowly to the door. Behind it he heard wind songs. From an open window? He had been in this very room only hours ago. In fact, he had fallen asleep by a white telescope. Sands gripped the knob, almost recoiling from the gnawing hot-cold of the brass handle. He steadily turned it. The door groaned open after considerable effort on Sands' part. The cold slapped his face before he could articulate what had happened. He tried to turn, tried to pivot on his heels and race back the way he had come, but the door slammed shut with a thunderous force.

37

The weight of a dark sky bore down upon him. He scurried across the road and into the forest unseen. A flashlight and the weight of an imaginary 9mm handgun were all that he carried. The air was clear and cold. His shoulder throbbed from the pain when he swung his arm.

Thankfully, the sky held a moon tonight. It hung on the horizon, but the light was sufficient to guide him without having to have the flashlight constantly on. Sands walked unhurriedly for close to ten minutes before glancing back. The road he was on was dirt—gravel, completely hidden by the thick foliage of the forest on either side. The trees were dense here, and often he lost sight of the moon, needing to turn on the flashlight to ensure he didn't walk into a tree.

He found a river a good hundred yards to the right of him. Actually he heard it first, the steady trickle of water; his mouth and lips were chaffed; he licked them incessantly as he made his way toward the sound, keeping his bearing by listening to the drum of the current splashing against cold rocks. The sound was soothing; for a moment he forgot his throbbing shoulder, the pain in his stomach and fatigue; instead he enjoyed this time alone in the sudden freshness of cool evening air. When he reached the source of the sound, he bent down, cupping both hands and dipping them in the water before placing them to his lips.

Night sounds invaded him at every step. This was nature's domain and a wealth of animal sounds abounded. Bird calls pierced the night along with the sound of buzzing insects and nocturnal mammals. Sands walked along at a brisk pace stopping suddenly when he heard a sound to his left: an animal scurrying to take cover from the intruder.

Thirty minutes into the hike the terrain began to get rockier and steeper. Sands stopped to take a breather and to gather his thoughts. He had no idea where he was going, but he continued walking, as if being pulled along toward some prearranged meeting place. Sands felt as if he was getting close, as if whatever he was doing here would soon be revealed to him. He could feel it in his bones.

Again, a sound off to the left caused Sands to suddenly drop to the ground and remain still. On his haunches, head cocked towards the noise, sniffing for scent like a hound dog, before rising slowly to seek shelter behind a large oak tree. A strange sound had disturbed the night air. A sound strikingly human.

Sands had switched off the light and held his

breath. He squinted his eyes trying to scan the darkness ahead for any signs of activity. He saw none, but again heard a low-pitched noise, muffled and unnatural sounding. Exhaling silently, he sucked in a deep breath and waited.

A beam of light cut through the blanket of darkness and arced toward him. Sands immediately shot to the ground and stopped breathing. It was way after midnight. What was someone doing out here this time of night?

The beam winked out before arcing back again. This time he saw three pinpoints of lights bobbing up and down and growing larger. Three persons, coming toward him.

Sands mind raced. He couldn't run without attracting attention, could he? What about hiding?

The oak tree shielding his body was large and full. Sands took a chance and shone the light directly upward, illuminating its branches, which were plentiful and fairly low to the ground. If he was going to make his move, he'd have to do it now!

Quietly, he got up and pressed his chest against the tree. The lights were still a ways off, but were gaining quickly. He could hear muffled laughter and the sound of crunching twigs and leaves. He glanced up, locked his gaze on to the nearest branch, and leaped. He caught the limb with his right hand, pulling himself up. Immediately the pain from his shoulder shot down his side, but he ignored it and he used the other arm to aid him. He gritted his teeth and almost cried out, but was able to relax his grip once he had hoisted himself up. Quickly he climbed upward until he had put a good thirty feet between himself and the ground. His chest heaved from the exhaustion; Sands concluded there was no way anyone would see him unless they stood directly under this tree and glanced up.

Sands propped his body against the trunk of the tree and waited. The sounds were becoming louder, the arc of light wider and closer. Soon now they would be almost below him.

"So?" he heard a voice stab the air, "When you gonna head back to the city?" Male voice. Sands gathered that they were less than thirty yards away. The sounds of boots crunching on ground was becoming louder. The men swung their lights in a sweeping motion as if searching for something or someone.

"Haven't decided yet, either day after tomorrow. Or the next day after that." Second voice. Female. Sands was in the process of rubbing his aching shoulder when he froze.

Female voice—familiar.

"Me, I could stay here forever . . ." Third voice— also female, also familiar— ohmygod!

Sands almost convulsed as the pleasure spread through him.

Almost lost his balance and careened headlong to the ground.

Almost screamed out her name, but something, something held him back.

OH MY GOD!!!

Could it be?

Three of them, one male, two females—both known to him. Through the branches and densely packed leaves Sands could barely see the outlines of them. They were coming closer toward the tree. For a moment it seemed they were going to pan to the right, but at the last moment they veered back toward him. Sands' heart was in his throat. The voices! Oh my God, the voices! Two of them, the women, passed directly underneath him, to the right of the large trunk, while the third, the man, circled to the left of the tree as Sands' eyes burned.

Moments later the trio was gone, their arc of white lights fading into blackness. Sands remained among the treetops for a few minutes more, chest heaving, mind and pulse racing as the images of the women's heads ground into his psyche.

Chantal.

And Nona.

She was alive!!!

He wasn't crazy.

She was alive.

THANK GOD . . .

38

Twenty long, grueling minutes later, after he had remained in the V of the large oak tree, scratching at his head, trying in vain to understand what Nona and Chantal were doing *here*—not that Sands knew exactly where here was—were they searching for him? Sands climbed and hiked a short distance until he came upon a narrow dirt track. He took the road, following its curves as rays of moonlight edged him on. Ten minutes later he crouched behind an eight-foot-high, wrought-iron fence, staring at a complex of buildings. It was quite an arrangement. He couldn't see clearly, but the sound of fluttering and flapping assaulted the air. From his vantage point, he could see a large modern greenhouse beyond a large rectangular pool. A main building off to the left was surrounded by lights. To the right appeared to be a stone pathway that disappeared into the shadows.

Sands stayed crouched behind the fence and continued his scan. He couldn't see any activity.

Except for the bright lights surrounding the main house, the place looked deserted.

He checked left, then right—nothing. Standing, he mounted the fence fairly easily, swinging his legs over the top. In seconds, he was on the other side, kneeling on the slate ground, slightly winded. Moving closer, scampering low across the ground, meandering around a long rectangular pond until he found himself peering through the side window of the main structure. Behind him a hundred yards away was the greenhouse. The realization of where he was flooded his senses and made him sick. Suddenly it was crystal clear.

Birds.

The sound of birds . . .

Coming from the greenhouse.

Hundreds of them.

Chantal had a bird. An exotic one. Hadn't she said her brother was a collector?

Was this his place?

Had to be.

She was here—and so was Nona! So it had to be his. Nothing else made sense.

"Hey, brutha!"

Sands spun around, coming face-to-face with the barrel of a twelve-gauge shotgun. He was forced back into the cool wall.

"This here is private property." Sands felt his heart go into overdrive.

"Calm down, man," Sands whispered, "I'm . . . I got lost, you know? Lost?"

"Yeah right." The man cocked his head to the side while removing one hand from the barrel of the shotgun, keying his mike that was attached to his left epaulet.

Sands hands were above his head. The long dark barrel of the shotgun didn't waver a bit. "I know the people who live here," Sands ventured. "Give me a break, man, I'm looking for *Nona*." Pausing, searching the man's dark eyes for a clue as to his identity, and for recognition in the man's eyes. "I'm here for Nona . . ." he repeated, but saw nothing. His eyes dropped to the man's attire— some sort of uniform. Security? Sands didn't have time to complete the thought.

"Ummn-hmmmn," the man responded, nodding his head, studying him. "Don't know no Nona . . ." he replied, the barrel of the shotgun wavering an inch or two as Sands seized the opportunity.

"Oh God!" Sands moaned. His body went limp, falling sideways and onto his good shoulder. He moaned in pain.

"What the fuck . . ." the man said, temporarily caught off guard. The shotgun tipped forward slightly . . .

Sands' leg moved up and forward with lightning speed, connecting with the man's crotch. He fell easily, the shotgun spinning out of his hand and clattering to the ground.

"Ohhhh shit!" the gunman moaned. Sands reached for the shotgun, gripped it tight in his hand as he jumped up. He pointed it at the man lying on the ground, but there was no need—he was balled up, fetal position, eyes scrunched shut, balls on fire.

Sands, his damaged shoulder spasming in pain, frantically glanced around. No one else appeared out of the shadows. He raced to the edge of the building and glanced around the corner. The complex was still. Raced back, kneeling down on the flat slate, he shone the flashlight into the man's dark face.

"Where is she?"

No answer.

"Don't fuck with me. Where's Nona? I know she's here!" This elicited a chuckle from the man.

"Told you, man, don't know no God damned Nona!"

"Chantal—she's here, too—I saw her! You must be her brother—the bird collector."

Another chuckle. "Chantal who? Man, you've been smoking something— this here's private property—besides we're closed." The man spit, a nasty ball that landed close to Sands' feet.

Sands considered the shotgun in his left hand. Almost pointed it at the prone form lying on the ground. But what would that prove? He was no killer.

The man still had not moved. But he was hurting. Bad. A blind man could see that. It would be at least a few minutes more before he was able to stand, then move.

Sands tossed the shotgun far into the bushes and made a run for it.

The rear of the greenhouse was bathed in shadows. Hundreds of birds cried out, as if frantically trying to escape their extinction. Sands searched for an entrance to the place.

The main entrance in front was locked. Sands pondered running back to the man lying on the ground—seeing if he had the keys on him—too much time to be wasted. His heart was racing. Glancing around, spying loose rocks on the ground by a back wall to the complex not far from where he stood. He grabbed one, hefted it in his hands before smashing it through one of the windows. Quickly, Sands cleared away the glass and climbed in. He stood still, listening for noise. All he heard was the steady flutter of bird wings.

Sands found himself in a wide room, extremely tall ceilings, damp and hot. Wild plants grew on either side of him. A walkway snaked from one end of the greenhouse to the other. He couldn't see the end of the room, since most of it was bathed in shadows. He followed the path, ignoring the flora before him. Birds fluttered in the treetops over head. He came to a doorway; he opened it, saw stairs that descended downwards. He took them without hesitation.

The downstairs was in subdued light. Sands found himself in a narrow corridor with several closed doors on either side. He flung doors open, searching for Nona. Both rooms, one a utility closet, the other housing a furnace, were empty. At the end of the hallway, Sands saw an opening into a larger room. It was the only one left.

Cautiously, he crept to the opening, careful not to let his footsteps announce his presence. He pressed his body against the wall and waited, hoping to hear some sort of sound. Here, downstairs, away from the birds, Sands heard only his breathing. He edged over to the opening and held his breath. With his good shoulder shielding him, he swung into the opening. What he saw made him blink with incomprehension.

He had found Nona. But his heart sank as he surveyed the scene around him. She was not alone. She stood against a bare wall, clad only in a pair of lacy panties that barely covered her sex, her arms bound with brown leather thongs to the back wall. Her face was beautiful in the half-light. Chantal sat in a recliner off to the side. She was smoking a joint, oblivious to his entrance behind her. Nona's eyes found his—and softened. She smiled.

"We have company."

Chantal's back lifted off the chair as she turned. Her expression turned sour. "It's him! Jesus!"

Sands moved cautiously into the room, his stare not leaving Nona's.

"It's me," he said quietly before elevating his voice. "Been looking all over for you . . ." A half-hearted chuckle elicited from his mouth before he became serious. "Thought you were dead or something."

"Man, Nona—this is that crazy-ass fool who broke into my house! Why are we standing around talking to his ass?" Chantal had gotten up, gone to Nona, shielding her body with hers. But as Sands made his way over to them, Chantal backed away.

Sands closed the gap between himself and his lover. She lifted her head slightly as he reached her, eyes moistening. Sands kissed her cheek and undid her wrists. His eyes watered and he had to force himself to shake the tears away.

"We should go," he whispered to Nona.

She looked at him quizzically. "Go where?"

"Don't know. Anywhere—away from here—get you . . . cleaned up . . . so we can . . . talk." He stared at her—the fullness to her cheekbones, the smoothness to her black skin. He reached out—and his fingers found her mouth— feeling her lips, moving up to her nose. He glanced down, her heavy breasts inches from his touch. He inhaled her scent—she smelled heavenly. This was no dream—no aberration—this woman in front of him was real. He sighed heavily feeling the waves of emotion roll through him.

All this time thinking I was going insane. My mind dissolving into lifeless matter . . . into nothingness.

And yet, here she is. Standing before me. Alive. Real.

It means that I'm okay.

"Just want to talk," he repeated, hands at his sides.

"Nooooooooo, Nona, don't go anywhere with this fool!" Chantal cried.

Nona considered him before her lips curled into an erotic grin. The action was incredibly sensuous, and Sands couldn't help but feeling aroused. But the overarching sensation was one of intense relief. The wave washed over him again and again and again . . .

He'd found her. Found her alive.

"All you wanna do is talk?" Nona asked, her lips

inches from his ear. Her breath was like feathers, tickling, caressing. It made his toes curl.

"Well . . ." He smiled sheepishly.

Nona looped her arm in his, turned to her friend, Chantal and said softly: "Girl, don't wait up . . ."

The words were lost on Sands. He was staring at her mouth—her lips curling into a smile that meant more to him than mere words could ever describe, feeling her nakedness against him, the warmth that enveloped him, radiating outward from her with a force that subsumed him.

They were finally together. And everything would be okay.

39

David Sands awoke slowly, his eyes adjusting slowing to the blue-gray haze that clouded the room. The floorboards creaked when he sat up and stretched, wincing as the pain in his shoulder returned…except…there weren't floorboards beneath his feet—instead it was cold ugly concrete. Quickly he spun around, searching the room for Nona. She had to be here. The night's events were like ice in his mind—crystal clear. He replayed the scene over and over; extremely proud of the way he had come through. But as he looked around, a sickening feeling began to seep into him. Like a numbing cold that chilled to the bone, Sands knew what was wrong. If last night had been real, then where was she? Where was Nona?

The pain spread to his arms and chest, numbing his hands and toes. A dream?

A dream?

NO!

Sands wailed long and hard, until his voice was harsh and raspy, the noise degenerating into an animal cry of pain and longing.

Wiping away the sweat, Sands finally realized he had crossed the edge.

"KEEP THAT GODDAMNED WAILING DOWN!!!"

The voice boomed, causing Sands to wince and immediately become quiet. He jerked his head around—and found himself in a cell.

A cell!

No more than twelve by ten feet—two bunks on one wall, one on top of the other—Sands spread out on the bottom, a stainless steel commode, no toilet seat. Thick black bars were mere feet from his own. Sands swallowed his fear and sat up, bumping his head.

It can't be.

"You best keep that shit down," a voice above him hissed. A scruffy black face, white eyes hovering in deep black sockets, appeared overhead. Sands jumped back, shocked.

"Where am I, please?" he croaked. His mind raced. Nothing made sense. Where was she? How could he have lost her? He had come so far—only to have her slip through his fingers . . . again . . .

"Negro, what? You locked the fuck up!" Laughter gave way to a coughing fit. Sands stood. Moved to the opposite wall. Light filtered in from the bars—otherwise dark. He shook his head morosely.

"Don't understand—I mean—"

Just then a guard sauntered by—stocky, white,

well built, muscles bulging under his pressed uniform. Glock semi-automatic at his hip; black baton in his calloused hand.

Sands leapt to the bars, fingers clenched around the metal as his eyes glared.

"Just what am I doing here?" he yelled, the voice unfamiliar—that of an animal.

The guard stopped walking, turned, pursing his lips. Tipped his head up to the ceiling, a smirk painted on his lips *thick*.

"Let me see—as I recall B&E, assault. Oh and that lady may press charges—too early to tell, son."

"B&E? Assault?" Sands repeated, incredulously.

"Yeah, dick-wad—that's what we call it when you scale a wall after hours of the Brooklyn Botanic Gardens. Assault is what it's known as when you beat a security guard down to near unconsciousness!" He eyed Sands for a moment before continuing on his way, satisfied he'd inflicted enough damage.

"But I DIDN'T DO IT!" Sands yelled, palms banging against the bars, the action having zero effect.

"Tell it to the fucking judge!" the guard yelled back.

Overhead, in the top bunk, his cell mate was balled up, having another lengthy laughing/coughing fit . . .

40

Mr. Whittaker sat on the stoop, his windbreaker flapping in the October breeze.

"Hiya, Dave," he announced, brushing back what little hair he had on his balding head. "This wind's a bitch, wouldn't you say?"

"Yeah." Sands cuddled the brown paper bag close to his chest. Inside were two fifths of Jamaican rum—his favorite. Lately he'd been drinking a lot. Lately it seemed there was nothing but him and his trusted Jamaican.

"So, how's things, Dave? Haven't seen much of you lately." Sands pursed his lips and concentrated on the sound of the wind. The old man's voice seemed far off and distant; not real at all. So much had happened. So much had changed. Why, in the past few months had he gone from a normal, relatively happy guy to . . . what had he become? A convict? An animal? Who knows? It didn't matter anymore. There was only the portrait left. Sands scratched his hairy face and sighed.

"Same old same old. You know how it is."

"Sure. How's the painting coming along?"

"It's coming, I guess." The image of the two-meter-by-two-meter canvas flashed inside his head. He tried to smile but found it required too much effort. So he turned to leave.

"Everything okay with your *situation*?" Mr. Whittaker asked, glancing up to look him in the eye. "You know, that thing with the police?"

Sands paused. Turned around and shrugged his shoulders. Waved a hand as if to say, "You know how it goes, shit happens . . ." He didn't want to talk about it. Still didn't understand it completely himself. Just let the lawyers handle things, is what he told himself every night as the thump in his chest became overbearing. Now, only a shot of Jamaican calmed his nerves, made the hurt and incomprehension go away . . . A week until he was due back in court—a week before he'd learn just what his punishment would be . . .

"Guess you haven't noticed our new neighbors?" Mr. Whittaker said, changing the subject.

Sands removed his hand from the guard rail and looked back at Mr. Whittaker. His clear blue eyes were fastened on Sands.

"No, I didn't know."

"Yeah. We got some new ones. This morning actually. They're in the process of moving in now. A nice couple. Young kids, but that's all right. They're moving into the house behind ours. Met the husband out in the yard. Seems like an awfully nice fellow." Mr. Whittaker paused to wipe his lips with his hand. Sands blinked once, his mind firing thoughts in and out of his consciousness like a piston. Had he heard right?

"You say the house behind ours?"

"Yeah," Mr. Whittaker answered. "You know which one I mean. The vacant house. The one with the crappy yard."

"Oh," Sands managed to say.

"A nice young couple," Mr. Whittaker continued. "Not sure if they're related to that brother-in-law or not. But it's an awful coincidence—the way they look." Mr. Whittaker chuckled to himself and looked up. Sands was closing the door behind him, a look of ghost-white terror on his face.

The place had been near perfect once.

Now it lay in shambles. Bottles were strewn over the carpet; plates with caked-on food lay everywhere; in the sink dishes and pots were piled up until nothing else could fit without toppling over. A steady drip from the kitchen faucet resonated against a crusty pan. Pizza boxes, cracker wrappers, and unread newspapers lay everywhere. In the kitchen puddles from melted ice were situated every couple of yards. Stains littered the floor from food and acrylic paints that had been flung in a fit of rage. And among the filth and stench of rotting garbage was the portrait. The enormous square canvas lay against a wall not far from the fireplace. On the ground were trays of paints and dirty brushes. Colorful splashes of reds, blues, and browns anointed the floor. Sands didn't care. It was almost complete.

He opened a new bottle of rum and put the fifth to his lips. The liquid burned going down, but soothed him. He glanced at the portrait, studying it.

"This thing sucks!" he yelled, flinging the brush at the canvas. His last work. Supposedly his best. But it wasn't coming out the way he planned it.

The portrait of Nona.

What had she been like? Could he even remember her face now?

The portrait was a reflection of his thoughts. Her face, soft, dark lines within shadows; hair—frizzy, super-sized afro, surrounded by colorful swashes of dazzling light.

Images came to him easily at first. The way her hair moved as she danced, her sensuous hips swaying in the moonlight. Later, those faded as well and he would be left with a blank mind, unable to use his gift any further. Sometimes, after he retired for the night, snatches of her would visit him in a fleeting remembrance of something small, no matter what time of night. Sands would rise, dip his brush into the paints and fill in the blanks. Other times, he would go for days without being able to lift a brush at all; all of his energy funneled into keeping him from smashing the painting to pieces.

"Some artist I am," he said aloud. "Can't even get her right." He took another swig and the alcohol made him calm.

Sands so wished he owned a gun. A gleaming 9mm like the bulky thing that had been in Chantal's hand. He'd keep it nearby, laying on the floor by the window, loaded, the safety switch off. He'd glance at it often. Sometimes he'd want to pick the thing up and fire off rounds at the goddamned painting. But instead, he'd turn away and take another hit of Jamaican. It wasn't time yet.

He ignored the churning in his stomach. No use in wasting time. He pressed on, oblivious to the discomfort. The painting took precedence over everything.

At sundown the lights blinked on in the dark house facing his. Sands put the brush down immediately and went to the large windows. He stared out as he took a long gulp, watching for movement. Noticed the detail of the house-face for the millionth time. Dark stone the color of mud. He shivered and felt incredibly tired.

A young woman came to the window. She glanced out, then faded from sight. It was getting dark. Sands checked the moon rising overhead and sighed.

The woman returned. Sands sat down and pressed his face against the cold glass. She was a young woman; couldn't be more than nineteen or twenty. She wore jeans, a button-down work shirt, rolled-up sleeves, and her head wrapped in a colorful head wrap. She kneeled at the window and looked out, admiring her new backyard. Sands watched her like a hawk— his body frozen in time, only his eyes shifting with her movement. He ran a hand through his hair and felt nothing. The woman got up, faded from sight, then returned. The husband or boyfriend, a man the color of midnight, walked past the window, reached for his girlfriend/wife. He pulled her close and kissed her. Sands closed his eyes and exhaled sharply. The couple relaxed their embrace and the husband receded. The woman remained by the window. Sands' own face was meshed with the glass, his breath flaring out and covering his view. He didn't move. He sat, mesmerized by the sight of this woman.

She reached for her hair and undid the wrap. Long dark hair tumbled free, spilling down her neck and shoulders. She flung it from side to side, glad to have it freed. She stood up, grabbed the window pane and with one movement, pushed the window open. Cold air raced in, blowing her hair back from her shoulders. She shivered slightly and fanned herself with her hand. She glanced back and then slowly unbuttoned her blouse. Sands strained against the pane of glass, his sweaty palms streaking them with his perspiration. The bottle beside him toppled over and dark rum began seeping onto the floor. Sands paid it no mind. The woman reached down and pulled the ends of her shirt out from her jeans. For a moment she stood there, the breeze blowing the shirt apart, teasing Sands by bearing her tiny breasts and causing her dark nipples to harden. Sands' jaw dropped and his lips fought to form a word that never emerged. The woman's husband moved in behind her and wrapped his arms around her, cupping her breasts in his hands as he teased her erect nipples. He pulled her to the floor and out of sight. The light blinked out a moment later.

* * *

The overturned bottle lay empty. A growing stain of dark liquor, soggy to the touch and stinking. David Sands glanced at the painting with tears in his eyes. It was over. Finally over. This was the end. Its meaning was clear. It was time to press on. Over. End of story.

If Sands owned a gun he'd pick it up with both hands as he sat down, his back to the painting. The canvas was still wet and sticky, the trays of acrylics open, the brushes scattered at his feet. He sat back, allowing his hair to touch the canvas and mix with the paint. He closed his eyes, musing about how he'd raise the gun to his forehead. With both hands, he'd placed the muzzle at the center of his forehead and run both thumbs along the trigger.

So, this is what it has come to, Sands thought. He opened his eyes and glanced around. Closed them again and increased the pressure on the imaginary trigger. Relaxed his fingers and let the gun tumble into his lap.

No last words. Just a portrait. A fucking painting that didn't even do her justice. They say a picture's worth a thousand words. *Well, look at it,* Sands thought, *and you tell me . . .*

No words.

If he owned a gun he would have picked it up right now, leveling it at his forehead.

He cried while imagining what it felt like to jerk the trigger.

41

It would take a split second for the bullet to travel through flesh and bone into his brain and out the back of his head, piercing the canvas behind him. And in that blink of an eye, Sands imagined he'd see everything. Images whirled past him at breathtaking speeds. Events that he had forgotten about years ago invaded his psyche, each one in turn saying their final good-bye. They made him happy and he found peace.

Suddenly everything slowed down. Sands was petrified and he lashed out with his arms, reaching for anything that would support him. There was nothing there. His vision dimmed and the window in front of him became foggy.

A moment later he stood on a rain-slicked street corner. A single street lamp illuminated the night. Sands sighed.

Thank God, he thought to himself, *I'm not dead yet.*

Not dead yet . . .

His vision had cleared and he turned in the direction of a storefront window. Fifteen yards away, in the midst of a wide expanse of glass: a portrait in a window.

A woman.

A beautiful woman.

Nona.

Sands staggered toward the painting, in awe of the portrait. The painting was Nona. Not his, but perfect. Sands could not have done it better.

He reached the window and spread out his hands, embracing the glass with his rain-soaked body. Blood smeared down the front and Sands jerked back in terror. Nona's portrait blurred as he fell back in slow motion, her image receding from sight. All at once he was on his back, the stars tiny pinpoints of light high overhead. Millions of raindrops cascaded down upon him, blinding Sands with their intensity. He pawed frantically to reach the portrait, to touch her one last time, but she was forever from his grasp. Sands tried to scream, and at that moment everything went black.

Moments later, Nona was there, as he prayed she would be. No excuses or explanations, just Nona, her face as fresh as sunlight and a smile that made you want to die.

Sands felt his face warm when she breathed.

Nona took his hand silently and led him out of the black . . .

EPILOGUE

The sun shown down brilliantly on the expanse of grass, warming everything in its path—the grove of towering oak trees, the row of pink and white azaleas rimming the buildings, the picnic tables that spotted the property. He sat alone on one of them, away from the main building, head down, sketch book in his lap, charcoal pencil in hand, working diligently, tuning out all distractions, the way he worked best—filtering out all of the external noise until his mind focused on one thing only, zeroing in on the subject at hand.

Her.

It had been a little more than six months since that fateful morning when he awoke, his surrounding nothing more than a bleak concrete jail cell— Autumn had come and gone. Winter too— Spring was now in the air—a lot of rain these past few weeks, flooding the ground, sprouting new life from damp earth, turning everything a washed-out gray—but not today. Today flowers bloomed; birds were chirping, filling the air with their song.

He neither heard their chatter nor paid them any mind.

Nor did he sense them as they neared—two of them, the doctor that had treated him since he'd been admitted, and this new one—a stranger. When they were slightly less than ten feet away his fingers ceased to move, and his head rose a few inches, as if sniffing the air for a scent.

"Morning, Mr. Sands."

He recognized Dr. Rollings' voice and smiled. Glanced up, placing his charcoal pencil beside him. Turned to stare at them. Sucked in a breath, excitedly.

"You recall the doctor whom I told you would be working with you? May I introduce Dr. Aaliyah Waymans."

Sands wiped his hand before extending it, eyes locked with hers. "A pleasure."

"Mine too." Soft, yet firm handshake.

Sands took her in: medium height and weight, olive skin, shoulder-length, golden-brown hair, hazel eyes—littered with flecks of green. Eyes that engaged. A comforting smile.

"Dr. Waymans comes to us from the Weill Medical College of Cornell, and we are privileged to have her here at The Center. I'm sure you will find her a delight to work with."

Sands heard everything, but focused on "delight" as his smile matched hers. Yes, he mused, Aaliyah was already a delight . . .

Dr. Rollings patted his shoulder and said, "Well,

I'll leave you to it, then." Walking away, Sands watched him for a moment before returning his gaze to her.

"May I sit?" she inquired.

"Please." Sands took his pad and placed it on his left; she took a seat to his right. Turning to him, she brushed the hair from her face.

"I've been studying you, Mr. Sands; studying your case file, and I don't mind telling you, I find you intriguing."

"David, please." His eyes locked with hers, yet he allowed his gaze to stray imperceptibly—just a millimeter—to her aquiline nose, the rise of her cheeks, the color, texture to their form . . . lovely . . .

"And as I'm sure you've been made aware by Dr. Rollings, my goal is for you to progress to the point where this Center is but a fleeting memory— get you back into the throes of civilization, so to speak—get you back to your endeavors, that creative engine that is, I'm sure, raring to throttle up."

Sands smiled, but said nothing. She, like Dr. Rollings, wore a white lab coat, name embroidered in blue with white letters across her left breast. The coat was buttoned closed, but Sands could not help but marvel at her form *beneath*; he could sense the curves hugging the fabric without fully seeing them—part of it stemmed from spying her angular calf muscles, fully displayed in all of their glory. She wore a skirt and matching mules, but her calves were like works of art—*sculpted* is the word that came to mind—and he conjured up what the rest of her must look like, splayed nude before him, just the two of them, alone in his studio—a place he could only visit in his dreams now.

Her voice raised. "Are you with me, David?"

"Absolutely." Missing not even a beat, his stare once again locked onto hers, flecks of green within hazel orbs dazzling him with their brilliance. "Nothing," he continued, "would please me more."

"I'm delighted to hear that," she responded. A pause. A beat or two before she gestured to his sketch pad with her chin and said, "What are you working on?"

Sands shrugged. "Portraits. It's what . . ." and he chose his next word carefully, "*consumes* me lately."

"I see. May I?" She held out her hand. Sand glanced downward, taking in the slender forearm, her upturned palm, manicured nails that extended from thin digits, wondering what her touch must feel like against his skin, before reaching for his sketch pad and handing it to her.

The face that stared back was all too familiar.

Dr. Waymans nodded and handed it back. "I'd like to talk about her, if you don't mind."

"Okay."

"I've recently spoken with Nona."

The weight of her words crashed headlong against him. Sands' eyes flashed wide for a split second. Otherwise he was still. She was surprised by his control; his lack of outward emotion when it came to what she had just uttered, but she didn't show her astonishment.

"Just the other day, as a matter of fact. We had

an interesting chat, the two of us—she sends her well wishes, by the way."

Sands was, at this exact moment, a man of extreme contrasts. On the one hand, he could feel his face burning—knew how he must look to her—ready to ignite—on the other, his fascination with the lovely Dr. Aaliyah Waymans was this very minute overshadowing anything else, like an eclipse of the sun—blotting out all sunlight. Ready to ignite over news that Nona was indeed alive, and yet, smoldering inside over this new *creature*, Aaliyah—just repeating her name over and over in his head caused a sweet sensation to erupt within . . . oh so lovely . . .

Of course, he had been told that Nona lived—his attorney, the judge, and his doctors all had said as much. But somehow those words had seemed hollow up until now. For here was someone who had actually *spoken* to her—and they had chatted seemingly about *him*, a day or two ago—too much to process—too much to consider . . .

"She wishes me well?" he found himself asking.

"Yes. She carries no ill will toward you—she wishes you no harm."

"I see." He didn't, but remained quiet.

"I probably should back up." Dr. Waymans straightened her back as she spoke. "After reviewing your file and holding numerous conversations with Dr. Rollings, I felt what would be most beneficial to you would be to talk to the people—the key players in your realm, to hear their stories, their point of view as it relates to you."

Sands waited a beat before saying, "And?"

"Well, what I learned was this: the object of your attention and affection is not some figment of your imagination—you're not hallucinating—she does really exist. Nona Scott-Walker. She's a real person, although you and she have never met." Dr. Waymans let the weight of her words settle in.

"We haven't?" Sands asked. "But what—"

"No, you haven't. That much is undisputable. You've never met— regardless of what your mind is trying to tell you."

"We . . . we had something . . . shared something special . . ."

"Yes," Dr. Waymans continued, not wanting to interrupt, but not wanting to lose the rhythm, the flow to her words. She'd consulted her notes, discussed her approach with Dr. Rollings several times. "But it did *not* occur. In your mind it is vivid…like the smell of those flowers, like the color to those leaves," she gestured overhead, "but the reality is this: what you *think* you shared did not exist. It's not real."

Sands considered her words—of course, he'd heard this countless times, too—but, somehow, hearing it from her, Dr. Waymans, a fresh new lovely face, somehow gave it new weight, new meaning.

"Okay," he said.

"The question, of course, is why? Why is your mind doing this—conjuring up vivid images, interspersing them with real-life events so as to confuse you?"

"Do you have an answer?" he asked.

"No, but I aim to find out. You've made a great

deal of progress here, David. Dr. Rollings tells me you're a model patient—very willing to participate— eager to get back to your old life."

"Old life," Sands repeated, and for a moment he was thrust back to his top-floor loft on Park Place in Brooklyn, the expanse of window-glass, smoldering red-orange glow to his fireplace, his easels, his paints . . . the building beyond . . . shapes behind a yellow shade . . . Lisa—those wire-frame glasses, mocha-brown complexion. She'd visited him here often—the only one—she knew everything now—he'd bared his soul to her over the past half-year, and she'd loved him for it, Lisa putting on a few extra pounds, probably from the stress of worrying about *him*—but it suited her—he liked the way she looked now, seemingly comfortable in her own skin—and he found that he was thinking about her often now—like, when he finally gets out of here, he'd like to spend some time with her—perhaps settle down, if that's even possible after all of this—the two of them—make a go at it . . . there just might be that chance.

Dr. Waymans watched him intently.

"My old life . . ." he repeated once more. "Yes, I'd like that back." Said it with firm conviction, and the doctor had no doubt that he meant every word.

"Then you and I have much work to do." She rose, pressing her hands against the fabric of her lab coat, smiling. "Nona has to cease living here," she said, pointing to her temple. "You need to recognize that she's just an aberration, nothing more, and move on. In time, we'll discern why she visited you the way she did, but the important point is to let her *go* . . ."

Sands sucked in a breath and exhaled.

"I can do that."

"Can you?" she asked. "I hope so. So does she—as I've said, Nona wishes you well."

"What did she say?" he asked, voice barely above a whisper.

"That you and she never met. That you probably ran in the same circles—you know she's living with that well-known painter, Brehan—actually they have a child together—that the two of you may have met at any number of art gatherings, gallery exhibits, parties, and the like, but that you two have certainly never met."

Sands nodded his head, mind racing.

"Her husband?"

"Shot himself after leaving her for dead. But she survived. Three days in a hospital with a shattered jaw. But that was then. That's history. Now she's very happy, and very much alive."

Sands considered every word.

"Her friend, Chantal?"

"Chatted with her, too. Nice woman—very talented. Runs a fashion label that I dare say is up and coming—talk of the town. Incidentally, she and Nona have gone their separate ways." Dr. Waymans cocked her head in his direction and said, "We need to work on you staying out of her house—no more breaking and entering," she said with a firm smile. "Are we clear on that?"

Sands nodded. "I'm not trying to hurt anyone, you know," he said.

It was Dr. Waymans' turn to nod. "I believe you—but we need to be two hundred percent sure on that point! That's the deal, David. Because you *did* hurt people. You hurt that Botanical Garden guard; you hurt Chantal—and you could have inflicted irrevocable damage to yourself. We need to be absolutely certain you're no longer a threat to anyone, including yourself."

Dr. Waymans smiled, and instantly the pent-up tension, which moments ago was thick like mountain fog, evaporated. "Then, David Sands, you get your life back . . . it's really that simple . . ."

With that, Dr. Aaliyah Waymans sauntered away.

Sands watched her leave; his mind raced, considered everything that she had said. All of it—the power to her words, the depth to their meaning—rolled around in his brain for a long while. He nodded once, then again. A smile adorned his face. *Yes,* he thought to himself, *I'm going to get my old life back.*

Picking up his sketch book, he flipped open to a fresh, new page. Smoothing out the sheet with his palm, he reached for his charcoal pencil, hovering it inches above the blank paper.

Aaliyah, his mind pronounced.

Ahhh-Liy-Ahhhhhhhh.

Marveling at the way their eyes connected.

Sands smiled again as he pressed charcoal to paper, beginning with her hazel-green eyes . . .

THE END

Accokeek, Maryland

Please turn the page for a sneak peek at

AWAKENINGS

On sale wherever books and e-books are sold.

One

The snow drifts lazily to earth, the way leaves flutter to the ground caught in an autumn breeze, descending in a haphazard fashion, see-sawing back and forth, each oversized, water-laden snowflake following its own course immune to the path of others. Taj presses his nose and cheek against the dual-pane window and exhales gently, observing his breath fan out across the sheet of cold glass before fading quickly, as if an aberration—a bubbling well in a sea of sand dunes. He glances down forty-something stories to the Manhattan street below, which one he isn't exactly sure; they are staying at the W hotel at Times Square—it could be West 47th or Eighth Avenue. Taj never has possessed a keen sense of direction. One thing is clear: it isn't Broadway that he is staring at. He is certain of that.

Taj presses his cheek again to the glass. The cold feels good on his smooth dark skin. He glances upward, marveling as he does each time

he returns to the city at the diversity of structures
and their architectures—like the city itself, a mi-
crocosm of multiplicity—granite, steel, brick, aluminum, old and new in peaceful coexistence, like
hip-hop and jazz. He never grows tired of exploring her structures—the details, fine lines, and
craftsmanship that speak to him of art, creativity,
and a way of constructing things long since retired. He subscribes to this mode of thinking, this
way of life.

"These are some big-ass snowflakes," Taj re-
marks softly. He turns slightly, taking in the brown
couch, low coffee table, wall unit, and entrance to
the bedroom. A single lamp by the couch is illuminated. Soft music emanates from the clock radio
in the bedroom. The two-room suite is small, yet
comfortable. Perhaps the mood has something to
do with the snow—the way hundreds of flakes
each second collide with the tall windows, opening
up, smearing their contents on the glass.

"Please. I hate it when you talk like that."

"Like what?" he asks, already knowing the answer as he turns toward her. He stares at Nicole.
She is on the couch, her legs folded underneath
her, shoes off, with thin square-frame glasses
perched atop a perfectly shaped nose. Her dark
eyes, enhanced by brown caramel skin and rosy
cheeks, flick over to him briefly before turning
quickly back to her book—a leafy hardback, James
Baldwin no less.

"You know, trying to talk like that. 'Big-ass?' It
doesn't become you." Taj runs a hand over his
chocolate baldhead and smiles. He loves his woman.
Precisely at such times he knows this with the cer-

tainty of a Swiss quartz timepiece—watching her
the way he is just now, thinking to himself how
lucky he is to have someone like her in his life.
And so Taj sighs, captures her wink, and turns
away. As he returns his stare to the window, glancing down once again at the street, the stream of
traffic, and warmly dressed people, he feels a sudden urge to be out among them.

Taj and Nicole walk hand in hand (more accu-
rately, glove in glove), the two of them bundled
against the deepening cold. Nicole's wool ear
warmers keep her head somewhat shielded; her
red ski parka seems to attract snow the way a summer barbecue attracts mosquitoes. Taj wears a
long dark wool overcoat, collar turned up, that
reaches nearly to his ankles, and one of those Rus-
sian military-style hats that submarine captains wore
during the second world war, with real fur that peeks
out as if a squirrel or rabbit were seeking refuge
underneath. The snow is swirling around them, at-
tacking from all angles, getting into their nostrils
and eyes, pelting their heads and thighs. Nicole
reaches for Taj's arm and intertwines hers with his,
enjoying as they always do the closeness—the
warmth that can be felt even now, on this bitter,
New York evening. It is eight p.m., several weeks
until Christmas. The streets are lined with holiday
lights, decorations, and shoppers: courageous
souls like them who have braved the elements in
search of a sale or last minute gift item or, in the
case of Taj and Nicole, have a chance to walk in
one of the greatest cities in the world (just ask any-

one in Manhattan!), marvel at the architectures, take in a museum or two, or just enjoy the magic and romance of this snow-covered evening.

The sound of music is everywhere, emanating from speakers hung on lampposts every hundred feet. Christmas favorites are cycled, ones that they sang as children, and Nicole can't help but hum along as Taj points upward at the carved molding on the top edge of an Eighth Avenue apartment building or co-op. Intricate patterns carved in stone are interspersed with decorative corbels; eighteenth-century faces gaze downward. An unending sea of taxicabs glides along choking the entire avenue, and Taj notices that not a single one is unoccupied.

Going nowhere in particular, they turn right at the corner and dash into a coffee house, as much for relief from the cold as to get something to eat and drink. They settle into a high table by the window, amazingly vacant at this exact moment, after ordering a pair of lattes and jelly-filled pastries. Nicole removes her ear warmers, shakes the snow from her thick hair with a quick zig-zag movement of her neck, and attacks the pastry with her fingers, tearing at the flaky bread as though it were wrapping paper. She watches Taj closely, reaching out as he removes his hat and wiping the moisture from his smooth dark head with her hand. His eye begins to quiver—again; the third or fourth time today (that she's noticed), the lower eyelid trembling as if to its own eclectic beat. She passes her fingers over it to cease its movement. He catches her left wrist as she pulls back, brings it to his mouth, and gazes at the ring silently before kissing her fingers gingerly. Nicole blinks back tears and stares at Taj for a long time. Their eyes are unwavering before movement outside their window releases their concentration on each other.

Nicole is speaking about *Giovanni's Room,* Baldwin's acclaimed novel set in Paris in the 1950s—a young man grappling with his sexuality and the pain of choosing between a man and a woman, and how she intends to weave next week's reading into a discussion with her students on sexuality in literature. Taj listens intently, watching her eyes animate as she speaks of her work—associate professor of American literature at Howard—adding Baldwin to his already extensive to-do list.

Redressing in their coats, hats, and gloves, the two reemerge forty minutes later, appetites satisfied and freezing limbs thawed, ready to brave the elements once again. They cut across the street during a momentary lull in traffic, Nicole in tow as Taj heads for a brownstone with a lone sign in the shape of a saxophone, pulsing blue neon. They stand for a moment discerning the jazz that escapes, deciding whether or not they wish to check it out. In the end, they decide to move on, still warm and cozy from the coffee and pastry, feeling the night air, the temperature seemingly on the rise.

Onward . . . past Christmas lights and the serene nativity scenes in store-front windows, then on to the neon madness and excessiveness of Broadway. Taj just shakes his head, attempting to quickly calculate how much power is expended in this four-block radius on signage alone. He gives up, recognizing it is of little consequence to him or others.

Back onto side streets where life seems to move at one notch back from normal—third gear instead of fourth—down tree-lined blocks whose

canopies are blanketed with fresh snow. Past resi-
dential homes that sport fully decorated trees in
their parlor windows, each one more beautiful
than the previous, as if the whole spirit of Christmas has been reduced to a competitive sport. Taj
and Nicole walk hand in hand, drawing it all in,
like smoke, inhaling the scent and the vapors—the
very essence of the city.

They come to a dark stone church on the corner of a busy intersection—a three-building structure that is out of place among the steel and
aluminum skyscrapers that tower toward the heavens, their top floors obliterated by the falling
snow. The church is eighteenth century, Gothic in
its design, embellished with cathedral spires and
thick wrought-iron gates. A crowd of onlookers
stands on the stone steps leading to enormous oak
doors that are held open as though they are wings
or outstretched palms, the bright warm lights inside inviting. Song can be heard spilling out into
the night—Christmas carolers singing "Silent
Night." Nicole turns to Taj and grins. He leads her
up the stairs, past the onlookers, and into the sanctity of the church's interior.

Inside it is warm. Nicole shakes off the snow and
Taj respectfully removes his hat. The pews are in-
termittently filled with folks who have come to
hear the choir sing. They are diverse: blacks, whites,
Asians, Africans, young and old, each putting aside
their cultural differences on this night to sing
songs that toll of the night Jesus Christ was born.

Crowds of people gather at the rear end of the
church, as if afraid to move closer to the singers,
or still deciding whether to stay or go. Taj leads
Nicole past the throng, thick coats and jackets cov-

ered with melting snow that runs down the fabric
and pools at their feet. Inching closer, Nicole behind him, his hand clasped in hers, fingers intertwined, they move past folks who have joined in
with the carolers singing "O Holy Night," the sweet
sound reverberating off of domed ceilings and
stained glass windows. And then, as Taj is consumed by the sights, sounds, and smells within this
church, his ears discern one strain that is unique
and stands alone—and he pivots to search for the
source: a woman's voice—distinctive and hauntingly familiar—sensual in its smooth delivery, a
soulful melody that interlaces itself amidst the
choir's song. Taj turns, first 180 degrees, then in
the opposite direction. Nicole senses the change
in him, like a flame extinguished from a sudden
change in pressure, and asks if everything is okay.
Taj ignores her, not in a disrespectful way, but
some things can only be dealt in a serial way, one
at a time, in order of priority. And so, Taj gives *this*
his full attention.

Before the first row of pews is a black couple facing forward, their backs to the others. The woman,
with her thick twisting hair tied back and head
moving to an unknown beat, is accompanied by a
tall, bald gentleman wearing an expensive camel-
hair coat. Taj is certain this woman is the source of
the familiar melodic strain. Taj moves parallel with
them and turns, releasing Nicole's hand as he
does, looking past the man and observing the
woman in profile. He watches her as the words of
the song waft from her lips. A tidal wave of recognition rises up and crashes onto him with a force
that stops his heart cold.

Twenty years.

Can that be right?

Yes.

Twenty years.

His movements are now beyond his control. He is being choreographed and flows along, his mind outside of himself as he shifts closer to the couple. And then without conscious thought, Taj opens his mouth, leans in, and says softly, "Jazz, look into my eyes . . . focus only on my eyes . . ."

Cheyenne is raptured by the sound, the way this choir has come together and filled this holy space with their sweet voices. She raises her head to the vaulted ceiling overhead and closes her eyes, matching their words but with a melody all her own. When Cheyenne is singing, she is in her element— it is what she is passionate about, what moves her, what makes her blood course through her veins with a sudden rush. She spies her husband Malcolm quickly glancing at his Movado. Yes, she knows they need to watch the time—there's a CD release party later on that evening at one of the city's hottest clubs. Malcolm, record executive and producer *extraordinaire* and currently one of the hottest and most powerful forces in urban music today, needs to be there at precisely the right moment. Cheyenne knows this all too well, the routine repeated many times during the last year. Not that she's complaining. The life they lead is storybook, no two ways about it. And yet tonight, what is most important to her right now is completing this song, singing these words that take her to a special place—many, many years ago, before she grew up and when her mamma was still here.

She leans into Malcolm, rubs his arm as he turns to her and smiles. He loves to hear her sing. It brings him comfort and joy. And so he reaches for her, placing his arm around her waist as he flashes her a smile, and he reminds her that they need to be going soon. Cheyenne silently nods.

"Jazz, look into my eyes . . ."

When she hears those words, uttered from behind her, the color drains from her face. Cheyenne ceases to sing. Her mind is racing, connecting thoughts with long-filed-away images.

" . . . Focus only on my eyes . . ."

She is already turning, a mixture of pain and pleasure filling her so quickly that she fears she will drown. And in an instant she is facing *him*. She raises her eyes slowly, as if not wanting the confirmation that is sure to come. But then their eyes meet, and she *knows*. One look at the eyes tells all. It's Taj.

"Oh–my–God," she mouths, so softly that no one, including her husband or Taj for that matter, can discern a single word. Tears freefall down her beautiful face. Never in a million years did she ever expect to see him again. And yet, staring into those amazing eyes, the ones she recalls with sudden clarity—hazel colored (the yin/yang of *that* color against his dark skin), their piercing yet calming intensity and almost magical qualities—Cheyenne is speechless. Suddenly, the air is being drawn out of this enormous room and she is finding it difficult to breathe. She is dizzy. Her husband turns back and flicks his stare between his wife and this stranger standing far too close.

"Baby?" he says, reaching for her. "Are you okay?"

Behind Taj, Nicole is watching the scene unfold. She hasn't heard the words that he spoke to this woman, but she has witnessed the reaction. Nicole, like Malcolm, has figured out (in the short time that has elapsed—five or six seconds) that something is not quite right.

Cheyenne continues to stare at Taj.

Taj silently returns her stare with his.

"Baby?" Malcolm says, louder this time as he turns to Taj. Malcolm and Taj are roughly the same size, Taj being a half-foot taller, but both possess similar characteristics—baldheads, dark-skinned complexions, and piercing stares.

Nicole reaches for her man, tugs at his shoulder as Cheyenne sobs louder. Taj waves Nicole off with a shrug and reaches for Cheyenne's face. He strokes it (cheek to chin with a single finger), smiles, and asks softly, "Have you remembered our pact, Jazz?"

Cheyenne opens her trembling mouth and responds, "Yes."

Taj smiles. "Good. I see life has treated you well." Cheyenne readies to respond, but Malcolm has wedged himself between his wife and this man.

"Look—I don't know who the hell you are," Malcolm says, his face twisted into a snarl, "but I don't appreciate your stepping to my wife like this."

Cheyenne steps forward and pulls on Malcolm's coat as she momentarily loses sight of Taj. "Honey. Don't!"

Taj, on the other hand, remains still with eyes forward, his gaze boring into Malcolm's forehead. Nicole reaches for Taj's elbow again, connects with it, and tugs him backwards. Taj continues to smile.

"Are you well?" he mouths. Cheyenne nods and sobs harder.

"Taj? Taj?" Nicole yells, pulling harder on his sleeve. "What is going on?"

Malcolm shrugs off Cheyenne's attempt to control him. He steps forward, this time inches from Taj's face. Beads of sweat have appeared on his forehead and baldhead. He wipes at his head forlornly.

"Listen, asshole. Who the fuck are you, and why are you calling my wife Jazz?"

Taj breaks his stare with Cheyenne and locks onto Malcolm. He remains silent.

"I'm talking to *you*, asshole!" Malcolm's finger juts twice into Taj's chest.

Nicole's voice is behind them, rising in pitch and intensity. "Taj, what's going on? Taj, tell me what's going on!"

Taj looks down slowly at Malcolm's fingers, then back up. He considers his surroundings and steals a glance at Cheyenne, who is pulling on her husband with one hand while wiping her eyes with the other. Mascara is smearing along her full cheekbones. Taj feels a sudden twinge of sadness and turns to leave.

"Where do you think you're going?" Malcolm says loud enough that some of the carolers cease their singing and begin to crowd the space, wondering what the commotion is all about. Seeing that Taj is not paying him any respect or attention, Malcolm grabs for his elbow. Nicole has gripped the back of Taj's coat with her hand.

Taj spins around so suddenly and with such intensity that Nicole has no choice but to loosen her grip on his coat. Again, he bores into Malcolm with those hazel eyes and leans into him until mere inches separate their faces. Taj opens his mouth and whispers to Malcolm: "Don't ever touch me again," he hisses. "You have no idea who you are dealing with. You need to be fearful and walk away."

Cheyenne has attached herself to her husband, pulling and begging him to back off. Nicole is yanking on Taj and becoming frantic. Both men refuse to budge, but Malcolm blinks first.

"Be fearful," Taj repeats, lowering his voice a notch further. "Walk away." Taj breaks his stare with Malcolm, rotating his head slightly so that he can see Cheyenne.

Their eyes meet—briefly.

They lock—then disengage.

And then, Taj turns and leads Nicole through the crowd.

Malcolm remains where he is, nostrils flaring, chest pounding, recalling the intensity of his adversary that has suddenly chilled him to the bone, wondering as he collects his wife and stares her down, *who* was that man?

Two

The thing Taj recalled first—when he dug deep into the recesses of his mind—was the heat. He remembered the terminal, Norman Manley International, a place so small and backwater that he knew for sure he was in a foreign country. Well, yeah, what did he expect?

Here he was, in Kingston, Jamaica, just landed after flying nearly two thousand miles—a journey that took him from the Eastern Shore of Virginia north to New York. He and his pop had looked in the encyclopedia he had borrowed from school to get a sense of where he was going—and where he was going was south, not north. So why then, did he have to travel by air from Norfolk, north to New York's Kennedy, only then to head south? It never made any sense to him.

While deplaning in Kingston the heat had hit him fast; as he walked down the metal stairs from the jet's belly to the tarmac, the heat had smacked him dead in the face so hard that it took his breath away. This wasn't a little bit of heat—this stuff was downright oppressive!

The second thing that Taj recalled, which had always

stuck in his mind, was the soldiers with their weapons—large, black automatic rifles and semi-automatic hand-guns—big, bulky things that would scare the shit out of any sixteen-year-old—especially one who hadn't been raised on guns.

He was from the Eastern Shore of Virginia, a narrow tract of land between the Chesapeake Bay and the At-lantic Ocean. His father was a waterman. His father's father had been one too. They didn't play with guns or associate with them. Didn't have the inkling to. Han-dling fish was what Taj's family did—day in and day out.

In the shade of the terminal lobby, a corrugated alu-minum building with Coca-Cola signs displayed every hundred feet or so (the branded red and white logo that is internationally recognized), Taj waited among the hordes of Jamaicans—black people with downtrodden eyes. Taj had seen blacks before—his father and relatives are dark-skinned as well—but here there was a sea of them. A few stared back at him, a few nodded silently, their long dreads swaying as they moved, but most ignored him. Which was okay with him.

Taj's very first plane ride had gone fairly well. He had been scared—had talked to his pop about it—asked him the night before he was to leave whether there was any-thing to worry about. And Pop had looked him in the eye and said no, there was nothing to fear. Taj nodded, con-sidered his pop's response for a time, and then asked if he had ever taken a plane. Pop regarded him silently for a moment before shaking his head.

They had encountered some turbulence just past Miami, up around 37,000 feet. The plane had been buf-feted around a bit, not very much, but enough to scare Taj into thinking he was going to die—until the woman sitting two seats away (a quiet white woman with glassy blue eyes) reached over and patted his tense knuckles, told him that what they were feeling was normal, and that everything was going to be alright.

He felt like kissing the ground when they finally touched down in Kingston, but as he headed for the tarmac the heat had slapped him silly. Then he suddenly was aware of the guns and soldiers. Well, he momentarily forgot all about turbulence and that kind of nonsense.

Taj was part of a church mission, a small group of folks who were heading to the mountains of Jamaica to help build a community. He had been selected from hundreds of teenagers in his congregation. Why, he never really knew—but he was honored to be going. His guidance counselor at the high school had told him that this was indeed a once-in-a-lifetime opportunity to see how other people in a different part of the world lived. Okay, he wasn't traveling half way around the world, but Taj got the point.

A very small group was to go on this trip and remain for a month. Taj had very much wanted his pop to go with him, but that just wasn't going to happen. Pop couldn't afford to be off from work for one single day, least of all thirty. Besides, in New York they would be joined by four other individuals—two other high schoolers, like himself, and their guardians from their respective churches. In addition, there were supposed to be a dozen or so folks already there in the mountains. Taj and these new people were cycling in; others would be cycling out over the course of the upcoming month.

Sitting in the terminal, wiping the perspiration from his forehead (wishing like hell he had had the forethought to corn roll his afro), his knapsack and oversized suitcase beside him, Taj glanced around, trying to ascertain which folks were in his group and making the final leg of the journey with him.

And then he saw her—coming around a corner, a shiny blue Samsonite trailing behind her, bell-bottom jeans, sandals, and a flowery patterned shirt that accentuated her burgeoning breasts. She was about five seven, with a thin waist, a golden bronze complexion, and thick frizzy dark hair that hung halfway down her back. He put her at no more than seventeen—Taj had never seen anyone so beautiful in all of his short life. He sat there, enthralled, watching her, unable to move, his limbs glued to his sides, feeling the adrenaline surge through him. His mouth dried up, even though he had no intention of speaking.

She walked with an older woman who Taj guessed was her mother (who was shorter, a bit plump, and wore her hair in a much more conservative, shorter style) but had the same face—half Indian, half something else—probably black. The girl was beautiful like he had never seen before, with high cheekbones, a thin nose, and sculpted features—a hint of American Indian, but with a skin tone that told Taj she was mixed.

Taj spent the next forty-five minutes watching her every move—the sketchbook that he had brought with him laid in his lap, untouched. (Taj knew that he wanted to be an architect, so he carried a sketchbook with him wherever he went, capturing ideas on the white pages.)

By the time they announced his flight (he overheard some Jamaicans call it a puddle jumper) he had completed three separate fantasies with this stunningly beautiful girl as his co-star. Of course, Taj never spoke to her—he couldn't actually go to her and just say something. Taj wasn't confident around girls, never had been.

He was well liked in school, but never found the right words to say to girls—so he, for the most part, left them alone.

And then she was rising along with her mother as they called the flight—his flight—and Taj felt his stomach burn. The same queasy feeling that had come over him at 37,000 feet returned—yet he was on solid ground. He watched her as she gathered her things and headed for the plane. He followed slowly, his mind and heart racing, mesmerized, like a lamb to the slaughter.

The tarmac was on fire—or so it seemed. The asphalt appeared to be smoldering. Taj guessed it was just the heat. Beyond the gate was a Beech King Air Turbo-prop. As he trudged toward it, his bags trailing behind him, he watched the girl—the sensual way her hips swayed and the way she ran her hand down the side of her face, pushing her thick hair behind her ear. It would remain that way for a good half-minute or so before falling out of place again—and just that simple act, of raising a bronze arm to her face, was driving Taj crazy. What it was, he couldn't figure. But it made him feel . . . very good . . . .

The plane wasn't large—Taj counted five round port-holes on the side of the white fuselage with red and black trim, so he figured it would seat a dozen passengers at the most. He glanced behind him and saw no one else except a Jamaican with long black dreads held down by a yellow bandana, carrying a single black bag, slowly limping toward him. A thick black walking cane was used for support, and Taj noticed that the handle was intricately carved; the bottom, however, was as smooth as a blade of grass. The man wore an expressionless face behind black sunglasses. The pilot, Taj guessed, was already on board.

At the doorway, a dark woman with bright teeth

smiled and, in a thick accent, directed everyone to leave their bags by the rear of the plane. A well-muscled Jamaican was stowing those in the cargo hold.

Taj reached the tiny steps that were built into the fuselage. He climbed slowly, conscious of his head—he was already over six feet tall. The stewardess smiled and motioned for him to take a seat. Taj glanced around the tight cabin, saw that the girl and her mom had taken one set of cracked leather seats two rows up from the door. She was reaching for something in her knapsack when he entered—and glanced up momentarily. Taj stopped, sucked in a breath, as her gaze roamed over him, stopping at his eyes. He decided to smile after some slight deliberation and gave her a weak one, but the girl neither returned it nor held his gaze for a moment longer. She went back to what she was doing—rummaging through her knapsack, as if he weren't even there.

Deflated, Taj took a seat at the back of the plane and next to the window, pushing away thoughts of this girl, replacing them instead with thoughts of his pop.